TWISTED

DYSTOPIAN URBAN FANTASY

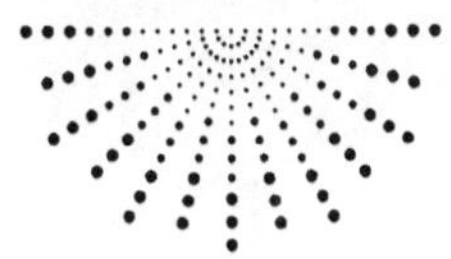

ANN GIMPEL

Edited by

KATE RICHARDS

CONTENTS

Twisted — v
Copyright Page — vii
Twisted: Book Description — ix

1. That's Impossible — 1
2. Just Like Old Times — 13
3. Collateral Damage — 25
4. Weirdness Squared — 41
5. Evil's Not Dead Yet — 53
6. Best Laid Plans — 67
7. Bargains — 79
8. A Newer Evil — 93
9. The Sea Keeps You Humble — 107
10. A Cat's Tale — 119
11. Hell's Gateway — 131
12. The Only Good Vamp is a Dead Vamp — 145
13. Love's not on the Menu — 159
14. Chances and Changes — 171
15. Warnings — 183
16. Monsters on the Loose — 197
17. Let Me Go — 213
18. As Green as Shifters Come — 225
19. An Honorable Death — 237
20. Affair of the Heart — 249
21. Hijacked by the Future — 261
About the Author — 273
Abandoned: Book Description — 275
Abandoned, Chapter One: Borrowed Trouble — 277

TWISTED

BITTER HARVEST, BOOK TWO

Dystopian Urban Fantasy
By
Ann Gimpel

TWISTED: BOOK DESCRIPTION

A runaway spell is the most dangerous weapon of all

The sea is the only life Juan's ever known—not counting the decade he spent as a Vampire. Those years gave him a healthy aversion for anything supernatural, but he's a shifter now. It's way better than being one of the undead, but he still doesn't trust magic. Paired up with Aura to teach him, he falls and falls hard, but she spurns his advances.

A history professor before the cataclysm, Aura deals in prophecies for her shifter pack. Juan is one hell of an attractive package, but he left a string of broken hearts during his years as chief navigator on cruise ships. She'd be an idiot to sign on for a fling. She has enough problems without adding a broken heart to them.

What began as an exploratory mission to see if anything is left of the world turns sour fast. A Vampire attack, a possessed priest, and a gateway to Hell mean fallout from the spell gone bad that pinned them in South America is far from gone. Retreat is tempting, but nowhere is safe. Surrounded by hardship, they sail on. Evil is leaching in from somewhere, and they have to find the breach.

1

THAT'S IMPOSSIBLE

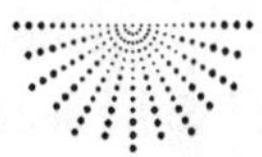

AURA MACKENZIE ROLLED her shoulders to get the kinks out of her back. She hadn't had much space to roam in Ushuaia, but *Arkady*, a sturdy Russian research vessel that once ferried tourists through polar waters, was smaller by far than any other place she'd spent much time.

She'd retreated to her cabin to shower since the vessel wasn't pitching and rolling quite so much. The journey south from Ushuaia had grown rough once they left the Beagle Channel and turned southeast. If it hadn't been for a healthy dose of magic, she'd have been horribly seasick right along with several of the dozen female Shifters aboard. As it was, she'd been queasy the entire time.

Four men traveled with them. Men who'd once been Vampires but were now Shifters, courtesy of a powerful spell that had nearly killed them all. Viktor and Juan had worked together for years, and this was their ship. Pre-Vampire, Recco and Daide had been veterinarians in Ushuaia, and both men had a hell of a time with the transition from animal healer to animal killer. For whatever reason—maybe some leftover Vampire juju—the seasickness gene had bypassed the men, and she was jealous.

Until about two months ago, they'd all been trapped in Ushuaia, and she still couldn't quite believe their gambit to escape had paid off. The wicked enchantment holding them prisoner had lasted ten years, and she'd been certain they'd all die in the remote location at the tip of South America. Between increasingly toxic water and a lack of food, their fate didn't require her skill with prophecies to predict.

Yet, they'd broken free. Whether it was permanent or a momentary respite remained to be seen.

Back home in Wyoming, she'd been a historian. Unlike many tenure-track faculty, she'd enjoyed her comfy academic position where the hardest thing she had to do was deal with unruly graduate students. A cat Shifter, she was bonded to a mountain lion, and it missed Wyoming's mountains and the forests where they'd roamed. She did too. Ushuaia had mountains, but they were nothing like the Rockies towering above her erstwhile home.

She rolled her eyes. It would be a long time before she saw Wyoming again. And a strong possibility existed she never would. The reason they'd left Ushuaia was to explore the Southern Ocean in gradually widening arcs to determine if the Cataclysm—the wickedness that had held them prisoner—was wreaking havoc elsewhere.

Or if their counter spell had wiped it out for good.

One thing was certain. If the Cataclysm lived anywhere, it would be out for blood. The evil was sentient, and it knew good and well who was responsible for its destruction around Ushuaia. A shiver tracked down Aura's spine.

"Yeah," she muttered half aloud. "Not much point pining for home. Maybe I'd do well to label wherever I am *home* and call it good." The thought pleased her, and she chuckled. It was an improvement over the fear that gripped her whenever she thought about the Cataclysm. She'd survived those years in Ushuaia by leveraging denial and cunning, useful traits she'd do well to keep front and center.

"Get moving," her cat urged. *"Don't you want off this boat?"*

"You bet," she told her bond animal.

Aura tucked her blonde hair under a thick, wool cap and grabbed a pair of gloves. That done, she slipped into a waterproof jacket and popped out of her quarters. Bundled to the gills in warm clothing, she was already sweating, but the momentary discomfort was worth it. They'd pulled into a sheltered bay a little while ago, and Viktor had activated the PA system to announce that anyone who wanted could go ashore.

Ketha, a wolf Shifter and Aura's closest friend, rattled down a nearby staircase, buried in her own pile of winter gear. Her long, dark hair with red and gold streaks was covered by her parka hood, and her golden eyes shone with excitement.

Ketha beamed at Aura, cupped a hand around her mouth, and addressed the empty corridor. "Anyone else want to go?"

"Me!" Rowana shuffled into the passage. Strands of silver hair had resisted her efforts to cover everything with her hood, and her brown eyes sported dark circles beneath them. "Sheesh. I've never had to wear so many clothes. My eagle wanted to fly, but I didn't figure it would be any warmer than me outside this ship. They're not usually cold weather birds."

Ketha shot an indulgent smile Rowana's way. "You're overprotecting your bondmate. Eagles live in Alaska."

Rowana puffed out her chest. "Next to the Chilkoot River because it runs *warm* all year, which means a ready supply of salmon. I wouldn't presume to tell you how to take care of your wolf—"

"Fine." Ketha waved the other woman to silence. "I apologize."

"Where exactly are we?" Aura cut in. All of them were edgy from the rough transit of the Scotia Sea. It had taken six days, three more than normal according to Viktor and Juan.

"A deserted whaling station on South Georgia Island called Grytviken," Ketha replied.

Aura sent a speculative glance at her friend and sister Shifter. "I'm going to bet you read up on it."

Ketha shook her head. "Nope. My secret weapon is Viktor. He adores this part of the world and regales me with stories."

Rowana snorted, her eyes sparking with mirth, and her usual good humor apparently restored. "And here I thought all you did was paw at each other."

"Oh, we do plenty of that too." Ketha grinned.

"Don't leave without me," Karin called, slamming her door behind her. Once plump, her face showed the ravages of the hell they'd lived through, but her shrewd copper eyes didn't miss much. Today, her snow-white hair was covered by a wool cap and a hood. "Good news! I found a stock of promethazine in the infirmary."

"What's that?" Aura asked. "I wish you MD types would speak English."

"We do." Karin leveled her gaze Aura's way. "It's trade name is Phenergan, and it's a seasickness medication, among other things. Means I won't have to use as much magic once we get underway again."

"Don't those things have expiration dates?" Rowana asked.

Karin made a noise between a grunt and a snort. "Yes, but they mean nothing. The pharmaceutical industry wants to make sure you keep spending money, so they slap 'use by' dates on everything."

"Good to know," Rowana muttered.

Aura tossed her shoulders back and tried to forget how miserable she'd been. "Maybe I won't need anything next time."

Karin shrugged. "We'll see."

"Come on, gals. Let's go." Ketha headed down the corridor toward a door leading to one of the outside decks and a gangway. "Viktor told me two of the rafts are still seaworthy."

"What happened to the other ones?" Rowana asked.

"They're rubber. They rotted."

Aura's cat made a low, hissing noise inside her and said, *"We can swim to shore. Let's do it."*

"Maybe you could," Aura countered. "I'd drown wearing all these clothes. They'd drag me right to the bottom."

"What was that all about?" Ketha asked and latched the door open. "I only caught the tail end of it."

Cold air blasted through, bracing after the warmth of the ship. "Just my cat weighing in. Not sure it liked the idea of a partially rotten raft."

Ketha trotted the length of the ship to where a metal staircase led down to water level. "This one isn't rotten, silly." She ran lightly down the swaying stairs.

Aura followed, but she held onto the handrails. When she reached the bottom, she gazed across an expanse of water at falling-down buildings and the hulls of wrecked ships partially submerged near shore. Ketha had identified it as a deserted whaling station, and it certainly looked the part.

The whine of an engine caught her attention. Viktor motored around the side of *Arkady*, standing in a large, black raft with pontoons curving around every side. He helped Ketha aboard and then Aura. She sat on one of the pontoons while the two other women got in.

A large-bore rifle was propped next to Viktor. "What's the gun for?" Aura tipped her chin at it.

"Never know what we might run up against," he replied. "It was my weapon of choice to guard against polar bear attacks in the Arctic."

"What are you expecting?" Rowana asked. "There aren't any polar bears here."

"I'm not expecting anything, but I like to be prepared."

"Thanks for taking care of us." Ketha glanced fondly at her husband.

"Welcome. No one else wanted to go?" Viktor furled his tawny brows. Tall and broad-shouldered, he still held the ungodly beauty common to Vampires. Aura guessed he'd always been movie-star stunning with brown-gold hair and eyes the shade of uncut emeralds. Defying the chill, he'd tossed his hood back, and his hair blew every which way in a stout breeze.

Ketha shrugged. "Guess not. I put out the call in the corridor."

"Seasickness can be a real bitch," Karin spoke up. "Between all the magic I ran through some of you and not having the stomach to eat anything for a few days, my bet is everyone else is sleeping."

"I wanted to make sure we weren't waiting for anyone." Viktor sat next to the idling engine and engaged the throttle. They hit the wake dead center as they motored toward shore.

"Do you suppose we'll find anyone here?" Ketha eyed him. "I meant to ask you before I got all duded up to spend time outside."

"I have no idea. The far end of this cove"—he pointed—"has barrack buildings built by the Brits after the Falklands War. They're substantial, like everything British. Big enough to house maybe five hundred men. As I recall, they were reasonably self-sufficient, with solar-powered desalination machinery and solar electricity generators."

"What about in the winter?" Rowana asked. "When there isn't any sun?"

"No one lived here in the winter," Viktor replied. "The war only lasted a couple of months, and it's been over since 1982. As I recall, Argentina didn't exactly roll over and agree to British sovereignty, hence the barracks to house enough men to discourage further hostilities."

"Winter," Rowana prodded.

"Yeah, winter." Viktor smothered a snort. "Thanks for the redirect. There used to be a skeleton force in the barracks and people to man the post office and museum during tourist season. That was about it. They all went home to the Falklands around April, so I'd be surprised if we found anyone here. Anyone alive, that is."

Aura chewed her lower lip. "Mmph. Let's see. The eclipse was in late November, which is the Antarctic summer, so the Cataclysm hit this part of the world when there were likely folk here."

"True enough," Viktor said. "We can hope for something beyond corpses, but I don't expect we'll find anyone."

Karin frowned. "Maybe I should have brought the medical bag I cobbled together from supplies in the ship's infirmary."

"Nah." Ketha shook her head. "If we find anyone and they're in such bad shape they require your services, we'll haul them into the raft and—"

"Maybe," Karin broke in. "The Cataclysm created isolated pockets of humanity. We all developed the same immunity to the bacteria and viruses that incubated in Ushuaia. The place we're about to step out of this raft is its own petri dish of bugs, and we'd do well to take normal biohazard precautions. Our Shifter magic will help, but it's not a guarantee we're protected from everything."

"But I never had any problems," Viktor protested. "And I've spent months on South Georgia Island. Hell, I spent three weeks here, once, when a bad series of storms blew through and it wasn't safe to leave."

"That was before the Cataclysm," Karin said and turned to Ketha. "Feel like providing a microbiology lecture about mutation and natural selection?"

"Not right now," Ketha replied, "but I'd be happy to gin something up later, once we're all back aboard *Arkady*."

Viktor swung the craft around so its stern end hit the beach. "I'll get out," he told the women, "and drag the raft ashore. Perch on the pontoon about where I am and time the waves. Wait until the tide is moving out before you jump down."

"Before anyone goes anywhere," Karin said, "exercise reasonable caution. Don't touch anything. Don't collect anything to bring back to the ship."

"Don't drink the water, and don't breathe the air," Rowana muttered.

The lyrics from Tom Lehrer's song, "Pollution," struck Aura as humorous, and she laughed.

"I wasn't trying to be funny." Rowana looked askance at her.

"I know," Aura said, "but I was thinking about the life we left behind. What you said reminded me of another aspect of it: music."

Ketha followed Viktor's direction and jumped off the pontoon, wading through the surf to shore. Aura and the other women followed her. All of them wore knee-high Wellington rubber boots. The ship's mudroom had been stocked with them and their waterproof jackets and bibs.

"Where to?" Aura asked Viktor once he'd tied off the anchor rope to some handy rocks.

"We should be methodical about this," he replied. "Maybe we'll walk down to the barracks, check them out, and then make our way back this way." His mouth twisted into a sad expression. "There used to be fur seals here. Lots of them. They'd block the road and bark at you, but I'm sure they're all dead. They lived on fish and krill."

"That way?" Aura pointed.

At Viktor's nod, she set out along a rutted dirt road that hugged the shoreline. The ocean was only a few feet away, so close it must wash over the road from time to time. She skirted an enormous hole easily, since the track was wide enough to accommodate vehicles, and passed a couple of crumbling buildings on her left. Rotting carcasses, probably the remains of seals and seabirds, dotted the road. She stepped over and around piles of them. Mostly bleached bones, they reminded her of Ushuaia's streets before they'd cleaned them up.

Caught up in the simple joy of movement, something she hadn't been able to indulge in on the ship, she breathed the chilly salt air, drawing it deep into her lungs. The air in Ushuaia had grown progressively more toxic, so she appreciated being able to breathe without assuming every breath brought her one step closer to her grave. She saw rows of tan buildings a quarter of a mile before she reached them. From long habit, she sent her Shifter senses ranging wide. If anything was alive out there, she wanted to know about it before she got too close.

"Watch it!" Her cat was near the surface, and a snarling hiss punctuated its words.

Aura ground to a halt. She'd pulled well ahead of everyone else with her leggy stride. Viktor and Ketha strolled with their arms wrapped around each other as lovers often did. Karin and Rowana brought up the rear, chatting.

"Watch what?" she asked her bond animal.

"I caught a whiff of wrongness. Check for yourself."

"What is it?" Ketha pulled up next to her. "Why'd you stop?"

"My cat thinks something's not right."

Viktor slipped the rifle off his shoulder in a fast, fluid motion that spoke to his familiarity with it.

Aura shut her eyes, urging her senses to preternatural sharpness. Something unpleasant and eerily familiar zapped her. She curled her hands into fists and dug deeper. She had to be wrong.

Before she was through dissecting what she sensed lay beyond, perhaps in the barracks a couple hundred yards away, Ketha muttered, "Shit! It isn't possible."

Aura opened her eyes and gripped the other Shifter's arm. "You picked up on Vampire emanations, right?"

Ketha nodded, eyes wide with disbelief. "How? They're all supposed to have transformed into humans or Shifters."

"Why are you talking about Vampires, dearie?" Rowana asked. She and Karin had finally caught up with them.

"I have no idea how," Aura gritted out the words, "but they're here."

Karin narrowed her eyes to slits. "Vampires? Don't be ridiculous. The Cataclysm altered them, removed the Vampire mutation in their DNA."

"Or not." Rowana twisted her face into a grimace.

"Check for yourself," Ketha told the other two women.

Aura scrubbed the heels of her hands down her face, urging rational thought, and then scanned the place that felt menacing one more time. "It's not quite right for Vampire, at least not the Ushuaia variety," she muttered.

"Not exactly," Ketha agreed. "But there are at least two of whatever they are, and their emanations are closer to Vamp than anything else."

"The question of the hour," Viktor said, "is whether we move forward or retreat. It's a group decision."

Aura thought about it, and when she spoke, her words came hard. "We left Ushuaia to figure out what was left in the rest of the world. If we turn tail and run the first time we encounter anything, we may as well never have set sail."

Viktor grinned wryly. "Spoken like a true explorer. Shackleton would have been proud of you."

"I remember reading about him," Aura muttered. "If this is Grytviken, isn't he buried here?"

"He is, indeed," Viktor said. "His grave is on the far side of the post office, but only because his wife told the ship with his remains to bring him back here. I guess he was quite the philanderer, and she wasn't interested in footing the expense of bringing his cheating ass home."

"Interesting," Aura said, "but we're stalling. My vote is to see what the hell feels like Vampire."

"Mine too," Rowana said.

"I'm in," Karin said. "If we could survive Armageddon against the Cataclysm, how hard could this be?"

Viktor cocked his head to one side. "Depends. If they're Vamps, only beheading with iron will do them in."

"Maybe they'll be friendly." Ketha screwed her face into what might have been a hopeful expression, except it came off more like a grimace.

"Friendly and Vampire in the same sentence is an oxymoron,"

Viktor said in a flat, dead tone. "It appears we're all game, so all of you get behind me and stay close. Deploy your magic. It's still far more finely honed than mine." He shouldered the rifle. "If I have to, I'll use this. It should at least slow them down."

"Do we have any way to communicate with the ship?" Ketha asked.

Viktor slapped his forehead with an open palm. "Crap. It's been too many years since I ferried Zodiac rafts ashore. I'm not thinking. Hang on." Reaching inside his insulated parka, he withdrew a two-way radio and depressed the push-to-talk switch.

"Juan. Come in."

The radio crackled. "Juan here."

"Possible Vampire sighting. Secure *Arkady* and come now."

"Aw Jesus! Really?" Juan's words held a strangled note. "I'll drop the other decent raft in the water and bring Recco and Daide with me. Where are you?"

"By the barracks. Don't waste your time stopping in the town."

"Roger that. Be there in half an hour. Maybe less."

"The iron saber is in the equipment locker. Bring it along and make damn sure it doesn't puncture the raft."

Juan chuckled. "Aye, aye, Captain. Your faith in me is touching."

Viktor rolled his eyes. "By the time you get here, we'll either be dead or turned or breaking bread with the bastards."

More static. "You're sure it's Vamps, and they're alive?" Incredulity underscored Juan's question.

"Affirmative on the alive part. See you soon."

"Roger that. Over and out."

The radio sputtered to silence. Viktor clicked it off and dropped it back inside his parka. "Let's get moving."

"Don't you want to wait for Juan and them?" Aura asked.

He shook his head. "No. They'll bring the Zodiac to the beach down there." Viktor pointed at the barracks. "Vamps have ears like lynxes. They'll hear an engine even over the roar of the surf. We need to be near enough to do some good once they figure out we're here."

Aura was still trying to make sense of how the demise of the Cataclysm could turn Vampires into Shifters in Ushuaia and leave them untouched a few hundred miles away. Maybe it had something to do with Karin's mutation theory.

"Guess we're about to find out," she muttered.

"What'd you say?" Ketha asked.

"Nothing. I'm with Viktor. Let's get this show on the road."

2

JUST LIKE OLD TIMES

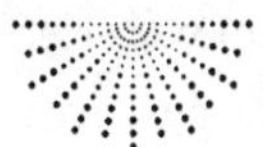

JUAN TORRES LOUNGED in the glassed-in bridge, sipping a cup of coffee. They were at anchor, so he didn't need to bother with the wheel or navigating. Not until they were underway again. His chair was tilted back, and his feet rested on the rail spanning every wall. The command center was his favorite part of *Arkady* because of its expansive windows. Five feet tall, they lined the entire bridge on three sides.

The coffee was hot and thick and bitter, exactly the way he liked it. He'd been pleasantly surprised to unearth a trove of beans in one of the food lockers. Some cook must have stashed them during *Arkady's* last voyage because Juan had taken inventory before they left port.

Arkady had been in dry dock for eight months before the Cataclysm hit. Skirting too close to rocks had damaged her hull. Not badly, but enough to require repairs. Those were completed in short order by a competent shipbuilder. Normally, they'd have ferried the boat back to Germany in October for a thorough overhaul to make certain it was ready for the Antarctic tourist season, but unusually rough seas and a lengthy winter meant neither he nor Viktor had been able to finesse a round trip to the shipyards peppering the Baltic Sea.

It wasn't the end of the world. They kept the second ship in abeyance in case something happened to the other vessel. He recalled a particular conversation—the one where he and Viktor decided to stop worrying about *Arkady's* annual checkup. They'd been aboard *Gavrill, Arkady's* sister ship, on their way back from the summer season where they ferried tourists through the Canadian Arctic as well as swinging through Svalbard with its scenic fjords.

A host of hardy passengers had signed on for the voyage from Norway across the Atlantic and down South America's eastern coastline, a decision that had cost all of them dearly.

A hurricane spawned by the Cataclysm—except he hadn't known anything about magic then—drove *Gavrill* into deadly rocks south of the Strait of Magellan. The boat sustained major damage, and they'd lost half the people aboard along with the ship. Juan unclenched his jaw. The memory still haunted him, made him wish he'd somehow done more even though he'd come within a hairsbreadth of drowning.

The seas had been high and the wind shearing in ninety-knot gusts. Thirty-foot swells crashing against sharp rocks had destroyed two overloaded rafts. The occupants struck out swimming for shore, but most never made it. Life jackets didn't do much good when waves battered you over and over.

After the disaster with the first two Zodiacs, he and Viktor switched up their strategy. The boat was lost anyway, so they'd fired the engines full throttle and forced the vessel closer to shore. It was sinking, but not very fast. Unlike Hollywood portrayals, big ships took their sweet time heading for the bottom. The crane that lowered the rafts broke off at deck line, so everyone else donned life vests and made for shore.

When he and Viktor gathered the group who reached a narrow, rocky beach, they counted forty-nine. Less than half their number. Given what happened afterward, though, it might have been better if the lot of them had perished in the Southern Ocean. At least drowning would have been clean.

Juan slapped his feet on the deck with a resounding *thud*.

He dropped his coffee cup on the chart table and paced from one side of the bridge to the other. Why the fuck wouldn't that memory leave him be? It had been ten years, for chrissakes, but their struggle first through the ocean and then across the Tierra del Fuego range could have happened yesterday. No one else died, but it was probably because only the hardiest had fought their way through the brutal sea to shore. The storm that had driven their ship aground raged on once they left the shoreline. Most of the time, he and Viktor navigated through the mountains by compass since they couldn't see more than a few feet.

He'd thought about Shackleton more than once during those three days it took them to cross the Tierra del Fuego. Juan wasn't a praying man, but if Ernest Shackleton's ghost protected mariners and fools, he did his damnedest to channel him. Many of the early adventurer's quotes still rattled around Juan's head, notably:

"Superhuman effort isn't worth a damn unless it achieves results." And "Difficulties are just things to overcome, after all."

Juan had been relieved, jubilant even, once he realized they'd made Ushuaia. They had another ship there—*Arkady*—and they'd recover from their losses. He'd been in shipwrecks before, but nothing as vicious as what he'd just lived through.

His elation was short-lived. They'd no sooner marched into Ushuaia, still battling forty-knot gusts, hail, and sleet, when a group of Vampires waylaid them.

Vampires.

What the unholy fuck?

Raised in Buenos Aires, Juan was no stranger to superstition, but he'd never believed in anything magical. Until Raphael turned him. The years he'd been a Vampire had been odd and horrible. It was like the man he used to be gazed out through uneven glass at a distorted world. On the rare occasions he wasn't lusting for blood, he used to pretend he was still human. It worked for a while when he caught something and roasted it for his dinner.

But his illusion of normalcy went up in smoke every time he cut into something's jugular vein, and hot, coppery blood slithered down his throat. The elation—almost a sexual high—that went along with drinking blood disgusted him, but he couldn't turn it off or stay away. Not for long, anyway. When he couldn't stomach what he'd become, he'd sneak aboard *Arkady* and lie on his bunk, breathing the familiar scents from when he'd still been human.

During the early years, he hatched plan after plan to escape, but a barrier spawned by the Cataclysm made travel beyond Ushuaia impossible. No. If he'd been set on leaving, the time would have been the couple of weeks after the Cataclysm hit. Once it gained a toehold, no one else arrived, but no one left, either. Juan had spent the first few months after Vampires snagged him, in a cell. By the time he was free, he'd been turned, and the die was cast.

No going back from the choice he made when Raphael offered his streaming wrist.

Viktor had occupied the cell next to him, and the two of them tried every trick at their disposal to spring themselves. Eventually, Raphael showed up and dragged Viktor into the corridor right outside Juan's cell.

The crafty, old Vampire had focused the full force of his hypnotic blue-gray eyes on Juan. "Watch. This is a great honor, and you will be next."

Juan hadn't wanted to watch, but he hadn't been able to tear his gaze away from the grisly specter of his closest friend being drained to the point of death. He silently urged Viktor to turn his head away when the Vampire offered his wrist, flowing with dark-red blood. Death was better than being a Vampire. Surely, Viktor knew as much.

For a long, agonizing moment, Juan thought Viktor might have the strength to refuse. His normally tanned face was ashen, and he lay limp in Raphael's arms. Damn! Viktor was going to beat this. Yeah, he'd die, but some things were far worse than death. Juan had just sucked in a relieved breath, when an agonized moan ripped from Viktor, and he glommed onto the Vampire's wrist, throat working while he drank.

Disgust and hopelessness vied with resignation. If Viktor hadn't had the strength to resist, Juan probably wouldn't, either. He felt Raphael's gimlet gaze locked onto him and raised his own, staring defiantly.

A small smile played around the Master Vampire's profanely beautiful face. "No one can withstand the pull of Vampirism. You'll see when it's your turn."

"And when will that be?" Juan had asked.

"Soon. When I need to feed again."

Color had returned to Viktor's face, but his green eyes held a flat, dead aspect. He wrenched his mouth away from Raphael's wrist. Bolting upright, he'd raced down the corridor and out of the cave system holding the prison cells.

"Aren't you going after him?" Juan demanded. He curled his hands around the bars of his cell and shook them.

"No. No reason. Newly made Vamps are always hungry. I'll catch up to him once he's fed."

Juan's stomach had twisted into a hard, painful knot. He tried to remain silent, but a question forced its way out. "Will he hunt people?" Juan stopped shy of adding, *like you just did*.

Raphael tossed his head back and laughed. It made his luxurious dark hair dance around him. "Who knows? He may begin with animals, or maybe he'll dive right into the real thing." Still laughing, the Vampire turned and sprinted down the corridor, moving with superhuman speed.

"Hey, man! You're going to wear a hole in the linoleum." Recco stepped into the bridge. The door swung shut behind him.

Juan stopped dead. He shook his head hard and then turned to face the other man. Recco was a wolf Shifter now, but he'd been a Vampire right along with Juan.

"Thanks. I get lost sometimes, and not in a good place."

Recco drew his dark brows together. His native heritage showed in his high cheekbones, deep-brown eyes, and beak of a nose. Straight black hair fell untidily around his face to shoulder level. Like all of them, he'd borrowed heavily from clothing stowed aboard the ship. Black woolen pants hung off slender hips, and a warm red jacket was zipped to his chin.

"What were you chewing over?"

Juan shrugged, suddenly uncomfortable. "When I was turned. It's not one of my better memories."

Recco snorted. "Mine, either. Daide and I mourned for months. We limited ourselves to rat blood when the hunger grew so overpowering it was all we could think about. Mostly, we tried to find real food. Got harder as the years went by, though."

Juan held up a hand. "It's okay. We don't need to dig any deeper into trading war stories. How come you decided not to go ashore with Viktor?"

"I would have, but I was asleep. Was there an announcement?" At Juan's nod, he went on. "Must have been out pretty good. Any chance of floating another raft? It's not like we're on any kind of schedule."

"It could probably be arranged." Juan smiled. "Let's wait until Viktor gets back."

"Who went with him?"

"Four of the women. Ketha, Aura, Rowana, and Karin."

"Good. Means Zoe is still here." Recco glanced away. "Never mind. Didn't mean to open my mouth."

Juan quirked a brow. "Interested in her, are you?"

"You might say that. She's incredible with her lilting Irish brogue and those masses of red hair." Recco's copper cheeks developed a rose tone, but he didn't look away. "Her eyes remind me of a doe. All soft and brown and gentle."

"Do you know what kind of Shifter she is?" Juan asked.

Recco nodded. "Coyote. They're sacred to my people."

"This might be a great opportunity to talk with her," Juan said. "Ship's quiet. You don't have to scream to be heard over the wind."

"Maybe I will." Recco angled his head. "How about you?"

"How about me, what?" Juan had understood what he meant, but the question brought up a welter of uncomfortable feelings. States of mind he hadn't had to think about for years.

"The women. Do you like any of them?"

Juan chucked. "Why? Are you considering a double date?"

Recco's gaze sharpened in speculation. "You're hedging. Why?"

Heat moved slowly up his chest and neck to his face, and Juan cursed his fair skin. "Because I only have time for the ship right now."

Recco rolled his eyes. "Spare me. We're all working our asses off. You can tell me. I won't blab."

A likeness of Aura blasted into Juan's mind, far more pleasant than his earlier imagery of Raphael and Vampires.

"Aha!" Recco made a thumbs-up sign. "There is someone. If you ever want to talk about it, I'll be around." Spinning on his heel, he strode out of the bridge.

Juan retrieved his coffee and drained the cup. It was cold, but it didn't matter. He'd been meaning to find some surreptitious way to learn more about Aura, the blonde mountain lion Shifter who was Ketha's closest friend. Like if she'd left a husband back in Wyoming. Or a fiancé. Or even a boyfriend. All he knew was she'd held a teaching post at some university and was an expert on magical prophecies.

The sway of her hips when she walked and the curves beneath her layers of clothing had caught his eye. Once he'd begun to pay attention to her, smitten followed fast. She'd become a favorite fantasy object when he lay in his bunk, but he felt guilty for stroking himself to orgasm while constructing visions of what she might look like naked. His cock swelled to fullness when he thought about her, and Juan rearranged it so it wasn't bent at an uncomfortable angle.

Vampires were plenty capable of sex, but Juan had borrowed a page from Viktor's book and remained celibate. The female Vamps never appealed to him, and he'd be damned if he'd take a human against her will—if he could even have located one. They'd barricaded themselves into strongholds right after the Cataclysm. Shifters had helped, hiding the locations with their considerable magic.

"One more walk down memory lane," he muttered. Not much percentage in looking back, but once he'd kicked the door open, it didn't close easily.

He'd wanted to engage Aura in conversation several times, but the trip across the Scotia Sea had been hard. When he wasn't at the helm, he was either asleep or eating. And she'd been seasick, right along with many of the women. She'd get over it. Everyone did, eventually—or they gave up on going to sea.

"You should approach her," his cat spoke up.

Juan almost dropped his coffee cup. The whole Shifter gig was so new to him, he didn't often think about his recently bonded mountain lion. He'd had a hell of a good time shifting and running before they left Ushuaia, but since they'd been aboard *Arkady,* he hadn't had spare time to do much of anything not directly involved in moving the ship from Point A to Point B.

"Why might that be?" he asked his bond animal. Talking out loud to it still felt odd, but he was alone on the bridge so he didn't have to explain anything to anyone.

"I know her cat. We've roamed together for a very long time. It would be a good mating for both of you."

Juan strode to the window and glanced out at the remains of Grytviken with its collection of enormous cylindrical storage towers. Raphael had no sooner turned him than he'd force-fed him more information than Juan ever wanted about being a Vampire.

So far, he knew less than nothing about being a Shifter.

"Help me understand," Juan said. "If I hook up with a woman, do you and her animal mate as well?"

"Not the way you mean," the cat replied. *"I have a body. You know because you've shifted into it, but mostly we're creatures of spirit."*

"Just because you get along with Aura's cat, is it a reason why she and I might…" Juan struggled to find words, but the cat saved him the trouble.

"Yes."

The radio crackled to life. Juan vaulted to where it lived in its cradle attached to the wall and snapped it up.

"Juan here."

"Possible Vampire sighting. Secure *Arkady* and come now." Viktor's deep voice crackled with fury.

Breath whooshed from Juan as if someone had socked him in the guts. "Aw Jesus! Really? I'll drop the other decent raft into the water and bring Recco and Daide with me. Where are you?"

"By the barracks. Don't waste your time stopping in the town."

"Roger that. Be there in half an hour or less."

"The iron saber is in the big equipment locker on Deck Three. Bring it along, and make damn sure it doesn't puncture the raft."

Juan sucked air through his teeth; madness trod close to the surface. He'd die before he let another Vampire turn him. "Aye, aye, Captain. Your faith in me is touching."

"By the time you get here, we'll either be dead or turned or breaking bread with the bastards."

The radio clutched in Juan's white-knuckled hand spat static. "You're sure it's Vamps and they're alive?" Incredulity underscored his question.

"Affirmative on the alive part. See you soon."

"Roger that. Over and out." Juan tucked the two-way radio

into his jacket in case Viktor needed to communicate something critical before he got there.

Running on autopilot, he pulled the keys needed to engage the ship's engine and dropped them into a pocket. Pirates had never been a problem this far south, mostly because no pirate in his right mind plied the Roaring Forties and Fifties. They were more a scourge around Australia and Polynesia. The Arabian Sea and Indian Ocean too.

But if Vamps lived on South Georgia, they may well have been searching for an escape route for years. His muscles felt like rocks. He'd hoped to the bottom of his soul he was done with Vampires for the rest of his natural life.

"Get over it," he muttered and pushed the button on the PA system.

"Recco. Daide. Meet me on Deck Four next to the crane immediately. We're heading to shore. All women will remain on board. I'll explain later."

If there is a later...

He piled into his outdoor gear, layering a waterproof bib and jacket over his insulated jacket and pants. A pair of knee-high Wellingtons came next.

He patted the pocket with the ship's keys, wondering what to do with them. The hard truth was, if he and Viktor didn't make it back, *Arkady* would sit in King Edward Cove forever. Perhaps a fitting end for a ship that had spent much of her life in these waters. Juan hung onto the keys. He'd be damned if he'd make it easy for anyone to commandeer the boat. After pelting down three decks, he scooped up the saber. It was right where Viktor said, but Juan would have been surprised if it wasn't. Organization had always been Viktor's middle name.

Sword in hand, he clambered up one flight and ran to the large crane that moved Zodiac rafts in and out of the water. Some of the newer, fancier Antarctic cruise ships had helicopters. He and Viktor had been on the verge of buying one until the Antarctic

Tour Operators' Association ruled ships had to have two. In case one ended up stranded.

It would have meant two pilots and a whole lot of expense, so the project ended up on a back burner.

Recco and Daide were waiting for him, bundled against the cold. "What's up?" Daide asked. "Hey! What are you doing with Raphael's saber?"

Juan activated the crane. "Viktor and the others need help."

"What kind of help?" Recco chimed in. "If it's bad enough you need a sword, should I bring medical supplies?"

I wish it were that simple.

Juan turned to face the other men. "It appears what we did in Ushuaia didn't eliminate all the Vampires."

Shock and horror bloomed on Recco's face. "Jesus. I want to puke."

"How is that even possible?" Daide choked out the words.

"I have no fucking idea. Look. I'll ride the raft down to the water. You two scurry down the gangway. I'm sure it's still deployed. I'll meet you there, and we'll go find out."

The men ran for stairs leading to the gangway level. Juan watched them flee as if the dogs of Hell were after them.

Who am I kidding? Vampires are worse than a whole horde of Hell hounds.

Juan laid the saber carefully in the bottom of the raft and climbed in after it. He gripped the upper end of the sling, set the crane to its down position, and waited until the raft settled onto the water. When Viktor left earlier, Juan had manned the sling apparatus, hauling it back into *Arkady*. For now, he unclipped the raft, secured the loose ends of the sling to a bolt, and called it good. Seawater eroded everything, but it was the least of their current problems.

Forcing a calm he was far from feeling had become second nature during his years at sea, and he borrowed shamelessly from his past life. What he wanted to do was get the hell out of this bay, but he couldn't leave Viktor and the women who'd gone ashore with him.

Besides, the whole purpose of this trip was to assess what was left of the world. If Vampires still prowled, they needed to know about it. An unsettling thought slammed into him. If Vampires were alive anywhere, it had to mean the Cataclysm wasn't dead, either.

3

COLLATERAL DAMAGE

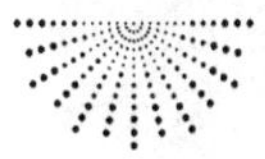

AURA JUDGED the distance between them and the barracks. Perhaps a hundred yards remained. Within her, the mountain lion prowled restlessly. It wanted out. If there were Vampires to face, it viewed itself as a more capable adversary than she was.

Viktor drew to a halt and dropped the rifle to his side. The four of them formed a semicircle in front of him.

"What? Why'd you stop?" Ketha shook herself from head to toe. "Sorry. Wolf is giving me a raft of grief."

"Yeah, my cat is too," Aura muttered.

"We probably should wait until Juan gets here," Viktor said. "He'll have the saber. It's far more effective than my rifle. Whatever's out there still has a Vampire feel to me. Did any of you discern anything more definitive?"

Aura paid a thread of seeking magic outward. The information she'd collected earlier hadn't changed. "Vampire, but it's not quite right." She narrowed her eyes and stared at Viktor. "What happens to Vamps who don't have anything to eat?"

A blank expression washed over his face. "I suppose they'd die eventually, but I don't know for certain." He winced. "I was the only one who failed to pay attention to Raphael's lessons because

I was more focused on finding a way out than maximizing the hand I'd been dealt."

Ketha elbowed Aura. "You're thinking it's why they feel different? No food?"

Aura swung in a circle, taking in a landscape littered with bones. Seal bones. Smaller, lighter carcasses might have belonged to birds. "Beyond Vampire, I don't sense anything else alive here. Maybe on the other side of those mountains"—she pointed upward—"but not along this stretch of shoreline. I didn't bother to check the buildings near where we landed the Zodiac. My cat agrees with my assessment, or it would be champing even harder at the bit to come out and hunt."

Karin made a noise between a snort and a grunt. "I'm pretty sure those Vampire fuckers don't die in the way we understand it. Their DNA undergoes some serious rearrangement when they're turned."

"What I wouldn't give for a lab," Ketha muttered. She cast a speculative glance Viktor's way.

"Since you brought it up," he said, "all the research stations have microbiology labs, but they're mostly located on the Antarctic continent."

Aura furled her brows. She knew Ketha well enough to intuit where she was going with her line of inquiry. "First, we have to catch a Vampire." She leveled a pointed glance at her friend. "Then we need a way of preserving tissue samples."

"Would beheading and dropping the whole mess into a deep freeze do the trick?" Viktor asked.

"Maybe, but I'd need a well-fed Vamp for comparison."

"Ewww. Good luck with that," Aura muttered. "I hoped I'd never see another one of those bastards—ever."

Ketha's nostrils flared. "Makes two of us. Hey! I hear an engine."

Aura did as well. The waiting versus not waiting conundrum had solved itself while they talked. She swept the barren landscape again, alert for anything that could help them. Between falling-down buildings and dead marine life, it was far gloomier than Ushuaia had been. At least the city had retained life within its boundaries.

Viktor waved an arm and covered the few feet between the roadway and the shore. The Zodiac veered toward them. Moments later, Juan flipped it around and threw the anchor rope to Viktor. Catching it one-handed, he dragged the craft onto the small rocky beach and tied it off to a good-sized granite boulder.

Juan, Recco, and Daide clambered out, and then Juan reached back inside for the saber. He offered it to Viktor, but the other man shook his head. "Not yet. We need to think this through."

"I figured by the time we showed up, you'd have a plan in place." Juan directed a meaningful look Viktor's way.

"The plan was to wait for the saber," Viktor retorted.

Recco tilted his head back, scenting the air. "It's not quite right for Vamps," he announced.

Aura nodded slowly. "Do any of you know what happens to Vampires when there's no more food? Or blood?"

"Sure." Juan nodded. "Viktor should know. How come you didn't ask him?"

"She did." Viktor set his jaw in a tense line. "I'm the one who didn't pay any attention to Raph. Remember?" He made come-along motions at Juan. "Spit out whatever it is, so we can get moving."

"Vampires go into a kind of stasis without food," Juan said. "Since they aren't exactly alive, they don't exactly die, either. From what Raph said, they can remain viable with zero sustenance for centuries."

"What?" Karin sneered. "Waiting for blood to show up?"

"About the size of it," Recco cut in.

Daide frowned. "If I recall correctly, Vamps coming out of stasis are vicious. Even more so than normal. We'd do well to proceed with caution."

"I'm not doubting Raph said that, but whomever we sense must know we're out here." Juan spoke slowly. "They'd have heard the boat—and us talking."

"Good point," Aura said. "Why haven't they stormed us?"

"We'll never find out from here," Viktor muttered. "This isn't much of a strategy, but let's trade." He gave the rifle to Juan, taking the saber in return. "Are we agreed whatever we sense is coming from the center building?"

After everyone nodded, he went on. "We'll pair up. Ideally, I'd like to approach the building on the three sides with doors, but we all need to be close to the saber."

"How about if we form a line with you in the middle?" Juan suggested. "And me on one end with the gun. If I have to shoot, none of us will be in the way."

"Sounds good to me." Viktor reached into a pocket and drew out a handful of shells. Juan made a grab for them, checking the rifle to see if any were chambered.

"It's loaded, and the safety is off," Viktor said curtly. "I should have told you that up front."

"Thanks, *amigo.*" Juan dropped the ammo into his own pocket.

Viktor eyed the women. "Can you spin or weave, or whatever the term is, protection around us if we're spread out in a row?"

"Sure," Ketha said, "but it might not mean much to a determined Vampire."

Viktor moved to the center spot and took off at a rapid pace. If looks could kill, anything they ran into would shrivel up and die from fright.

Everyone else fanned out to one side or the other and ran to keep up.

Aura trotted next to Juan. Ketha was on her other side. The closer they got to the barracks, the stronger a disgusting smell grew. Vampire raised to the nth degree, but ones who'd been rolling in their own shit—and vomit. Decaying vegetation mingled with the sickly-sweet rot of putrefied meat. Rotten-egg stench overlaid everything, along with the sharp sting she associated with formalin. Her eyes watered, and her lungs burned.

"At least two. Maybe three or four," Aura muttered.

"My take as well," Ketha said. "Jesus, breathing is painful."

"What I don't get is where the greeting party is—and why they smell so godawful." Juan punctuated his words with a disgusted grunt. "Worst Vampire sloth I ever saw was after Jorge beheaded Raphael and ended up coated in dried blood he didn't bother to wash off."

Aura breathed shallowly through her mouth. They'd reached the front of the building. Viktor twisted the door handle. "Goddammit. It's locked."

Ketha moved in front of him. Power flared from her fingertips. A rusty, squealing sound battered Aura's ears as the lock reluctantly gave way.

Viktor grabbed Ketha's arm. "Stay back," he instructed, and gave the door a good, hard kick. It swung open, and he trotted inside, cursing in German, sword raised and ready.

Aura gagged. If she'd thought the smell was bad before, it was nothing compared with now. "What the fuck?" she blurted. "It's cold here. Far too cold for anything to decay. Hell, I've come across carcasses in the tropics that didn't smell this bad."

"Yeah. I wondered about the stench too." Juan angled his body between her and the building and raised the gun to firing position. "I'm going after Viktor. The rest of you remain here."

Before she could lodge a protest, mention the women's magic trumped the men's by a good big bunch, he vanished through the darkened doorway. A long, low whistle followed.

"Safe enough," Viktor called, his voice gruff. "You all should see this."

Aura tugged the front of her parka up so it covered her nose and called a mage light. It flickered a soft violet next to her. As prepared as she'd ever be, she followed the other women inside.

Grimy windows let in enough light, she didn't need her

magical one so she extinguished it. Breath clotted in her throat at the scene spread before her. Three men ravaged by various stages of deterioration lay on a scarred beige linoleum floor, but they weren't the source of the stench. A battered oak desk and two chairs were the only furniture in the room.

Karin crouched next to one of the men. "Pretty sure these animal bites"—she pointed—"happened before he died. Which means he's been dead for a considerable time."

Ketha flipped another of the dead men over. "I don't believe this one was ever a Vamp."

"This one wasn't, either," Karin confirmed. "And when these men died, there was still wildlife here. Hungry seals, like as not."

"Which probably means Mr. Unlucky Number Three wasn't a Vampire, either," Aura gritted out and jerked her chin at the third body. Where the hell was the smell coming from? She still sensed Vampires, but where were they?

Viktor rifled through the desk with a dusty computer terminal sitting atop it. He pulled out an assortment of pens and pencils followed by a yellowed envelope.

"What do you have there?" Ketha asked.

"I have no idea." Viktor walked over to a window where the light was better. Balancing the saber so the tip rested on the floor between his boots, he extracted a sheet of paper from the envelope.

"What does it say?" Juan clicked the rifle's safety to on and lowered it before he moved closer to Viktor.

"We want to know too," Recco and Daide said almost in unison.

"Hang on. Probably nothing beyond a requisition list, but I'll read it." Viktor cleared his throat.

"Here we go." He smoothed the paper in front of him, and his eyes widened.

"Not a shopping list, after all?" Ketha asked.

"Nope. It's not. Listen up. This looks interesting."

"Come on, *amigo*, the suspense is killing me." Juan craned his neck to peer over Viktor's shoulder as he began to read.

"In the unlikely event anyone finds this—or our bodies—my name is Richard Laurie. My companions are Chris Stott and Harold Johnson. We're British citizens, and we're the last survivors on South Georgia Island. Something hideous happened, and a dark barricade held us prisoner here. No ships could penetrate it, nor could we leave.

"Our communication with the outside world faded after a few years, and we knew we'd die here. Fifteen others died before us, and we buried those we could in the cemetery on the far side of the post office, a courtesy I'd request of anyone who finds us. There's something odd happening inside the church, so a simple burial will suffice. No need to try for anything like a service.

"But I digress. After we'd been trapped here for about four years, three abominations crawled over the Allardyce Range and into Grytviken—"

"Are those the mountains behind us?" Rowana broke in.

"Yes," Juan answered.

"Sorry, go on." Rowana crooked two fingers Viktor's way.

Viktor nodded and turned the page to its other side. "There's no easy way to say this, and whoever reads this probably won't believe me, but those three creatures were Vampires. I had no idea such a thing even existed outside of legends and bad television, but I got over it damned fast.

"They grabbed two of our number, drained them of blood, and resurrected them as creatures of evil, of night. Chris and Harold and I knew we had to do something. One thing Grytviken had was a well-stocked laboratory. It's one building down from this one and locked tight—"

"Hey! Great news!" Ketha crowed. "Bet the air's cleaner there too."

"If you all don't stop interrupting, I'll never finish," Viktor protested.

"Sorry. Got excited at the prospect of test tubes and micro-scopes." Ketha might have been smiling, but she had her jacket pulled over her nose and mouth the same way Aura did.

"Watch it. I'll get jealous." Viktor rolled his eyes. "Last bit here." He ran a finger over the page, probably hunting for where he'd left off reading.

"We mixed an infusion of silver powder and iron since folk tales suggested supernatural creatures were sensitive to one or both elements. I'm not proud of this next part, but one of our research team was very close to death. She had cancer. A ship had been on its way to pick her up and take her to Argentina for medical treatment when the barricade closed us in. In any event, she agreed to serve as bait and drank the infusion knowing it would kill her.

"The predictable happened. All five Vampires closed in on her as she walked the ocean-side road. We watched from the sidelines to make certain everyone drank from her. They were hungry enough, they all did, after a huge argument about whom she belonged to. Thank God no one suggested turning her, maybe because she was so sick. The next part happened fast. So fast, Linda was still alive when the five of them collapsed.

"We moved like lightning and dragged them into a sub-base-ment beneath this office. It's partially sunk into the ground, and the small windows have iron bars on them. We bound the Vampires with iron chains and barred the door from this side, also with iron.

"To be on the safe side, Chris, Richard, and I traded off keeping watch with a shotgun at the ready. You see, we'd made special shells with silver powder and iron filings in the casings, but we never needed them.

"By the time we went back for Linda, she was dead. Ground was too hard to even try to bury her. You won't find her body. Something got her. Probably seals. I tried to keep track of time, but I may have missed a day here or there. We lived for another year or so after we captured the Vampires. They kicked up an unholy fuss for the first few months but then grew quiet. They never stopped stinking, though.

"Maybe they died? I have no idea, but none of us were willing to go back down there to check on them.

"This is about it. I'm the last. Chris and Richard are gone. We still had food, but the water went bad. It's what did us in in the end."

"Jesus." Viktor glanced up and exhaled briskly. "That poor sod."

"No kidding," Juan said. "Is there more?"

"No. His writing got wavery. I suspect he penned this right before he died."

"At least it explains why we sense Vampires," Aura muttered.

"Yup, and why we'll leave the bastards right where they are," Rowana cut in. "They've been here for years, which means they can't get out."

Recco crossed to the desk and attacked the lower drawers.

"What are you hunting for?" Daide joined him.

"These!" Recco withdrew two boxes of shells. "Must be the ones they cooked up with silver and iron. It's a great idea. We'd be stupid to leave them."

"They probably aren't the correct caliber for this gun." Juan raised the rifle he'd never let go of.

"No, but I bet they'll work in the old-fashioned firearm on the floor over there." Daide loped to the back of the room and picked up a dusty rifle, slinging it across his shoulders.

"Nice work." Viktor nodded approvingly.

"Come on." Juan led the way out of the room with its air-stealing reek.

"Are we going to bury those men like they asked?" Aura asked once they were all back outside. "I didn't see Linda on our way up from the town, so Richard was probably right about an animal dragging her into the ocean or its lair."

"An animal that died from heavy metal poisoning after its

meal," Karin mumbled.

"Recco kicked at the ground. "Pretty frozen after ten years of perpetual winter. It would be hard to get a shovel into it."

"We could haul them into the harbor and give them to the sea," Juan suggested.

"We could," Viktor agreed. "The part I don't understand is why the demise of the Cataclysm didn't strip whatever's in the basement of their Vampire essence. By my count, they should have turned into Shifters or back into the humans they once were."

"I was thinking about it," Juan said, "but you won't like what I came up with."

"Which was?" Viktor leveled his green eyes on his friend.

Juan shrugged. "It's clear enough. We may have beat back the Cataclysm around Ushuaia, but its energy is alive and well elsewhere. Not at full strength, or we'd never have been able to sail into King Edward Cove, but the world truly is one ocean, and we've barely covered one percent of it between Ushuaia and here."

"Makes it even more important for me to see what's left in the lab," Ketha said. "According to Richard, it's one building over."

Karin narrowed her copper eyes. "I still think it's a risk. Touching anything here may well bring contamination aboard the ship."

"Too late. We already laid hands on the corpses." Viktor rattled the letter still clutched in his hand.

Recco held up the boxes of shells and shrugged. "Not leaving these here."

"At least if I found a decent microscope and some chemicals, I might be able to identify stray microbes," Ketha argued.

Karin tossed a hand skyward. "Fine. If you come up with some mutated bacterium we don't have an antibiotic for, it's on your head."

Ketha made a sour face. "What are the odds?"

"Maybe two or three percent." Karin shrugged. "Don't mind me. I have no idea why I'm so crabby. I spoke out of turn when I inferred you might bring doom down on us. My wolf is giving me hell over it."

"Thank God for the bond animals." Ketha grinned and headed toward the neighboring building. "I'll be quick about this," she called over her shoulder.

"Need help?" Viktor ran after her, the saber still clutched in one fist.

"Sure. Two of us can carry twice as much stuff." Ketha turned to wink at her husband.

"Daide and I will take charge of those bodies," Recco said. "Once we've deposited them into the harbor, we'll bring the raft back for Viktor and Ketha."

"Excellent," Juan said. "The women and I will go back for the raft Viktor left on the beach near town. At least we all have a weapon. Vik has the sword. I have this rifle, and you two have the other one."

Daide glanced at it. "It's an old bolt-action Remington. Nice gun. I'll clean it up once we're back aboard *Arkady*."

"Let's get moving, Bud. I want to get this over with." Recco walked back inside.

Daide followed. "We won't be able to lock it up once we're done," he called over one shoulder.

"See if Ketha can't secure it," Juan replied.

"Will do." Daide vanished inside the barracks building.

The road was wide enough for them to walk four abreast. For the first half mile, no one said much. Aura enjoyed Juan's solid presence by her side, but he probably wasn't aware she'd been casting surreptitious glances his way since the lot of them fought the Cataclysm.

"I'm not sure quite what I thought we'd find beyond Ushuaia." Rowana's voice lacked its usual sarcastic edge.

"Me, either," Karin said. "But I didn't expect imprisoned Vampires."

"None of us did," Juan agreed. "I've been puzzling through

what it might mean for other locations. And trying to figure out where the three Vampires came from in the first place."

"Are there other settlements on this island?" Rowana asked. "Seems big enough."

"It is," Juan said. "And sure, there were other settlements. Lots of them. Leith Harbor. Stromness. Godthul. Ocean Harbor, to name a few. They're all lined up on the northeast aspect of the island because it's the lee side. The southwest coastline is an absolute bitch. It's where Shackleton ended up before he engineered his heroic crossing to get help for the men he'd left on Elephant Island."

Aura smiled. "You sound like a tour guide."

"Sometimes I was, in a pinch." Juan grinned back. "Anyway, I figure the Vamps showed up here on a ship. Maybe the same storm that drove our other boat aground at the very front end of the Cataclysm nailed them too. This is all conjecture, but once they ran out of food on the windward coast—or got sick of the storms—they crossed the mountains and came out in Grytviken."

"The smell of human blood would have drawn them." Karin nodded agreement.

The small group reached the other Zodiac.

"Does anyone want to explore the town before we go back?" Juan asked.

"What's here?" Aura took in a series of buildings in various stages of disrepair.

"The museum and gift shop are in the same building, and it appears to be intact." Juan jerked his chin at a whitewashed structure. "Even if it's locked, that doesn't stop you guys. And the church up the hill was in decent shape."

"Richard mentioned the church in his letter." Rowana frowned.

"Yeah. He said there was something odd about it." Karin rolled her eyes. "All churches are a wee bit odd, if you ask me. Modern organized religions never approved of Shifters."

"So we stick with the museum." Juan smiled. "I'd like to see it again. We may never get back this way."

"Given the Vampires, it's a sure bet." Aura snorted. "Never was a lock a determined Shifter couldn't defeat." She scanned the harbor and saw the other Zodiac headed for the middle of the bay, presumably with Chris, Harold, and Richard's bodies. "I feel sad for those men, the ones who sat guard over the Vamps," she murmured.

"Why?" Karin drew her brows into a thick, thoughtful line. "I wish we'd thought of poisoning Vampires with silver and lead. Might have made the last decade easier."

Rowana shook her head. "Nah. Too many of them in Ushuaia. Once we'd lured one group and destroyed them, the others would have gotten wise to us."

"Maybe so." Karin twisted her mouth into a grimace. "Those years in Ushuaia would have been ever so much better with only us and the humans, though."

"Even I agree with your assessment," Juan said. "And I used to be one of the enemy. Come on. Let's see what's left in the gift shop. If they have warm clothing the mice haven't turned into Swiss cheese, I say we move it aboard *Arkady*."

Aura followed him up from the beach to a network of branching dirt streets. They'd held up better than the one leading to the barracks, probably because the ocean hadn't had as much of a chance to erode them.

Juan turned to her. "If the museum hasn't been plundered—and there's no reason to believe it was—there's a stuffed wandering albatross suspended from the ceiling. Sucker had about a fourteen-foot wingspan. Those birds could travel thousands of miles."

"You love this part of the world, don't you?" Aura cast a sidelong glance his way in time to see him nod enthusiastically, hazel eyes glittering with excitement.

"That I do. We spent summers—northern hemisphere summers—in the Arctic because we couldn't afford not to work half the year, but I couldn't wait for winter to return. I was born in Buenos Aires and spent my entire boyhood yearning to travel south." He stopped in front of a wooden door with the varnish peeling off in ragged strips.

Aura reached for the knob, turning it to check if it required magic. It rattled but refused to turn.

"I've got this," Karin announced, and a quick, hot jab of magic pulsed from her. The knob turned of its own accord, and the door creaked open.

The smells of camphor and lemon wafted out in a blast of stale air. "Whew! This place has been closed up for a while." Rowana slipped through the open door.

"Careful," Aura called after her. "We don't know—"

"I'm sure it's fine." Karin followed Rowana inside.

"Do you sense anything?" Juan asked and closed his fingers around Aura's arm. Heat from the contact seared her, and she leaned closer.

"I'm not sure. My cat's been quiet. If something bad were here, it would warn me."

"Good to understand how being a Shifter works. I'm still getting to know my bond animal. I figure it will take years at the rate I've been going." He tugged gently on her arm. "Come on. Let's have a look at the albatross."

He led her through the door and into a small museum. Time slipped by as they examined old log books and clothing and accoutrements left over from the 1800s. Everything was covered with years' worth of dust. Juan was a veritable treasure trove of information, and she could have listened to his deep, rich voice forever.

"Wonder what happened to Karin and Rowana?" Juan glanced around.

Aura had been thinking the same thing. "They both love to shop," she said. "Bet they got lost pawing through things."

"Let's round them up," Juan said. "The gift shop isn't very

large." Worry lined his words, and a frisson of discomfort frittered down Aura's spine.

"Rowana! Karin!" she called, but they didn't answer.

Her discomfort turned to fear, and she ran through the building, hunting through the gift shop and a couple of storage rooms and meeting areas. Juan remained by her side. When there was nowhere left to look, she spun to face him. "Where else could they be?" she demanded.

The skin around his eyes pinched with apprehension. "I don't know. Can you deploy magic to hunt for them?"

She slapped her forehead with the palm of one hand. "Of course. I'm still rattled from those Vampires." Aura raced outside, hoping against hope Karin and Rowana would be lounging against the side of the building swathed in spells, but they weren't.

Her throat thickened with foreboding. She shut her earth eyes, surveying the landscape with her third eye as she paid out power, hunting for her friends. Ley lines formed, showing her the charged grid connecting sacred sites all over the world.

Juan's energy pulsed next to her, but he held silence.

Aura battled fury and disbelief. As well delineated as the ley lines were, she couldn't find Karin or Rowana. Aura kept searching, determined not to miss any clues. When she finally dropped her casting and opened her eyes, Juan demanded, "What did you find?"

She inhaled raggedly, feeling jittery from a walloping dose of adrenaline. "Nothing. I found nothing. It's like the earth swallowed them up."

He grabbed her shoulders and stared hard at her, looking worried. "People don't just disappear. Something must be masking them from you."

Her head snapped up. "No other explanation, now, is there? The masking element has to be magical. I've been barking up the wrong tree. Seeking their emanations when I should have launched a far more global search."

4

WEIRDNESS SQUARED

Juan pulled out his radio and keyed in a pattern.

"What are you doing?" Aura demanded, her voice shrill.

"Alerting Viktor to show up as fast as he can with Ketha, Recco, and Daide. We should be together to deal with whatever this is."

"Why not use telepathy?"

"Because I'm not very good at it yet." He pocketed the radio, and it rattled when it landed atop the nest of rifle shells. Breath hissed through his teeth, and he shook the rifle. "Damn thing isn't worth the metal it was cast from. Not against something magical."

Aura ground her teeth. "Let me try this once more."

"Try what? What exactly are you doing?" Juan didn't want to bother her, but he needed to understand how her magic worked. Even though he shared the same supernatural ability, he'd barely scratched the surface of what it meant to be a Shifter.

"Deploying power again, but differently. Last time, I opted for a psychic view where I visualized ley lines. They should have identified Rowana and Karin's location, but they didn't help. Now, I'm hunting, plain and simple, for anything fueled by magic."

He wanted to ask what she meant by ley lines. As he under-

41

stood them, they were hypothetical alignments between sacred places in ancient landscapes. Things like cairns and beacon hills and the like. Making a mental note to ask her later, he remained silent.

She turned in a full circle, arms extended as if she were willing clues to drop into her outstretched fingers. Multihued light swirled around her until she looked like an Old-World deity, her fair hair streaked golden and her green eyes on fire.

He slung the rifle across his chest, so his hands would be free, and mirrored her actions. His fingers prickled when he faced the jagged mountains rearing above the townsite, but it was subtle.

She repeated her circle, and he did the same. This time, the prickling was more noticeable, but maybe because he was expecting it.

Aura nodded sharply. "This way." She hurried uphill in the direction he'd picked up the unusual sensation.

The rifle banged against his chest as he bolted after her. When she angled right, he knew they had to be heading for the church. It was the only structure up this way that hadn't been crushed by avalanches.

"Wait." He grabbed her arm.

"Let go." She shook him off and kept moving. "All living things have a particular energy flow. It's like music with pitch and cadence. What I feel is twisted. Like someone—or something—altered the natural world. It's the same way the Cataclysm felt to me. Not something you ever adapt to. It's like listening to fingernails scratching down a chalkboard over and over until you want to put your hands over your ears. Or puncture your eardrums so it stops permanently."

"Aura. Stop. We need a plan. You can't go barreling into some-thing neither of us understands." A fierce need to protect her raged through him, and it was all he could do not to drag her back to the Zodiac.

Christ! I'm thinking like a Neanderthal.

Or not thinking at all.

She ignored him, but she did stop about ten feet in front of the old church. It had ended up a library when none of the seamen showed the slightest interest in baring their souls to God.

"It's here. What I detected is here." Aura narrowed her eyes to slits. "I'd bet anything Karin and Rowana are inside."

The only reason it made sense was because they hadn't found the women anywhere else. Juan marshaled his primitive and largely untested magic, focusing it on the church. The air around the building developed a black tinge, and a perimeter came into view, pulsing with foul enchantment. It was how Raphael had always appeared to him.

Profane.

Broken.

Wicked.

He sucked in an uneven breath. "Why the church? Wouldn't it have been safe?"

She spun to face him. "Why? Who would have protected it from evil? There's no such thing as God. Not the one this church was dedicated to, anyway. The living gods and goddesses didn't require buildings to round up their followers."

His Catholic roots rebelled. "Fine. You can skip the lecture on theology."

The planes in her face hardened still further. "No time for this. Open your magic to me. I'll leverage power from us both and blast through the wall separating us from whatever's inside."

"What happens if we try to walk through it?"

"You don't want to know." Her nostrils flared. "Crap. I hope Ro and Karin are inside because if they're not, I'm fresh out of ideas."

She extended both arms and instructed, "Take my hands, and then hang on no matter what happens."

Questions must have danced behind his eyes because she added, "It's the easiest way for me to link with you."

He slipped the rifle over his head and laid it on the ground, flipping off the safety. If he needed it in a hurry, he didn't want to be tangled in the shoulder strap or grappling to find the safety switch. Turning until he faced Aura, he gripped her fingers. Heat sluiced through him; desire riddled with power seared his nerve endings.

Deep within him, his cat purred and made little, satisfied mewling sounds, as if Aura's magic were like mother's milk. Who knew? Maybe it was. Power raced through him in a blistering tide, dangerous and exhilarating. The black shielding around the church shuddered and moaned, as if it were alive and they'd injured it.

"What's doing that?"

She angled a pointed look right at him. "I don't know, but Vampires aren't the only wickedness in this world. Far from it."

Juan thought about the Cataclysm and the Archangel who'd helped them break its chokehold on Ushuaia.

There's a whole hell of a lot I know nothing about.

No time like now to begin addressing my shortcomings.

He stretched his boundaries, reaching through layers he hadn't explored since his transformation from Vampire to Shifter. When he'd been a Vamp, he'd never wanted to study his ability. The less he did that screamed Vampire, the better he liked it. While he'd enjoyed hunting in mountain cat form, it was as far as his foray into Shifter-hood had gone.

Aura tightened her grip on him, nails cutting into the backs of his hands. "Give me more," she gritted. "All you've got. It's weakening."

He opened his mouth to ask how she knew and how much more output they'd need to defeat the thing. Part of him shied away from such a sloppy undertaking. He was a navigator. Charts and maps and trajectories were where he lived. They offered precision.

Not always.

His thoughts provided a grim reminder of storms scouring the Southern Ocean. And oft as not the Arctic seas as well.

"Your mind is wandering." Aura's voice cut like a whip. "Help me."

He locked gazes with her and visualized his magical well expanding and flowing into her.

A fey smile split her full lips. "Yes. Perfect. Keep it coming."

The blackness grew denser, more visible. It shimmied like a bellows beating in and out. The air thickened with the stench of sulfur, almost as if the weathered church had turned into a portal to Hell.

"Hold fast. We have this." Aura shouted words in Gaelic.

Two more pulses and a piercing roar pounded against him. He would have slapped his hands over his ears, but he couldn't extricate them from Aura's death grip. Besides, she needed him. They were doing this together. He bellowed in pain as the growling, tearing noise escalated.

It sounded like the earth was folding in on itself, and he expected to see a crater ripped out of the rocky ground, one deep enough to suck them into the underworld.

The shadow around the church blew outward, showering them with sharp particles. He pulled Aura against him, shielding her face and head with his hands. Blood trickled from where shards cut him, but they were superficial. His ears ached, but they'd settle out.

She writhed in his arms. "Let go of me. The worst of this part is done. We have to go inside."

"Are the women in there? Can you sense them now?" He smoothed bits of shrapnel out of her hair and released her. She'd felt amazing locked in his arms, like she'd been born to be part of him. Did she feel the attraction as keenly as he did? Or at all?

"Yes. Something's still holding them prisoner, but they're inside." She eyed him. "You okay?"

"I'll live."

"Karin's a gifted healer. She can patch you up once she's free." Aura trotted the few feet to the door and splayed her fingers across it. She made a sour face. "What the fuck is inside? It feels like I ran my power through a vat of demon shit."

"Probably the same entity that built the thing we just crushed. Damn! No wonder Richard said the church felt odd. Talk about British understatement."

Aura lowered her hands until they hovered around a brass latch. It turned without a hint of protest as soon as her magic ignited, almost as if its mechanism had been well-oiled in anticipation of today. A shiver rattled down his spine. Mariners were a superstitious lot, and he had a bad feeling about what lay on the other side of the door.

Juan snatched up the rifle and pushed between her and the weathered wooden door. "I'm going first." Without waiting for her to tell him he could piss up a rope, he tripped the latch and kicked the door open.

Two big strides brought him inside. He was familiar with this building. He'd led many, many groups of tourists through it. Not much familiar was left. The pews were turned on their sides and the crucifix ripped from the wall. What had always been a quiet, peaceful spot bore the ravages of destruction and revenge.

Who the hell would have done such a thing?

Aura strode to his side. "Show yourself," she commanded in a voice ringing with authority.

Juan stared at her. "Who are you talking to? And where are Rowana and Karin?"

She skinned her lips back from her teeth. "We're not alone. I don't understand how, but there's a guardian here."

"What's—?"

"I'll explain later. Show yourself," she repeated. "I command you in the name of Gaia, mother goddess of the world."

A snarling roar tore at Juan's damaged ears. From the far end of the sacristy, a man rose from nowhere. He hadn't been there a moment before. Juan was certain of it. The church had been empty except for them.

The man wore stained vestments. Dark hair hung in matted snarls to his waist, tangling with a straggly beard. Screeching in a language Juan had never heard before, the man shambled toward them on bare feet that held stigmata as if he'd been nailed to a cross. Blackened holes, a mockery of Christ's markings, defiled his palms as well. Madness rained from the priest as he hurtled toward them, dark eyes brimming with an otherworldly light.

"What is he?" Juan ground out and raised the rifle to his shoulder.

"Once upon a time, he was human. Not anymore. Don't shoot him."

"Why not?" He relaxed the finger curled reflexively around the trigger.

"He might hold the key to releasing Ro and Karin."

Juan wanted to shake her, demand how she knew.

"Steady," his cat spoke up. *"You're new to this. She's not. Trust her."*

Aura raised her arms. Power crackled from her fingers in an arc. It stopped the mad priest in his tracks. Words still spewed from him, and he raised one hand. Black light pulsed around the dark, jagged hole in his palm.

"None of that!" Aura shouted and switched to Gaelic.

Juan had no idea what was going on beyond some fundamental battle between darkness and light. Strain carved deep into Aura's features. Now wasn't the time to engage her in a primer on how Shifter magic worked.

"What can I do to help?" he asked his cat.

"Find the women, and do what I tell you to free them."

"I thought we needed the priest."

"Are you going to argue or help the woman you love? The one I hope we end up mated to someday."

It went against the grain, but Juan turned his form over to his bondmate. He'd merged with its body but never ceded control of his own. At first, he fought the sensation, but it took too much energy, and the cat snarled its displeasure.

Juan reeled in his need to be master of his body, backing off until he sat in a metaphorical theater, watching action unfold on the screen. They moved across the rear of the church and down the far aisle toward the small space converted into a library. The door was closed. Locked. The cat raised one of his arms and shot power through his fingertips. It burned and stung, but the door sprang open.

"*You're still fighting me,*" the cat said. "*It's why your fingers hurt.*"

Excuses sprang into his mind; Juan smothered them. "*Sorry.*"

The cat pushed their body through the doorway. Sure enough, Karin and Rowana were there. They stood stock-still, eyes unfocused, as if in a kind of suspended animation. "*What's wrong with them?*" he asked the cat.

"*They've been ensorcelled. I already told you as much. You don't listen very carefully.*"

Juan winced. He deserved the rebuke, but it still didn't sit well. "*Who did this to them?*"

"*Not sure. Something evil took over the church and turned the priest into a demon.*"

"*How do you know?*"

"*He's talking in demonspeak. No more questions. No misplaced bursts of independent thought, either. Let me do this.*"

Something snapped inside Juan, and he didn't bother with telepathy. The cat could hear either way. "No. I'm going to do this. You tell me what to do. No one has run my life since I wore short pants."

A chuckling purr filled his chest. "*Very good. I wondered if you had any gumption. Wrap the women in power and imagine their prison breaking from the inside out.*"

Aura's Gaelic rose in intensity from the other room.

Juan clacked his jaws together. He wanted to strangle his bondmate for testing him, but it could wait. He raised his hands and visualized white light flowing from his fingers. It wrapped around the two Shifters, cradling them in its glow. Juan pushed harder, but nothing changed. Aura's shrieks battered against the faux priest's bellowing.

"Help me," Juan urged his cat, beyond caring about his misplaced pride.

"Envision water. Lots of water. Big waves. Pull them into your spell, and then splat it against the glowing light from the inside perimeter."

Water was easy. Juan knew it intimately in all its iterations, and he visualized a restless sea driven by gusts of wind. He instructed a wall of seawater to spend itself against the light, pushing from the inside out.

Nothing happened.

He tried again, shepherding an even bigger wave. It crashed against the light and bubbled away to nothing.

"What am I doing wrong?"

"Nothing. Try harder. Dark magic fights back hard."

He stared at Rowana and Karin. Were they slumping from their unnatural upright stance? It might be his imagination, but their eyes didn't appear quite so bleary. Maybe his efforts were working after all.

Juan shut his eyes. To his surprise, a new vista spread before him complete with shining lines stretching through the church and its walls. Ley lines. He was seeing interconnections within the magical world. They had to be what Aura had mentioned. An idea bloomed; he concentrated on the line closest to him. The next time he called water, he drove it along the ley line.

It followed it like a hound intent on prey and smashed against the white light.

Karin and Rowana fell to the floor and rolled upright immediately. At least they weren't in that hideous, unnatural trance anymore, but they were still trapped. Rowana nodded his way, but Juan didn't waste time. The ley lines potentiated his magic. He sent one more tsunami of a wave along the same trajectory.

When it crashed against the glowing light, everything exploded. His already-damaged ears throbbed in protest, but the women were free. They ran to him, talking. Their mouths were moving, but he couldn't hear them.

He couldn't hear anything. Not yet.

"Thank you," he told his cat. Regular speech might be beyond him, but telepathy would work as a replacement.

"For what?"

"Believing in me and a good, swift kick in the backside."

"When the dust settles. And it will, at least this time. You will put in the time it takes to learn about me and being a Shifter. This isn't anything like being a Vampire. It's voluntary. If you continue to ignore your gifts and my magic, I'll break our bond."

"I deserved that. I will do better. I promise."

Karin grabbed his forearm and forced him to look at her. Her mouth was still moving.

"I can't hear," he told her. *"Too many loud noises too close together."*

Nodding, she placed her hands on either side of his head. A warm, soothing sensation flowed from her fingers. He could almost feel it setting damaged cells to rights.

"Better now?" She smiled.

"Yeah. Your voice is still garbled, but at least I can hear. How'd you repair the damage so fast?"

"How else?" Karin grinned. "Magic. Thank you. The trick you did with water was damned impressive."

He opened his mouth to thank her and say they had to hustle back to the main room where Aura was, but his words never had a chance.

"Get down. Now," Viktor bellowed.

A gunshot blasted through the church, followed by one more. They undid whatever healing Karin had done for his ears, but Juan didn't care. He ran through the door. Viktor stood holding the bolt action Remington amid the acrid stench of gunpowder.

The priest lay in a rapidly spreading pool of blood, and Aura was spread facedown, not moving.

Juan covered the space to her prone form in two leaping strides and threw himself atop her body. Pulling her into his arms, he felt for a pulse. "Aura. Jesus. God. Talk to me."

Viktor hunkered next to them. "She's all right, mate."

"Good thing we got here when we did." Ketha hurried over. "That hell-spawned priest almost had her."

Juan looked up, drawn by motion from where the priest sprawled on his back. In defiance to every law of physics, the man struggled to a sit, his chest still spewing blood. "Thank you." Blood burbled from his mouth, staining his beard, but his eyes were clear, dark pools. No trace of madness remained.

Ketha ran to him. "Karin. Help me keep him alive long enough to tell us what happened here."

5

EVIL'S NOT DEAD YET

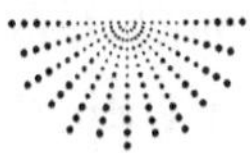

AURA CLAWED her way back from a world scoured by evil. Pervasive darkness had almost snared her. Marked by fire, which yielded heat but not light, and filled with hideous creatures she'd sensed more than seen. The priest's magic must have been driven by Lucifer himself to be so strong. Or one of the truly evil demons like Grigori or Ba'al.

She'd blown through so much magic, lethargy weighted her limbs. Even opening her eyes required gargantuan effort.

Relieved beyond words for her reprieve, she sensed Juan's arms around her and heard Ketha ask Karin for help. That last verbal exchange punched through her inertia. If there was information to be gleaned about her near miss with disaster, she wanted to be in on it.

"I'm fine." She thrashed weakly against Juan.

"Hush." He cradled the back of her head in his splayed fingers.

"I'm all right. Really. Let me go." She wriggled out of his embrace. It wasn't easy. She wanted to remain in those arms and cling to him. She may have escaped the hideous world that had her in its gunsights, but she'd remember what it felt like forever.

The sulfur stench—worse than a hundred Vampires—still burned her lungs and nostrils.

Juan's hazel gaze drilled into her, but he rocked back on his heels.

Karin was still chanting, so the priest wasn't dead yet. Aura lurched to her feet. Her head spun, and she shook herself from top to toe to focus her mind. Logical thought returned in patches, but she was having a hell of a hard time hanging onto anything for more than a couple minutes at a time.

She made her way to where Ketha and Karin crouched over the priest. A nimbus of glowing light surrounded the trio, which meant the women were bypassing speech, and tapping into the priest's mind and memories—while he still had them.

Did she have any magic left to join in?

Ha! Not very likely.

Juan's presence closed from behind her, and he placed his palms on her shoulders. "Let me help."

His distinctive magical signature probed the edges of her depleted center, the reservoir concentrating her power. No reason not to let him in, but she was slow on the uptake, still weak and worn down. Magic spiraled through her as soon as she opened herself. Her mind cleared along with her vision and her other senses.

Surprise spilled through her, companion to her newly heightened clarity. Somewhere between when she'd taken on the priest, challenging the spirit that had taken up residence in his soul, and now, Juan had learned a few things.

Aura joined Ketha and Karin's casting, careful not to disturb them. Considering the spreading pool of blood soaking into the priest's cassock and running across the floor, she didn't understand why he wasn't dead yet. His dark eyes were closed, and the drawn, crazed expression had departed, leaving his features peaceful, serene.

Compassion for her adversary tightened her throat. The priest had been a vessel for evil, nothing more, nothing less. He may have fought at the front end of his possession, but playing host to such wickedness would drain far stronger men than him.

Hell, the demon had almost snatched her up. She'd felt its pull and been well on her way along the downhill slide toward possession and obliteration of her free will. She'd misjudged the strength of the evil she stood against and nearly trapped her bond animal in Hell right along with her.

"Apologize later." Her cat's tone was laced with acid.

Deep in her mind, she felt Juan's shocked intake of breath; his fingers tightened on her shoulders as if he never planned to let her out of his sight. She was still tapped out enough she'd forgotten he'd be privy to her thoughts. Apparently, he hadn't realized how close she'd come to ruin.

Aura refocused fast.

"The priest is gone," Karin said. "Sorry. I did the best I could."

"It was enough." Ketha pushed heavily to her feet. "We got the gist of things."

"Which was?" Aura asked. "Sorry. I'm not at my best."

Karin laid a hand over the priest's forehead and recited the Celtic prayer for the dead before she stood.

"Come on." Ketha headed for the back of the nave where Viktor, Recco, and Daide waited. "I'd rather only say this once."

Aura trotted after her, but focused her words on Juan. "I appreciate the infusion of magic, but you can withdraw your power."

He moved his grip from her shoulder to circle her upper arm. "You took quite a chance."

Aura stopped and shot a sidelong glance his way. "So?"

A complex array of emotion played over his face. Fury. Relief. Determination. "So. Next time be more careful."

She ground her teeth. "I'll do what I think needs doing. We were stuck. We couldn't walk away from the demon using the priest's body."

"I was close. You could have called me."

"I had things under control," she insisted.

"Yeah. Until you didn't." He let go of her abruptly. "Sorry. Didn't mean to be quite so heavy-handed."

She swallowed around a closed place in her throat. He cared. Worse, she wanted him to care, but now wasn't a good time. For any of them. The world wasn't any safer now than when the Cataclysm had them pinned in Ushuaia. Bigger maybe, but not any less threatening.

"It's okay," she mumbled to cover her discomfiture.

One corner of his mouth turned up, forming an enigmatic smile. "My cat says we need to practice blending our magic—once we return to the ship."

Aura furled a brow and continued to the far side of the church where everyone waited for them.

"What?" He walked by her side as they joined the others.

"I bet your cat's been talking with mine." She tilted her chin toward Ketha. "What'd you find out from the priest before he died?"

The wolf Shifter narrowed her eyes. "About what I suspected. Once Vampires showed up here, they kicked a path wide open for other types of evil."

"But why the church?" Recco asked.

"Yeah," Daide chimed in. "I'd have thought this would be the safest place in Grytviken."

Ketha shook her head. "It's actually the opposite."

"I don't understand," Recco muttered.

"It is counterintuitive," Karin agreed. "See, you have to believe in something for it to affect you."

"I don't think so," Viktor growled. "I never believed in Vampires, and look how far it got me."

Karin scrunched her face into a frown. "I'm not doing a very good job explaining myself. Vampires are different."

Aura sucked in a measured breath and took a stab at clarification. "Even with Vamps, you have a choice. It might not be much of one because the will to keep on living—no matter how—is strong. But it's a choice, nonetheless. When Raphael—or whoever—offered lifeblood, you could have refused. It would have kept you out of evil's clutches."

"How does choice relate to him?" Juan pointed at the priest sprawled in a river of congealing blood.

"It doesn't. Not directly. He was a believer," Ketha said. "Which meant he believed in evil as well as good. It's one of the hallmarks of what it takes to become a priest. Not much point in holding up Christ's standard if you don't also recognize the existence of evil."

"The priest understood what was happening once the demon broke through," Karin cut in. "Poor bastard. He never wasted energy thinking he was going crazy, but he figured out damned fast he didn't have enough power to fight the darkness."

"It made him bitter," Ketha added. "He begged God for help. Prayed for all he was worth. Didn't do him a whit of good. He didn't last a week before the demon took over. The stigmata were a cruel joke. The demon nailed him to a cross and kept him impaled long enough to pound home there was nothing holy about Christ's trials. It's how the crucifix ended up on the floor. When the demon pulled the priest down—cross and all—he completed his possession ritual."

"It's how evil triumphs," Rowana spoke up. "By stripping us of our most sacred beliefs and hopes."

"How exactly does demonic possession manifest?" Viktor asked. "Is it like Vampire draining and resurrection?"

Aura shook her head. "No. For one thing, there's no mechanism to create new demons. And the person you were prior to the demon taking over gets lost in the shuffle."

"It happened with some of the Vampires. They drank the Kool-Aid lock, stock, and barrel." Viktor shrugged. "I never figured out why I didn't buy into Raphael's whole shtick, but it always made me feel dirty."

"Yeah, me too," Juan mumbled, with Recco and Daide echoing his words.

"It has something to do with how firmly grounded your sense of self was prior to being turned," Karin said. "With demonic possession, it doesn't seem to matter much. The priest's faith was solid, but it couldn't withstand the demon's onslaught. He might be dead, but we did him a favor killing him. It was his only way out."

Aura took a measured breath, still trying to sort and explain something so bizarre it was painful to think about. "Basically, demons weaken the veil between Hell and this world. If many of them locate vessels—like the priest—to dominate, they alter the cosmic balance and not in good ways. Lucifer has a far easier time promulgating his evil agenda when demons are loose in the world. You see it in escalations in violent crime. People lose the ability to be compassionate, but they don't realize they've changed, which makes it even more insidious."

"Bear with me for a minute," Juan cut in. "If the priest couldn't withstand whatever the demon did, doesn't it indicate most garden-variety men would have the same problem?"

"Of course." Aura waited to see where he was going with his line of reasoning.

"Which might mean an infinite number of demons have already jumped ship out of Hell," Juan continued. "With Vamps, there was never just one. Why wouldn't it be the same with demons?"

"It's possible," she replied. Juan's assumption was logical—and it chilled her to her soul.

"I hate to bring this up"—Viktor cleared his throat—"but what happened to the demon within the priest. Surely we didn't kill it."

"No, we didn't," Aura replied. "Absent a handy vessel, it retreated to Hell. It might have tried picking on one of us, but it probably didn't like the odds. One priest is child's play. Eight Shifters, something else entirely."

"Mmph. Any relationship between demons loose in the world and the Cataclysm?" Juan eyed her. "Something kept Hell's minions contained before, and that something changed."

Aura shivered and glanced at Ketha, Rowana, and Karin. "What do you think?"

"It's all interrelated," Rowana said flatly. "The Cataclysm made it easier for evil to flourish. Its energy propelled Vamps out of the shadows and into plain sight. Before, they snatched a person here and another there, but for the most part they remained hidden from human eyes."

"When Vamps showed up here, presumably after the Cataclysm was in full bloom," Juan muttered, "it must have opened some kind of channel for the demon that seized the priest."

"It's possible," Ketha said. "Either that, or the demon showed up here first, which lured the Vamps over the mountains."

"Damn!" Recco made a sour face. "And here I was thinking Vamps were shortlisted for the evil bastard of the universe title. Turns out they're not even at the top of the heap of badasses."

Aura closed her teeth over her lower lip, thinking. "We don't know how this works," she said slowly. "Not really." She stood straighter. "We understood how things fit together before the Cataclysm, and we believe we know why it happened. Developing a more complete picture of the post-Cataclysm world will have to wait until after we've gone a few more places, possibly found survivors with information."

"I agree," Ketha said. "We'll do ourselves a disservice if we make assumptions based on incomplete data."

"Jesus, but you sound like a scientist." Aura rolled her eyes.

"It's what I am, sweetie." Ketha leveled her golden gaze Aura's way.

"Look on the bright side. We all survived to fight another day. We should get him out of here." Viktor strode toward the priest.

"I'll help." Juan followed and grabbed the dead man's arms.

"What are you going to do with him?" Recco asked.

Viktor hoisted the priest's legs, and he and Juan shuffled toward the door. "Burial at sea, I guess. He can join the whale-bones littering the seabed in this cove. Be sure to grab the saber and the rifles."

Aura picked up the Remington and followed the men out the door. She didn't want to spend another minute in the church; it had nearly been her doom. Another shudder racked her.

"What's wrong?" Ketha fell into step next to her, the saber clutched in one hand.

"Nothing. I'll get over it. Was the hunt good?"

"Huh?"

"When we left you, you were headed for a lab to collect the esoteric equipment you love so much."

Ketha snorted. "Yeah, the hunt was good. Recco and Daide had just gotten back when we picked up Juan's call for help. Vik and I dumped everything we'd collected in the bottom of the raft. Damned convenient not to have to carry it all the way back here."

Breath whistled through Aura's teeth. "Crap! Speaking of rafts, we need to get back. The women on *Arkady* must be worried sick about us."

"They're okay. I used telepathy to let Zoe know."

"Did you tell her how bad things were?"

"Of course not. Only that we'd be a little longer than she might expect."

Aura screwed her face into a grimace. "We have to let them know what happened."

"Sure. We will once we're all back." Ketha's eyes developed an unfocused aspect, which probably meant she was talking with someone.

Aura considered listening in, but her magical well was still perilously low. "Who were you talking with?" she asked once Ketha's attention was front and center again.

"Viktor. He's become surprisingly adept with mind speech.

Anyway, he said for us to all get into the other raft, and they'll meet us at the boat."

Aura glanced around. Recco and Daide were a few feet behind them, but Karin and Rowana were nowhere in sight. "Goddammit! Not again."

"Not again, what?" Ketha asked.

"Karin and Rowana."

"They told us they were detouring through the gift shop," Recco said. "Sorry. Meant to say something, but Daide and I got caught up in conjecture about the Cataclysm." He grinned crookedly. "From a scientific perspective, it's a fascinating topic."

Rowana came into view, angling toward the Zodiac with her arms piled with clothing. Similarly burdened, Karin walked behind her.

"Talk about the hunt being good." Ketha smothered a laugh. Cupping a hand around her mouth, she called, "Did you leave anything behind?"

"Not much," Rowana yelled back.

"I never could resist a good shopping opportunity." Ketha flashed a thumbs-up sign. "Meet you at the raft in a few." She gave the saber to Recco and angled toward the gift shop, running fast.

Aura hurried to Karin and Rowana, holding out the arm not wrapped around the rifle to take some of the loot. "Neither of you ever said, but how the hell did you end up in the church in the first place?"

Color splotched Rowana's face. "Erm. It's kind of a long story."

"Yeah, we weren't careful," Karin said. "The demon laid a magical snare in the gift shop. Probably to assure himself nothing human would set foot in Grytviken he didn't have first dibs on."

"Do you suppose he knew the Vamps were imprisoned below the barracks?" Aura asked.

"I'd guess yes," Rowana replied. "Wonder why he didn't release them?"

Aura quirked a brow. "Maybe even demons don't care much for Vamp company."

"You're funny." Karin muffled a grim snort.

"Regardless," Rowana went on, "I fell for the oldest trick in the book. One of the necklaces was uber-shiny, far more than it should have been. If I'd been thinking, I'd never have touched it. Or I'd at least have tested it with magic first."

"The moment she closed her fingers around it, we got swept into a magical web." Karin continued the tale. "And ended up in the back room of the church, hamstrung with magic. Couldn't move. Couldn't talk."

"Damn!" Aura pushed air through her teeth. "Happened fast, huh?"

"Between the space of two breaths," Rowana said. "I knew the moment I'd tripped the bait, and I threw every bit of magic I had into breaking the spell, but I couldn't even slow it down."

Karin narrowed her eyes to slits and stared at Aura. "How'd you hold the demon off?"

"It's a battle I was losing." It was humiliating to admit, but better than false bravado. "If Viktor hadn't showed up when he did and shot the priest, it would have been too late. The priest would still be dead, but I'd have been swept into Hell."

"Why wouldn't the demon have jumped ship into your body?" Daide asked. They'd reached the Zodiac, and he bent to untie the anchor rope.

Aura dropped the Remington and her armload of clothes into the raft. The other women unloaded their clothes and clambered into the black rubber craft once it was back in the water.

"Do you know?" Daide persisted.

Aura shook her head. "Not really. It's one of the things I meant when I said we didn't understand enough about how good and evil function in a post-Cataclysm world. Demons have always left Shifters alone. Maybe that has something to do with it."

"What if it's not post-Cataclysm?" Ketha called. She ran toward them with her own load of shirts, pants, and jackets overflowing around her folded arms. In one nimble motion, she offloaded the items and followed them into the raft.

"Get in, everyone." Daide motioned with the hand not hanging onto the rope. "I'll be last."

"You'll get wet," Recco observed and gave the saber to Ketha.

Daide shrugged. "Wet's nothing. Today could have been so much worse."

Aura climbed over the pontoon and settled into the Zodiac. Daide was right. They'd escaped disaster by the narrowest of margins.

He tossed the anchor rope to Recco and followed it inside the boat. The tide was with them. Once the raft moved beyond the shallows, he started the engine.

"Maybe it was a poor choice of words," Aura mumbled.

"What was?" Ketha asked.

"Post-Cataclysm. My guess is we're in some intermediate gray zone where it's still out there, but not as strong as it was."

The raft moved toward where *Arkady* rode at anchor at the edge of the cove. No one said much. Aura didn't feel like talking, either. For all she knew, the Cataclysm could be resting up. Whatever face it showed next time might be even more ruthless than what they'd confronted in Ushuaia.

Worse, they'd exposed their strategy. To defeat it a second time —or a third or a fourth—they'd have to come up with something new. Something it wasn't expecting.

Juan waited for them at the bottom of the gangway. Blond hair blew across his eyes, and the chiseled planes of his face reminded her of pictures she'd seen of the old-time Vikings. He was heartbreakingly beautiful, as if he'd been born to conquer the seas. An ache settled behind her breastbone, but whether she yearned for him or simply for companionship eluded her.

"You two head on up," he told Recco and Daide. "I've got the raft from here."

"You sure?" Recco secured the Zodiac to cleats.

"Yup. Quite sure. Dealing with the crane takes practice."

Weariness dogged Aura as she waited to exit the raft. Nowhere near as debilitating as after they'd taken on the Cataclysm, but nor could she pretend she was at the top of her game. She needed food and sleep, not necessarily in any particular order.

One thing was certain. Waiting to see what the world had in store for them wasn't good enough. They'd gotten lucky today, but they had to be better prepared before they ventured much farther. An idea formed, pedaling in tired circles around her equally exhausted brain.

Viktor and the other raft were nowhere in sight, so he'd probably taken it to where the crane raised the Zodiacs out of the water, depositing them on the fourth deck where they lived. She scooped up armloads of clothing they'd stolen from the gift shop, nodded to Juan, and plodded up the wobbly gangway.

We didn't steal anything, she lectured herself.

Not exactly.

Ownership was a concept left over from her old life, the one she'd left behind in Wyoming. She balled her fists into the mass of fabric clutched in her arms until her hands hurt. Aura relaxed her fingers as she reached the third deck and angled inside the ship, headed for her cabin.

She'd do whatever it took to hedge their bets, make certain they survived. Pilfering a few items from a shop that hadn't seen a proprietor in years was small potatoes. She sent a small shot of magic—about all she was capable of—at the latch holding her cabin door shut. It swung open invitingly.

Walking through, she kicked it closed behind her and dropped the tangled mass of clothing onto the other bed, the one she didn't sleep in. She could sort out who got what later. Unzipping her parka, she hung it on a hook next to the door. Her next stop was the sink where she cupped water and dunked her face. Her head throbbed. Feeling dizzy and ill, she turned her attention inward for an overdue conversation with her cat.

"I really am sorry," she told her bondmate, painfully aware she'd almost trapped it right along with herself.

"Skip that part. The question is, what are we going to do so something like today doesn't happen again?"

Aura pitched facedown on the narrow bunk and burrowed beneath a wool blanket. *"I've been thinking about it."*

"Me too," the cat replied. *"You go first."*

6

BEST LAID PLANS

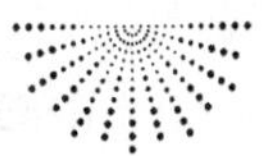

JUAN WAITED until everyone cleared out of the raft. The events in Grytviken had rattled them. He saw it in slumped shoulders, set expressions, and sparse conversation. If he were brutally honest, he was worried too. He was used to unexpected things coming up while he was at sea, though. Used to holding a pleasant expression and not letting anxiety seep through to where it might show.

Beyond the rest of the unsettling day, he felt sick and shaky—and furious—about the information he'd picked up while linked to Aura. Goddammit! The woman had almost sacrificed herself. He wasn't totally certain what it meant, but he'd rectify the gaps in his knowledge damned fast. Had she signed on for a one-way ticket to the underworld? Even if rescue might have been possible, her lack of judgment was damned disturbing.

Running on autopilot, he nosed the raft around to the boat's bow.

"Crane," Viktor shouted.

Juan readied himself to secure the craft. Once he'd centered it above a welter of cables, he tightened them from above until they held the boat firmly. He hung onto the crane's rigging to stabilize it as Viktor engaged the mechanism to lift the raft out of the water. Once the Zodiac settled onto the deck, he jumped out, reaching back to retrieve the few items left inside.

Viktor snatched up the saber and one of the rifles along with a couple of warm jackets while Juan freed the raft from the crane and its pulley system. Wind was picking up, a portent of vicious storms bearing down on them. Weather changed fast in the Southern Ocean, so fast he'd learned to run with even subtle cues.

Viktor looked tired, his face drawn and pinched. "You can finish up here," he said and turned to leave.

"Hold on a minute," Juan called. Reeling up the cables could wait.

"Yeah?" Viktor turned around and dropped to a crouch, laying the items in his arms beside him.

"What do you think about… Well, about today?" Juan trudged to his side and hunkered next to him.

Viktor shrugged. "Not sure. Of course, I'd hoped Vampires were a thing of the past. In terms of the mad priest and demons breaching the veil between Hell and here…" His words trailed off, and he tried again. "It's not like this is something any of us know much about. Supernatural phenomena weren't exactly a university course when I attended."

"The women know a hell of a lot more than we do," Juan pointed out.

Viktor pressed his mouth into a thin, hard line. "Too bad none of it is written down. Ketha has that big, old book but whenever I've tried to page through it, it's like reading gibberish. Plus, it's written in Gaelic."

He angled his gaze Juan's way. "What are your impressions about today? You asked me for a reason."

Breath hissed from between Juan's clenched teeth. "Yeah. Today. A wake-up call? A doubled-up fist to my midsection? I'd written Vampires off, put them behind us. Finding those fuckers alive—well, kind of alive—was a hell of a shock." He sucked in a tense breath. "We have to go back there and use the saber on them."

Viktor frowned. "Why? They can't escape. They're not bothering anyone the way they are."

Juan splayed one hand on the deck to stabilize himself as he played Viktor's question through his mind. "Not sure. Maybe it's stupid, but they give me the creeps. Beyond the creep factor, I hate them."

"It's what we were. For almost ten years." Viktor leveled his green eyes on Juan. "Or have you forgotten?"

"Of course, I haven't *forgotten*." Juan bit off the words. "But I'd love to move past that part of our life."

"We did. I'm far more concerned about what finding living Vampires means in terms of the Cataclysm."

"Maybe we didn't defeat it as thoroughly as we thought we did."

"No maybe about it." Viktor slid down until his butt connected with the deck and stretched his legs in front of him. "Since we're kicking this around, part of me wants to head right back to Ushuaia. At least we know what we have there."

Juan's eyes widened. He hadn't expected that.

"Yeah. I know." Viktor's nostrils flared. "If there was even a ghost of a communication system left in the world, I'd turn *Arkady* around."

"There's not. If we retreated to Ushuaia," Juan spoke slowly, "then we'd never know how the rest of Earth fared during the Cataclysm. I'm worried about what we'll find, but it doesn't mean I don't want to go look.

"Besides," he went on. "This isn't like when we used to ferry rich tourists around. We couldn't make any kind of major decision without putting it up for a vote."

Viktor rolled his eyes. "I suppose you're right. I'd certainly run this past Ketha, but I never considered tossing it out for open discussion."

Juan smothered a snort. "Because you're used to being captain and making decisions the rest of us have to live with, no matter how we feel about them."

"Really? How many times did you want to toss me to the fishes?"

"You don't want to know, *amigo*." Juan pushed upright. "Redirecting our attention to the next few hours, there's a storm afoot. I smell it, and the barometer's probably dropping."

"This cove is as safe as anywhere if a hurricane blows through," Viktor muttered.

"Let me check my instruments, and I'll give you my recommendations. No point setting sail if we hit big winds and huge swells."

"True enough. Some of the women got really seasick."

Juan looked askance at Viktor as he stood. "Seasick, hell. It's nothing but a minor inconvenience. We lost *Gavrill* ten years ago. I'd rather not sink another boat."

An odd expression crossed Viktor's face, disbelief mixed with anger. "Are you suggesting it was my fault *Gavrill* pitched up against those coastal rocks?"

Juan raised both hands, palms outward. "Not at all. Where the hell did you come up with that from what I said? If we hadn't crashed, all of us would have died. The Cataclysm would have killed us in the open sea."

Viktor squinched his eyes shut for a moment. When he opened them, he said, "Sorry. Today took a toll, and I'm reacting rather than thinking. The thing about the Cataclysm is we don't actually know what it would have done if we'd remained at sea. The only thing we know for certain is it formed a barricade around Ushuaia and probably every other population base in the world. Nobody in. Nobody out. Who knows what happened to areas where there weren't very many people."

"Good point. Didn't Ketha have some way to communicate beyond Ushuaia?"

"Yes. I did too, with *Arkady's* radio, but my ability to reach anyone petered out after the first few years. From what I gleaned, the Cataclysm appeared to be a widespread phenomenon."

"Have you asked Ketha what she found?"

"No." Viktor hesitated. "I can't wrap my head around every single ship at sea when the Cataclysm struck, sitting at the bottom of the ocean. Maybe some of them ran out of water, out of food, out of fuel," he went on. "If it's true, then they didn't fall prey to the Cataclysm, but to an inability to reach port."

"The end result is the same," Juan muttered.

"Yeah. Dead is dead, no matter how you got there. I'll ask Ketha who she talked with at the front end of the Cataclysm. Maybe she knows something I don't."

Before Juan could craft a reply, Viktor picked up the saber and the rifle and the clothing and vanished through a door leading inside.

Juan returned to the crane and finished straightening the cables so they'd be ready for next time. He flipped the rafts upside down. That way they wouldn't take on water if it rained—or if waves got high enough to wash over the deck.

Small actions like putting the Zodiacs to rights were soothing, but he wasn't fooled. No matter how many trivial elements he piled atop one another, control was the flimsiest of illusions. He clamped his jaws together. Even if Viktor floated his suggestion about returning to Ushuaia, Juan would argue against it. They owed it to themselves—never mind anyone else who'd survived the Cataclysm—to gather as much data as they could.

"I'm a resource. Include me in your plans."

Juan's eyes snapped open. "Caught me dead to rights," he told his bondmate, not bothering with telepathy since it felt clunky and awkward.

"Viktor ignored his raven too," the cat continued. *"He did recognize the women know more. Why do you suppose that is?"*

"Because they're more used to being Shifters?"

A rough, rolling snarl filled his chest until Juan opened his mouth to let it escape. "Not the right answer, eh?"

"It's not only about being a Shifter. It's about preparing for it and never, never forgetting to include your bond animal. Not for a moment. You wouldn't simply take a stab at moving this boat around," the cat went on. *"I've watched you. You're methodical. Careful. You check things many times before setting a course in place."*

Juan battered back a desire to defend himself. Of course, he didn't know shit about being a Shifter. Neither did Viktor or Recco or Daide.

"I can read your thoughts," the cat reminded him, sounding smug.

"And?"

"It's not so much about you knowing nothing about the magic foisted upon you. It's more that you've made little effort to learn about it beyond the fun parts where you become me, and we hunt."

"When would I have had time?" Juan winced. Self-justification had no place here. Neither did excuses. "Never mind. I could have made time. You're absolutely correct. Testing the boundaries of my magic never felt important—until today when you helped me free Karin and Rowana."

The cat was silent long enough, Juan wondered if it was done rebuking him. Not that he didn't deserve the reprimand.

"I'm relieved you acknowledged your shortcomings," the cat said. *"Gives me hope I chose well."*

"If something I do disappoints you, speak up when it's happening," Juan muttered. "This will take time. It's not like I embraced being a Vampire. Magic isn't second nature to me like it is to Aura and the women."

"But you will prioritize it," the cat pressed.

"Yes. I will. Promise. I told you the same thing back in the church," Juan replied.

"Good. Magic is like anything else. It becomes easier the more you use it."

The temperature was dropping, and Juan shivered inside his polar-insulated clothing. He couldn't work the crane with gloves on—not easily, anyway—so his fingers were white and numb. He stuffed his hands inside his pockets and flexed his fingers to bring blood back into them. During his years as a Vampire, he'd grown used to playing his cards close to the vest. He'd never talked about his antipathy for his Vampire-hood. Or much of anything else. Vampires weren't a chatty lot, and most lost their ability to introspect. Blood and sex drove them, interspersed with the occasional meal when blood wasn't available.

Today's conversation with Viktor had been intriguing—and disturbing. His discussion with his bondmate was also well-timed, and he offered silent thanks to the animal for reaching out to him. In truth, they knew less than nothing about the Cataclysm, other than the maelstrom had been spawned by a nefarious plot gone bad.

Shifters had schemed to rid the world of Vampires once and for all. The bait they'd offered was an infusion of Shifter power to strengthen the Vampires' abilities. The ploy was appealing enough to lure Vamps to a secret meeting in Siberia. They craved power, and adding the capacity to take on another form proved a heady incentive. Except the Shifters were lying. Their actual intent was to turn Vamps into Shifters and be done with the bloodsucking scourges forever. One of the Vampires had caught wind of the conspiracy at the eleventh hour. Since he was already involved in a forbidden love affair with a Shifter, he'd consummated it, knocking the enchantment off its axis.

The Cataclysm was the result.

After a final glance at the crane and the rafts—more to convince himself he hadn't missed something than anything else —Juan made his way two decks up to the bridge, his thoughts skidding in a million directions.

Concern for Aura.

Killing the Vamps lurking beneath the barracks.

Where to take *Arkady*. After the storm was over, that is.

What the Cataclysm would do next…

He pushed through one of the glass doors at the side of the bridge. Recco and Daide were bent over nautical charts spread across a wooden table behind the wheel. Recco raised a hand in greeting. "Hey!"

"Hey, yourself." Juan was surprised by how normal he sounded and blessed his tour guide training. He glanced at instruments clustered around the wall nearest the helm. Barometer, several types of compass, wind gauge, and the satellite feed, which had been dead for years. It didn't take long for him to verify his suspicions about the weather turning.

"Even I can tell a hell of a storm is headed our way." Daide glanced up from where he'd been drawing lines in pencil on a chart.

Juan straightened. "Nothing to be concerned about. We'll remain here until—"

Daide waved him to silence. "You don't have to do that. We're not paying passengers."

Juan's face warmed. "Sorry. Old habits die hard and other assorted excuses."

"Should we move the boat closer to shore?" Recco asked.

Juan shook his head. "This boat has a pretty big draft. We're fine where we are."

"I heard what you said." Viktor walked into the bridge. "So your recommendation is we remain here?" A formal note lay beneath Viktor's words. Maybe a carryover from their earlier discussion.

"Juan?" Viktor quirked a copper brow.

"Sorry. I'm tired. Yeah, it's my official recommendation."

"Where are we going when we finally do leave?" Recco asked.

"Not sure." Juan shrugged. "Viktor and I were just kicking it around."

Recco glanced from one to the other of them. "Feel like sharing?"

"We're not Vampires anymore. Means we can talk with one another," Daide added with a wry grin.

Juan waited for Viktor out of well-established habit. Besides, not much reason to launch into all the reasons not to return to Ushuaia unless Viktor was wedded to that option.

A corner of Viktor's mouth twisted downward into a grim expression, and he shrugged, appearing self-conscious. "Can't take the pressure." He took a measured breath. "I talked with Juan about returning to Ushuaia. I'm not ashamed to admit today was a good, swift kick in the ass not to underestimate the dangers of continuing."

"Is that what you want to do?" Recco crinkled his forehead into a thoughtful expression.

"In some ways," Viktor replied. "A better question, though, would be if I believe it's the proper course of action."

"Do you?" Juan turned to face him and crossed his arms over his chest. He was finally warming up in the overheated bridge.

"No. Only a coward plots a course to save his own ass at the expense of everyone else." Viktor inhaled sharply. "We could make a run back to Ushuaia, tails between our legs, but eventually it will be the wrong choice. If evil's still running amok in the world—and I believe it is—"

"The best we could hope for in Ushuaia would be defending ourselves from whatever face it shows next," Juan cut in.

"There have to be other people with magic left," Recco said. "Daide and I were just discussing that."

"Yes," Daide spoke up. "We're stronger with allies than on our own. While I'm delighted so many humans survived in Ushuaia, they wouldn't have been much good standing against the Cataclysm."

"Speaking of magic"—Juan cleared his throat—"my cat

reminded me the four of us have a huge way to go yet, learning how to maximize our new power."

Viktor shot him a pointed look. "Do you suppose it's been talking to my raven?"

"Or my wolf?" Recco said.

Daide rolled his eyes. "My coyote said much the same thing—just before it quit talking with me at all. Hearing the same message from all four of our bondmates can't be sheer coincidence."

"Probably isn't," Juan said, feeling marginally better about his recent dressing down at the paws of his bondmate.

"I'm one step ahead of you." Viktor adopted a knowing tone, the one that made Juan want to punch him.

"Well?" He unzipped his parka and slipped out of it, dropping it over a chair.

"I talked with Ketha. She agreed we could benefit from an intensive course in Shifter-dom. She was going to work out the fine points with the other women. We'll be here for at least a couple days—maybe more, depending how bad the storm is."

"Good use of our downtime?" Recco furled his brows.

"Something like that." Viktor had the good grace to appear slightly uncomfortable. "Sorry for planning out everyone's life. When I ferried paying passengers, they never minded. In fact, they expected a full-service operation, but this situation is different."

"Did you happen to ask Ketha who she communicated with beyond the barrier?" Juan asked, harkening back to their earlier conversation.

Viktor nodded. "News wasn't great. She did pick up broadcasts from inland areas, and they were just as trapped by the Cataclysm as we were."

Juan focused on the barometer. It was still dropping, and the wind had picked up. Waves chopped against the hull, making a hollow, booming sound. "I'm going to check all the decks. Make sure everything is battened down."

He snapped up his parka and headed for the door leading to his cabin across the corridor from the bridge. Before he left, he turned and let his gaze settle on each man in turn. "This keeps bothering me, so I'll toss it out there. Before we leave King Edward Cove, I'm going back to the barracks to take care of those Vampires."

Viktor opened his mouth, but Juan waved him to silence. "Hear me out. It's possible, actually likely, no one will ever set foot in Grytviken again. Ever. But if the world makes a recovery, and people come here again, we cannot allow those creatures to remain in stasis. Someone will discover them, and they'll end up turned."

He squared his shoulders. "Who knows? The event spawning the Cataclysm was fairly minor—maybe not from a magical perspective, but in the larger scheme of things. It's possible leaving Vamps here could turn into a lynchpin producing another disaster. My vote is for us to be thorough, and I'm willing to go alone if no one else agrees. How hard could beheading a few Vamps in stasis be?"

"We'll talk about it." Viktor's sentence held a closed-off aspect Juan recognized all too well. He'd decided the Vamps were more trouble than they were worth and was prepared to let them rot beneath the barracks forever.

"Nothing to talk about," Juan shot back. "I've made up my mind. Not expecting you to agree. Or give your permission. These aren't passengers"—he spread one arm to encompass Recco and Daide—"and I don't answer to you. Not anymore."

"Never said you did," Viktor sputtered, "but—"

"No buts. The only question is if you decide to come with me or not. You have some time to think about it. No one's leaving *Arkady* until after the storm blows through."

"I'll come," Recco called after him.

"Me too," Daide cried, his voice cut off by the door closing behind Juan.

Viktor didn't say a word.

Juan stopped by his cabin and traded the insulated parka for a rainproof, hooded jacket. He'd always gone along with Viktor's decisions when they were at sea. It was how things worked aboard ships. The captain gathered input from everyone and made all the important decisions.

On one hand, Juan felt vaguely guilty, like he'd done something wrong facing off against Viktor. On the other, he felt empowered, free. He headed off to make sure *Arkady* was ready to face the storm.

He and Viktor would figure things out. Their rapport was strong enough to withstand a few alterations in the status quo. If it wasn't, they'd never had much of a friendship at all.

7

BARGAINS

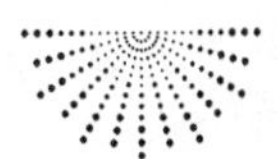

AURA SPENT the next hour floating pros and cons of various strategies with her cat. The discussion reflected a definite philosophical bent since neither she nor her bondmate had the vaguest idea what would show up next that wanted them dead.

Vampires. Demons. Or some perverse quirk of fate no one was expecting. Maybe Ketha could dredge up a few versions of the future with her glass. She was a seer, and information she'd gathered about the future was what made the difference and allowed them to take a bite out of the Cataclysm's hold on Ushuaia.

A big one. Big enough none of them had expected to see Vampires ever again.

Yeah. Won't make that particular mistake a second time. Aura pursed her lips into a sour expression.

"I've been in communication with the men's bond animals." The cat's words held an ominous undernote, and its comment felt like a shot out of left field.

"Why are you mentioning it to me?" Aura was confused. Usually relationships between Shifters and their bond animals were private, not topics of discussion.

"Because, and let me make this abundantly clear, none of them are pleased with how things have gone so far."

"Not pleased, how?" Aura's confusion changed to alarm at the clear departure from normalcy. If the animals were complaining about their bonded ones, trouble was afoot.

"The men don't understand what a gift and an honor it is to be selected by a bond animal."

Aura didn't have to think very hard to view the problem from both sides. "I'm not surprised," she said, treading cautiously. "Those men had Vampirism stuffed down their throats. None of this group ever warmed to it. Hell, none of them even knew magic existed before they were shanghaied by Vampires on the heels of the Cataclysm."

"Being a Shifter is nothing like being a Vampire. The comparison is disgraceful," the cat protested, punctuating its words with a growl.

Aura could almost see its whiskers twitching with annoyance. She inhaled briskly. "It's not the same."

"I just said that."

"What I meant was you can't draw a comparison between Ketha or me or Rowana and the men. We were steeped in magic from the day we were born. I dreamed you as a child, for chrissakes. I welcomed your visits to my dreams and couldn't wait for the day you broke through and I could actually shift. I've spent years studying and strengthening my magic. You can't fault the men for taking their time embracing the idea."

"Yes. I can. It's time we don't have. Juan's cat and I go back millennia. It's been waiting and waiting for him to pick up the banner and show some initiative with his Shifter magic."

"He did. Today." Protectiveness ran high, surprising her. Why would she feel the need to stand between Juan and the bond animal criticizing him?

"Finally. When his back was up against the wall, he solicited—and accepted— assistance from his bondmate." A low, hissing snarl filled

her belly. *"We—that includes you and me—were almost lost to darkness. If any of those men had made the slightest effort before today—"*

"Enough!" Aura snarled back. "They get it now. Blaming them for their shortcomings won't help. No one can fix the past."

The mountain cat subsided into whuffly snorts.

Aura swallowed around a tight place in her throat. "I truly am sorry about what happened earlier. I overestimated my magic—or underestimated whatever was driving the priest. I didn't realize I faced a demon until it was too late to break free."

"I know. I was there."

"Did you recognize the magnitude of what we faced?" Aura waited. The cat didn't have to answer, but if it did it was bound to tell the truth.

"No. I decided it was a human who'd been possessed by wickedness. I didn't sense Vampire presence, and I didn't dig any deeper. I should have."

"It's all right—" she began.

"No, it isn't. Part of my task is to use my senses, which are sharper than yours, to protect both of us. I was so focused on Vampires, I overlooked that they're far from the only evil walking in this world."

Love for her bond animal rushed through her.

"I'll make certain the men understand the most valuable part of being a Shifter is our partner's unquestioning loyalty, but that it must be earned."

"Promise?"

"You have my word."

"I'll let the other animals know."

Aura started to tell it not to but changed her mind. The animals had already broken an unspoken taboo with their earlier conversation. Maybe her cat could do some good, reassure the other animals of their mates' good intentions.

She hoped so.

Very little about becoming a Shifter was written down. Being born to it meant she'd taken a whole lot for granted. She stood and walked to where she could peer out the porthole. Juan strode along the walkway outside her window, looking like a man with a purpose.

His proximity on the heels of her conversation with her cat was fortuitous, something she should jump on. She wasn't under the impression she could make up for his and the others' lack of magical roots, but she could offer to teach them the basics about their animals and how to work in tandem with them.

Before she could talk herself out of it, she snatched up the parka she'd draped over a hook and hurried out her cabin door. When she pitched facedown on her bunk, she'd chided herself for being slovenly and not taking her sweaty clothing off, but it was convenient to not have to layer up again.

How best to approach Juan? She couldn't tell him his cat had been trash-talking him behind his back. It had to be one of the reasons such conversations weren't encouraged. Absolute trust was the bulwark upon which bonds were built. When you cut to the heart of things, if you couldn't trust your bond animal, why be a Shifter?

Aura winced. She and her cat had gotten into it more than once. They didn't always agree, and the resulting arguments left a bitter residue. It had made a strong pitch to make a run for it and leave Ushuaia during the leading edge of the Cataclysm. After conferring with the other women, she'd told her bond animal they were going to sit it out. Surely, the darkness and menacing energy would clear eventually.

Once it did then they'd leave.

Except, her cat had been right. The Cataclysm had done nothing but grow stronger, its rise empowering Vampires and propelling them into the light of day.

What if I'd heeded my cat and the twelve of us had left?

Aura didn't have an answer. She had no idea how Wyoming had fared. If Vampires had risen there as well, or if the Cataclysm had ever held the Rocky Mountain state captive. Plenty of Shifters lived in Wyoming. Hundreds. Surely, they'd had sufficient resources among them to stave off Vampires and whatever other evil rose to challenge them.

She pushed at the polished wooden double door at the end of the corridor. It didn't give, so she aimed a quick shot of magic its way.

Juan stood waiting when she walked through, eyeing her speculatively. "I was securing *Arkady* to ride out the storm. It won't be particularly rough in this harbor. It's why the old whalers built Grytviken here, but I'm still doing things by the book."

Aura smiled. He sounded so earnest, it touched her heart. "Why tell me?"

"Because part of securing the ship includes locking the sea doors. See there?" He pointed at metal doors standing open right outside the wooden ones. "You just unlatched them."

"Sorry. I didn't know. We should tell everyone to leave them alone. Does it mean we're confined to inside?"

Juan shrugged. "It's the safest place. We could get some unexpected gusts through here. Enough to knock someone who wasn't attentive overboard."

Aura narrowed her eyes and tilted her head back. Borrowing from her cat's senses, she scented the increasing wind. "Smells like snow."

"To me too." He smiled. "Want to walk with me while I finish this up?"

"Sure."

She fell into step next to him and searched for the best way to offer him lessons in magic and being a Shifter without alienating him. Men were touchy like that. They labored under the illusion they knew more than they did. It was a survival skill, but a hard one to work around.

"Today was a pretty close call," she ventured.

He stopped walking and spun to face her, gripping her shoulders. "Too close. You will never—" He let go abruptly and started walking again. "Sorry," he mumbled. "It's not my place."

Curiosity skewered her. "I will never what?" She caught up to him.

"I didn't like it that you came so close to being captured—or subsumed or immersed, or however you'd label it." His eyes glittered dangerously when he glanced sidelong at her. "Would there have been a way back if you'd been dragged to wherever the demon was herding you?"

Aura felt heat rise to her face. "Um. No. Probably not."

"Even worse," he gritted out.

"Look." She tried for a placating tone. "Nothing happened."

"This time. I have a feeling what we faced off against in Grytviken's church is the first of many warped curiosities lying in store as we continue our journey."

"*Warped curiosities*, eh?" She snorted. "Pretty fancy term for plain old evil."

"You're sidestepping the issue."

"Maybe I am, if the issue is my ability to take care of myself." Aura squared her shoulders. "This is a decent lead in to why I came out here. I saw you outside my porthole, and it seemed like a good opportunity."

"Opportunity for what?" Juan's tone was carefully neutral. They'd reached the broad, open decking area at the bow end of Deck Three, and he coiled large, thick ropes, securing them.

"The women and I," she began, "we knew we were Shifters from our earliest years. We didn't know right away what our bond animals would be. That information arrived when we were five or six, and they appeared in our dreams."

Juan straightened. "Yes. I understand that part."

"My point is"—she walked closer—"we were steeped in magic from birth. You never knew magic existed until Vampires removed your free will." Aura took a breath before hurrying on. "Leveraging power is like any other skill. It's learned and requires practice. I fully understand why you and the other men had little interest in immersing yourselves in being Vampires, but—"

"You can stop there." Juan's nostrils flared. "I already got a raft of shit about this from my cat. And I'm guilty as charged. I could have done a whole lot more learning about my new magical ability, but I didn't. My slipshod ways are about to change."

"Have you discussed this with Viktor and Recco and Daide?"

Juan nodded his head. "Yes, we just did. We'll have some downtime while we ride out the storm. All of us viewed it as a good opportunity to get started rectifying our sins." He narrowed his eyes. "I do wish we had books. I'm used to learning that way— by reading how something works and then putting it into practice."

An image of one of the Shifters' reference rooms in the basement of a hunting lodge outside Colorado Springs formed in her mind. "We have libraries, but obviously not here. Several are scattered throughout the United States, Europe, and the Far East in well-concealed locations where they'll remain safe from prying eyes."

"Good to know, but none of them will help me right now. Hopefully, your sourcebooks survived. Maybe someday, I'll be lucky enough to stumble across a few, but by then, I won't need them. Come on. One more deck to batten down, and then we can go back inside. Chilly out here, and that storm is nearly upon us."

As if his words bent the weather to his will, a snowflake landed on her face, followed by several more. The wind developed a howling, keening aspect, reminiscent of a devil child crying. Not to be outdone, waves slapped the hull.

"I hear the wind. Why isn't the water rougher?" She followed him up three sets of metal risers and along a walkway spanning both sides of the bridge.

"The geography of this cove protects it. The wind is above us. Most of it will remain there." He flashed a smile her way. "Those old seamen who built these whaling stations were tough, but they were smart too. They understood the importance of having a place to wait out storms and keep their ships from foundering."

Aura glanced at the huddle of buildings, what was left of Grytviken. Three ships were partially sunk in the shallow waters near shore, their masts rising from the bay like horns from prehistoric monsters. "Guess those boats weren't so lucky."

"Two were abandoned, and one ran aground."

"My own personal guide."

Juan shrugged. "Goes with the territory. You're not the first person to ask about the wrecks."

"I have an idea." Aura stepped in front of him before he could pull open the door that led inside.

He moved so close their bodies were almost touching. Having him this near was intoxicating. He smelled like wild things and greenery with the sharp tang of the sea mixed in.

"I have a few ideas myself." He latched his gaze onto hers. "You first."

Her belly tightened with wanting him, but it wasn't why she'd stopped him from going inside.

Focus!

Get a grip.

"I propose a trade." She tilted her chin upward to avoid the temptation of crashing her mouth against his and sinking her hands into his glorious hair.

"What exactly will we be trading?" His voice was raspy, thick with promise and need.

"Don't do that." She took a jerky step back. "Damn, but you're hard to resist."

"Don't do what?" The smoldering aspect fled from his eyes, replaced by a sly innocence.

"You know what. You're oozing come-fuck-me vibes."

Juan tossed his head back and laughed. "Oh, that. Good you noticed. I'm woefully out of practice. Sorry. I'll do my damnedest to behave better, but you're not making it easy."

Aura took a ragged breath—and one more step back. "You know a lot about this part of the world. I know a lot about magic. The trade I had in mind was swapping knowledge."

A broad smile spread across his face, turning his striking appearance into something so beautiful she couldn't look away. "Smooth. Very smooth." He tilted his head to one side. "I accept, but if we're going to turn *Arkady* into Hogwarts for adults, it should include all four of us brand new Shifters."

Aura giggled and then began to laugh.

"What's so funny, woman?"

She smiled back at him. "First off, it feels really, really good to laugh. There were years when I didn't so much as giggle. I was laughing because of your Hogwarts analogy. There used to be a world out there, one all of us took for granted. Shared fictional places were part of it."

Juan's expression became serious. He extended an arm and cupped the side of her face in one calloused palm. "We'll build a new world. Those of us who are left. And create our own mythologies, kind of like a phoenix rising from the ashes."

"I hope so."

She leaned into his touch. Maybe it was a bad idea, but he had the soul of a poet on top of all the other things she craved in him. For a tantalizingly delicious moment, she allowed herself to believe they might have a chance as a couple, that the world would hang together long enough to explore the attraction thrumming through her body.

Snow was falling harder, and the green-painted deck was almost white.

Juan pulled the glass door open and motioned her through.

"Why no sea doors up here?" she asked.

"Because the waves rarely make it to this deck. Now, the place you found me three decks down takes a real beating in rough seas."

Memories of being seasick engulfed her at the mention of

rough seas. Next time they ventured into the open ocean, she'd accept Karin's ministrations right away.

Viktor glanced up from where he stood next to the chart table. "Back, I see," he said to Juan.

"Excellent powers of observation." Juan stared back.

Aura shifted her gaze from one man to the other. What the hell? They sounded like two tomcats circling one another, spoiling for a fight.

"Did you change your mind?" Viktor asked.

"Nope. Nor do I plan to."

"Change your mind about what?" Aura was done keeping her mouth shut.

"We're going to go snag us some Vampire ass," Recco said brightly and punched Daide's upper arm.

"What? The ones in the barracks, or did some others show up?" Aura closed her teeth over her lower lip. Vampires hadn't been much of a threat to Shifters before the Cataclysm, but she'd be damned if she'd ever underestimate them again.

"Yeah, the ones under the barracks," Juan confirmed. "I can't see leaving them there. They'll never go away. If the world recovers and ships stop here again, it's not right for a gaggle of unsuspecting humans to fall prey to something we could have subverted."

"Do you honestly believe there's even one human left anywhere on Earth who hasn't developed a healthy respect for magic?" Viktor inquired.

"Beyond the point." Juan strode across the well-appointed space sporting polished wood panels and a nubby, non-skid gray floor. He stopped a foot away from Viktor. "Why are you so dead set against it?"

"We shouldn't take unnecessary risks." Viktor crossed his arms over his chest.

"I agree in principle, but it's not much of a risk, and it will clear Grytviken of any taint, make it habitable again."

The closed-off aspect in Viktor's face altered. "You always loved this old whaling village. I'd forgotten."

Juan nodded. "Yeah. I fell in love with Shackleton's heart and courage when I was still in short pants. He'd turn over in his grave"—Juan stabbed a finger at the windows providing a clear view of Grytviken—"if he knew we walked away from something that needed doing."

"Walking away definitely wasn't his style," Viktor agreed, his tone carefully neutral.

Aura recognized an opportunity and jumped on it with both feet. "Hey! What a great way to practice some of the magic you'll have learned."

The door at the back of the bridge swooshed open, admitting Ketha and Rowana and Zoe. Ketha's pleasant expression faded. "Jesus. You could cut the air in here with a very dull knife. What's going on?"

Instead of answering, Aura fired back a question of her own. "Have you scryed the future lately?"

"Yeah. It's why I'm here."

"I cast a tarot spread to help tack some parts down," Zoe added.

"I was only along for the ride." Rowana shoved thick silver hair back from her face.

The gesture told Aura the other Shifter was underplaying her role, and that she was worried. She must have been with Ketha when she dropped into a trance, possibly supporting her vision with additional magic.

"Looks to me like we need all of us." Aura spaced out her words for emphasis.

"I already said as much." Ketha sent a sidelong glance skittering across the space between them.

"No, you didn't," Aura protested. "You said you were here because you'd gotten a hit about what's coming down the pike."

Ketha trotted to the microphone mounted above the chart

table. Keying it, she said, "Bridge, everyone. Soon as you can." She set the microphone back in its cradle. "This was why I needed to be here. So I could use that."

"Focus, people," Viktor raised his voice for emphasis. "For starters, how many plans are out there for teaching us more about being Shifters? Ketha has her ideas, and it appears Aura is working on something different."

"Are you?" Ketha twisted until she faced Aura.

"I had something cooking." Aura bristled, not liking Ketha's tone or expression. "I have no idea if it's the same or different from what you have in mind."

"I was going to discuss it as a group—before I looked into my glass and got sidetracked."

"I was too, minus the being sidetracked part." Aura battled defensiveness. She inhaled raggedly to keep from blurting out words that would be even more divisive. Like telling Ketha to get lost. After all, Aura's bond animal had been the one to bring the problem with the men's bondmates to her attention—

Rowana stepped between them; soothing energy flowed from her, but Aura turned away. A part of her felt small, petty, but she didn't want to kiss and make up. The magical curriculum was her project. She should take the lead—

"*Stop it,*" her cat growled. "*This was never about you. You faced great evil today. Do not let its poison taint your judgment.*"

Its statements brought her up short, but she didn't trust herself to say anything. Not yet. Was residue from her skirmish with the devil affecting her? Making her suspicious of her dearest friend's intentions?

They were so few, and their survival so uncertain, the last thing they needed were internal squabbles. She took a deep breath, blew it out, and did it again. "It's all right." She aimed her words at Rowana.

"Is it?" Ketha sounded as friendly as a wolf guarding a fresh kill.

"Yes," Aura replied. "I'm sorry if I stepped on your toes. Let's try this one again from the top."

The harsh set of Ketha's shoulders deflated, and she shook herself. "I'm sorry too. I don't know what got into me, but we need to dissect and interpret the vision I had."

8

A NEWER EVIL

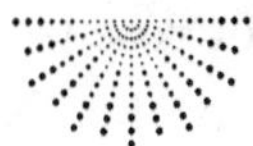

JUAN DIDN'T UNDERSTAND the increasing hostility in the room. Everyone was on edge. Had they picked up some magical virus in Grytviken? One that would urge them to turn on one another like a pack of feral dogs? The thought was disquieting.

Did it have something to do with the Vampires, since they'd ousted the demon?

He focused his attention on Ketha to calm her concerns. "Before we get to your vision, Aura wasn't trying to steal your thunder. She offered assistance, fast-tracking my Shifter magic. Earlier, Viktor mentioned you wanted to develop something along those same lines. I say the more the merrier. My cat's not very happy with me, and it has every right to feel disappointed—and annoyed. Up until earlier today, I fooled around with the fun parts of being a Shifter and ignored everything else."

Ketha walked to where Aura stood. "Why didn't you mention it?"

"Because I just came up with the idea in the last hour, and you never gave me a chance."

"Fair enough. Didn't mean to jump all over you."

"I know. Me, either." Aura glanced around the bridge. "Are we all in agreement about lessons in magic, no matter how they happen or who ends up teaching them?"

"I'm in," Recco said.

"Me too," Daide seconded. "My coyote quit speaking to me a while back. I've been worried it deserted me."

"Why didn't you let one of us know?" Worry sparked from Aura's eyes.

Daide looked away. Color rose from his neck to his forehead, making the sharp planes of his Native features even more pronounced. "I was ashamed. I understood what it wanted, and I kept promising it I'd do better. Except something always intervened, and I got tired of it nagging me. It's a weak excuse, but we were pretty slammed in Ushuaia."

"Did you tell it to leave you alone?" Rowana asked. The kind aspect left her face, and she could have passed for one of the Furies with sparks flying from her dark eyes.

"'Fraid I might have," Daide admitted. "I've tried to apologize, begged it to return, but the place it lives in my head has been empty." Naked pain carved into his features. "I miss it. I'd give anything to have it back."

"It will be all right." Aura grabbed Rowana's arm.

"How can you know?" Rowana demanded. "The bond is fragile when it first forms. Daide might have angered his bondmate to the point it—"

"I know because my cat's been in communication with the men's bond animals. All of them."

Ketha's eyes widened; so did Rowana's.

"I'm guessing that's unusual?" Juan ventured.

"Very," Aura replied, but stopped short of adding anything further.

"If you know something about my coyote, tell me," Daide pleaded. "I love animals. It's why I became a veterinarian."

"Sure wasn't for the money," Recco muttered.

"Truer words were never spoken." Daide elbowed him.

"The bond animals are willing to work with all of you." Aura moved her gaze from one man's face to the next. "But they need to see immediate and sustained effort on your parts. Actions to convince them they didn't choose badly when they bonded with you."

Daide's dark eyes filled with optimism. "I can do it. No. I commit to doing it. Please have your cat convey the message."

"No need," Aura said. "Your coyote never left, and it knows what's in your mind and heart."

Juan was encouraged by Daide's naked display of emotion. It gave him hope they hadn't damaged their relationships with their animals beyond repair. He focused on Viktor. "While we're waiting for the others, what's up with you?"

The other man dragged a hand down his face. "Not an easy question to answer."

Ketha moved to his side and wrapped an arm around him. "You haven't said anything, but your sleep's been restless."

Concern streamed from Viktor as he regarded his wife. "Have I kept you awake?"

"No, love."

A corner of his mouth twisted downward, and for a moment he seemed like the old Viktor with a sardonic sense of humor on display. He hadn't answered the question about what was bothering him, though. Before Juan could come at it from another direction, the eight other women filed into the bridge in groups of twos and threes.

"What was so important?" Tessa glanced around the small space. Her dark hair was in its usual collection of braids, and her dark eyes brimmed with curiosity. Like the rest of them, she was dressed in a collection of insulated outerwear appropriated from the ship's supplies. A rust-colored jacket was zipped to her chin.

Ketha walked to the windowed side of the bridge and turned to face everyone. "I did what I could to tease out what we'll face when we leave here. It's easier to only say this once when we're all here and can discuss what it might mean."

Viktor set his jaw in a tense line. "Discuss what it means? The last vision you had about the Cataclysm was clear enough."

She clasped her hands in front of her. "Each experience is different. Then I asked a very specific question about what would be needed to defeat the Cataclysm. Today, my search was more general. I wanted to know if the Vampires here were an anomaly, or if others survived. I also wanted some sense of what we might find if we sail farther east, as opposed to west toward Australia or north along the South American coastline."

Juan leaned forward, intent on not missing a word. "What'd you find?"

Ketha screwed her face into a frown. "It's not an easy question to answer."

"I'll say," Rowana muttered.

Viktor made come-along motions. "Start with the Vampire problem."

A flash of annoyance flared from Ketha's golden eyes, and Juan bit back a smile. Viktor might be her husband, but she didn't take kindly to being ordered about.

Viktor must have picked up on her irritation because he added, "Please."

Ketha nodded; a muscle twitched beneath one eye. "The place I searched first was our old home near Jackson, Wyoming. Figured since I had ties there, it might come into focus for me." A shadow flickered across her face, pain laced with resignation.

"That bad?" Juan asked.

"Worse," Rowana answered in a taut, no-nonsense tone.

"If my vision was accurate—and there's no way of knowing for certain—not much is left. I didn't see any of our Shifter kin, but I did see a Vampire."

"Only one?" Viktor asked.

Ketha rolled her eyes. "Where there's one, there are always others. Those bastards pack up. You should know."

Viktor winced. Juan felt for him. Neither of them had adapted to being Vampires, but nothing could erase the years they'd spent as Raphael's minions.

"How do you know what you saw wasn't in the past or the future?" Juan asked.

"I don't. The type of enchantment I summoned normally taps into real time, but it might not be accurate in a location over ten thousand miles away."

"Next question," Viktor spoke up, "is whether you not seeing Shifters means there weren't any."

"I don't have an answer for that, either," Ketha said. "Not much in the way of houses or any other structures were left. If Wyoming had perpetual winter too, snow avalanches could have wiped out those buildings, but it would take way longer than ten years."

"Earthquakes?" Tessa furled her dark brows.

"Who knows?" Ketha stood straighter, rolling her shoulders back as if the motion cost her. "What I did next was tag a different location, a closer one. Since I'm not very familiar with cities in South America, I settled for Buenos Aires. At least I've been there." She took a measured breath, either collecting her thoughts or buying time.

"It looks a lot like Ushuaia did. Piles of rubble from collapsed buildings. Rowana had to help me. My glass wasn't particularly cooperative."

"Is there a way you could share what you saw via telepathy? Or even better, go back for another scan?" Juan asked. "I was born there, and I know it well. What it used to be like, that is."

"Yeah. It's a great idea. I should have thought of it." She held her hands out, and the women closest to her took hold of them, extending their free hands in turn.

"Easier if we're touching?" Recco asked.

"Much," Rowana replied.

Once they were all joined in a large, ragged circle, Ketha said, "Clear your minds. Take a few deep breaths. Closing your eyes will help. I'll feel it when the energy is right." She began to chant, low and lyrical, in Gaelic.

Juan promised himself he'd prioritize learning it. He was good with languages; adding one more wouldn't be difficult.

The air around him crackled with power and drove thoughts of language lessons out of his head. He'd hated Vampire magic. It always made him feel like he'd been rolling in a vat of sheep shit. Shifter magic was clean, energizing, with a tang unique to whoever spun the spell. Ketha's magic smelled like Antarctic beech trees mingled with vanilla.

He shut his eyes and gave himself up to the heady energy swirling around him. Deep in his mind, his cat purred. Made sense. As a magical creature, it would be drawn to power. He sent gratitude inward, reassuring his mountain cat he valued and respected it and thanking it for not deserting him.

"You're welcome." It hesitated. *"You have no idea how close I came to relinquishing our bond."*

Unfamiliar emotion created a thick place in Juan's throat. He'd never been the praying type, but he vowed to do whatever it took to fulfill his part of the Shifter pledge. The cat was privy to his thoughts. It would recognize his intent.

Intent isn't good enough. This will require action, follow-through.

Clouds eddied across the blackness behind his closed lids. Silver-blue, they reminded him of the Arctic in high summer. He could have lost himself in those clouds. The cat seemed to agree, its purring growing in intensity. Or maybe it was happy and relieved he'd finally come to his senses.

With zero warning, the clouds fell away. Juan looked out at Buenos Aires, a deeply changed city from the one he remembered. The streets were crowded, like they'd always been, but similarities crashed to a halt there. Cars, trucks, and buses sat at odd angles, blocking every road. It appeared they'd run out of gas and been abandoned. Piles of rotting bodies were fair game for ravens, rodents, and black flies.

The stench must be horrible, and Juan was thankful smells didn't translate through Ketha's sending. He sent his consciousness ahead, pushing through what had once been a sprawling city of better than twenty million people. Roughly half the buildings still stood. Deep rubble piles spoke to the fate of the others.

Humans dressed in rags and looking malnourished as hell hustled this way and that. They might be hungry, but he didn't pick up on fear oozing from their pores. They might face problems, but at least they weren't expecting a Vampire to pounce at any moment.

So far, so good...

He moved upward and refocused the lens of his concentration, spreading it wide. Ketha and her sister Shifters could troll for evidence their kin had survived. What he wanted to know was if the Cataclysm still held Buenos Aires captive. His newly gained aerial perspective would accomplish that.

He hoped.

Juan panned out until he saw the Atlantic Ocean and the inlet for Rio de la Plata. Breath whooshed from him, followed by relief so profound his knees felt like jelly. If Buenos Aires had been trapped by the Cataclysm, its fell energy was gone.

"*Hold steady,*" the cat cautioned him. "*Do your part not to disturb the spell.*"

"*Got it,*" Juan replied.

Ketha was still chanting. If anything, the magic surrounding her had grown thicker, more compelling. Since he had the opportunity, he searched for the distinctive magic that meant Vampires were near. The alchemy was impossible to miss.

"*I can help,*" the cat spoke up. "*My senses are sharper than yours, and we'll be more efficient.*"

Juan breathed easier as they romped through sector after

sector of the old town and found zero hint of Vampires. Established by a Spanish expedition in 1536, the city had a rich and varied history marked by civil unrest, and Juan felt sorry to see so much of it lying in ruins. His old neighborhood was one of the hardest hit. Had his family escaped? He'd left a father, mother, and four brothers when he went to sea. Plus assorted grandparents, aunts, uncles, and cousins.

"*Your pack?*" the cat asked.

"*Yes, my family lived in this area.*"

"*No one lives there now. Will you ever return?*"

"*I have no idea. Not much to go back for.*"

The cat snarled, sounding fierce. "*Shifters are your pack now. It's how things work. Your family wouldn't understand.*"

Juan rolled his mental eyes since his earth eyes remained shut. Talk about an understatement. Like many families in Buenos Aires, his had been staunchly Catholic. For him to be able to take on an animal's body would scare the shit out of them. Furthermore, once they got over the shock, they'd shun him.

He hurried to complete his transit of Buenos Aires' spread-out geography. The city was huge, covering close to a hundred square miles. "*What do you think?*" he asked his cat.

"*No Vampires. I sense other, darker magics, but not theirs.*"

Juan waited until Ketha's chanting ceased; he opened his eyes to a sea of solemn expressions. Ketha released Viktor's and Rowana's hands, and the power swirling around the room dispersed.

The women exchanged glances, looking worried.

"Anyone feel like something hot to drink?" Juan asked.

"Sure. If you put a shot of whiskey in it." Aura raised her green eyes and zeroed in on his face. "It's been a bitch of a day."

Juan glanced around the room. Seeing nods, he walked briskly to the coffeemaker and got it going. He also plugged in the electric kettle next to it after checking it was full of water.

"I'll fetch liquor from the bar," Viktor said and ducked out the door.

Juan dragged a package of Styrofoam cups out, along with powdered milk, tea bags, and sugar. He'd been disappointed, but not surprised, by the damage in his home city. The world had gone through devastating changes this past decade. That anything remained was a miracle.

Viktor dropped two bottles—scotch and blended whiskey—next to the cups. Uncapping one, he took a swig, not bothering to add it to coffee or tea.

"Better?" Juan eyed him.

Viktor shrugged. "Too soon to tell, mate." He strode to the windows, and Juan joined him, waiting. Viktor had something on his mind, but prodding wouldn't make it happen faster. Snow and sleet battered the glass, and the wind howled around the ship, making him glad he'd battened everything down.

"What'd you see?" Viktor asked, still staring out at what remained of Grytviken.

"About what you'd expect," Juan replied. "Lots of rubble. No Vampires, but something dark and foreboding lurked in shadowed places. I couldn't identify it, and neither could my cat."

Behind them, rustling suggested everyone was helping themselves to the drinks Juan had pulled together.

Viktor curled his fingers around the grab bar running beneath the windows. "I picked up on a sense of foreboding." He pressed his mouth into a tight line. "It rattled me. Also, I was shocked to see so much of the city in ruins. It's been standing for hundreds of years."

"No, it hasn't," Juan corrected him. "It's been rebuilt many times. Fires. Earthquakes. The occasional flood when Rio de la Plata jumped its banks." Juan tapped Viktor's shoulder. "*Amigo.* Look at me. What's eating you? It can't be multiple opinions about how we proceed from here. Or that spat between Ketha and Aura about how to organize a curriculum."

Viktor made a sour face. "It's not."

"What then?"

"Lots of unrelated factors from insufficient crew to man this boat to the phalanx of unknowns we face. You know me. You worked with me for almost twenty years. I thrive on order. On having everything tacked down."

"Not true. You'd have opted for a desk job if you weren't addicted to the adrenaline rush of solving problems on the fly."

"Yeah, but I used to have a cache of resources." He shook his head. "That's not it. Not exactly. I'm still captain. Which means I'm responsible for the ship and everyone aboard. I sense danger no matter which direction we head. There's no safe harbor, and there never will be again. It's an adjustment."

Juan understood. They'd run into kickass storms before, but they'd always found somewhere to sit them out, like the leeward side of South Georgia Island or the South Shetland Islands off the Palmer Peninsula. Now their entire existence had turned into a storm, albeit a metaphorical one.

"Yeah. I get it."

Viktor angled his body so he faced Juan. "No. I don't think you do. You're what's left out of my cache of resources, which is why I'm not thrilled about you playing Vampire hunter under the barracks. What happens if you're killed? It takes both of us to keep *Arkady* going."

Juan straightened his back. "You'd manage, and I have no plans to sacrifice myself to those fuckers. It's enough they stole ten years of my life."

"What are the two of you chatting about?" Ketha walked to them and offered Viktor a cup of steaming coffee that smelled like it had whiskey in it.

Aura thrust a mug Juan's way. "Rather than Styrofoam, I thought you'd prefer your cup."

"Thank you. I could have gotten my own, but I appreciate your thoughtfulness."

Color spread across Aura's high cheekbones. "You're welcome."

Juan breathed in the welcome mix of dark-roasted coffee and spirits before taking a sip. He glanced at the others, gathered in small clusters.

"Come on back to the group." Ketha crooked two fingers. "We can share what we saw in our vision." She slanted her gaze at Juan. "No Vampires, right?"

"No Vampires," he concurred, "but—"

She held up a hand. "Wait and tell everyone."

Juan crossed the small space with Viktor, Aura, and Ketha right behind him. "Did you find Shifters in Buenos Aires?" he asked.

Zoe smiled. "Aye. Many remain, and they seemed to be flourishing. Makes my heart glad." She chewed on her lower lip. "Were there ever Vampires in Buenos Aires because I couldn't find a trace."

Everyone looked Juan's way, and he shrugged. "I'm scarcely the one to ask. I never believed in such things before the Cataclysm."

"Raphael supposedly came from there," Viktor said. "He relocated on account of some Vampire turf wars."

"Do you think he was telling the truth?" Aura asked.

"Now, there's a good question," Juan replied. "Raph's worldview was skewed. That's for damned sure. He believed his own hype, but whether it was grounded in reality was hard to verify. What do you think?" He elbowed Viktor. "You were closer to him than I was."

"The old bastard made himself the hero in his own stories. Every single one of them." Viktor's mouth turned downward. "I always figured he adjusted reality to suit his needs. After all, none of us were around in the 1600s in Europe to know what really went down. No matter what he said, he didn't risk losing credibility. I never believed his shit about Nosferatus being at the top of the Vampire heap until Ketha confirmed it."

"This is interesting, and I'm glad Shifters are thriving in Buenos Aires"—Juan sucked in a tight breath—"but what I want to know is if anyone else sensed evil. Darkness not linked to Vampirism."

"Yes." Rowana bit off the word.

Juan waited, but she didn't say anything further.

"Did you recognize it?" he prodded.

Aura drew her blonde brows into a thick, worried line. "Not precisely. In ways, it reminded me of what we ran up against in the barracks. Vampire but not."

"It was more closely related to the demon in the church than anything else," Ketha spoke up, but her words sounded strained.

Juan thought about it. "If demons invaded Buenos Aires, doesn't it suggest Vampires had to open some kind of gateway like they did here?"

"Maybe," Ketha replied.

"Could you say a wee bit more?" Viktor wrapped an arm around his wife.

"Och, and mayhap I could." She aped a Scottish brogue that made Zoe grimace.

Ketha snorted. "Sorry, sweetie. Couldn't resist." She creased her forehead into a mass of thoughtful wrinkles. "The world has changed. I know it's kind of a no-brainer, given what we lived through."

"The long and short of it is, we don't know what we face now," Aura cut in. "Vamps used to leave us alone. If there are far fewer of them, it's not unrealistic to expect another, different evil has risen to partially take their place."

"You said something similar." Viktor addressed his words to Ketha.

She nodded. "Indeed I did. Everything needs its opposite to exist. Vampires were our counterpart in the old world order. Even if we locate a few here or there, my sense is they're on their way out."

"So it kicks the door open for something else wicked to fill the void," Juan muttered.

"Exactly," Aura said. She turned the full force of her attention on Ketha. "We answered the Vampire question. Kind of. What did your vision reveal about where we go next?"

Ketha swept the bridge with her golden eyes. "Is there a whiteboard hiding somewhere?"

Viktor unwound his arm from around her waist and walked to the wall over the chart table. Reaching up, he unlatched two wooden cabinet doors. When they swung wide, they revealed a writing surface and an array of colored pens.

"Perfect." Ketha snatched up a green pen and began sketching out a rough map of the world.

Juan took advantage of the opportunity to reach inward. *"Thanks again for your assistance when we hunted through Buenos Aires."*

"No thanks needed." The cat paused. *"Hunting is one of my specialties. If you want to return there, we could find places to run."*

"I thought you said it was a bad idea, that my family—if any remain —wouldn't understand."

"They won't. That part is true, but I wasn't taking what you wanted into consideration. It was your home. I felt longing within you."

Juan didn't know what to say. Evidence of his bond animal's caring touched places in him that had been dead since the Cataclysm. Because he couldn't articulate his gratitude without sounding like a broken record—how many times could you thank someone?—he said, *"I'm looking forward to learning as much as you can teach me about Shifter magic."*

A deep, riffling purr filled his chest. *"Finally,"* the cat said, but stopped there.

Juan was relieved it was done with rebukes for his shortcomings. He'd do whatever it took and then some to hold up his end of their bond bargain.

"Ready," Ketha said. "All eyes this way."

THE SEA KEEPS YOU HUMBLE

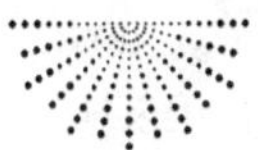

AURA WATCHED her longtime friend work. She understood the other Shifter was gathering her thoughts, and her chalkboard exercise gave her a ready cover while she decided what to share—and what to keep hidden. Once she was done sketching out the continents, Ketha picked up a contrasting color and made a series of Xs and checkmarks.

Lastly, she drew a red circle right around where Aura thought the 50th parallel might be. Placing the pen back in its tray, she turned and said, "Ready. All eyes this way."

Aura's gaze was already riveted to the schematic. She rolled her shoulders to dissipate an uneasy feeling about what was coming.

"Here"—Ketha pointed at the red circle—"felt safest to me. As I scanned north, things grew murky. About here"—she tapped the equator—"my ability to see anything useful dissipated. Did anyone have a different experience?" She folded her arms beneath her breasts, waiting.

Rowana frowned. "Yes. Me."

"And me," Karin added. "Even though I didn't find Vampires—

which should have reassured me—something out there felt even worse, but it was everywhere. North. South. You name it."

Ketha made come-along motions. "Something? Could you pin it down more precisely?"

Karin turned her hands palms up. "If I could, maybe this sense of foreboding would let up a bit."

"Nowhere felt safe," Rowana muttered in a flat tone. "Everywhere I scanned was bleak, dark. Evil even sought entrance among us when Aura and Ketha"—she looked pointedly at them —"squared off about teaching strategies."

"Glad I missed that part. I was relieved when ye pulled the plug on our group grope," Zoe muttered, her brogue thicker than usual.

"Aura?" Ketha stared right at her.

"My experience was a mixed bag." Aura searched for a precise, factual explanation, one she wouldn't dither through. But how could she assign facts to something as unexplainable as what she feared lay in wait for them? Ketha's gaze never left her face, almost as if she were hoping Aura would say something to countermand her worst fears.

Aura swallowed around a narrow place in her throat. "What we're all worried about is the Cataclysm, right?" Assent burned in the circle of eyes trained on her.

"Not so much worried," Juan spoke up, "as confused. How could we break it in Ushuaia and have it remain active elsewhere? I didn't see any evidence of it in Buenos Aires. Does it mean South America escaped? If that's true, why not the rest of the world?"

A crooked smile wanted out, but she pushed it aside. Juan sounded a lot like graduate students in the life that had been ripped out from under her. Serious. Dedicated. Intensely focused on the problem at hand.

"First off"—Ketha stepped in—"we don't know enough about what fueled the Cataclysm to answer any of those questions. My hypothesis was if we recreated the energy spawning it, the original casting would run through to its conclusion. I assumed that would fix things. It may have partially."

She glanced from one man to the next. "The four of you aren't Vamps anymore. Might mean the Cataclysm is in its death throes —if it remains anywhere at all."

"The ones beneath the barracks seem alive and well," Recco countered.

"Yeah. Why us and not them?" Daide added on the heels of Recco's words.

Juan furled his brows. "Maybe something happens to Vamps in stasis. Some alterations at the cellular level might have made them resistant to changing." He elbowed Recco who stood next to him. "What do you think? You have medical training."

Rather than answering, Recco focused on Ketha. "What exactly did you filch from the lab in Grytviken?"

"Two decent microscopes. Chemicals. Slides. A selection of instruments." She hesitated. "It's possible the reagents won't be particularly effective. They've all passed their expiration dates —by years."

"The ship's infirmary has a rather basic microscope," Karin spoke up. "Sorry. I should have mentioned it earlier. I'm still taking inventory. I'd have been done, except I was busy taking care of everyone who got seasick."

"Great. Means we have three," Ketha replied.

"Reason I asked," Recco went on, "is because we can compare biologic samples from the Vamps under the barracks with our own. Once we've taken them down, that is."

"Not sure how much good it will do," Daide broke in, "since we're not Vampires anymore."

Viktor made a noise somewhere between a snarl and a growl but didn't clarify it with words.

Rowana moved to Ketha's side and faced the others. "Science aside for the moment. I've been replaying the spell we hatched up to get rid of Vampires. What I fear is it altered the architecture of the world's magical underpinnings. Have any of you examined the ley lines? Really looked at them?"

Aura shut her eyes for a moment, recreating the pattern the ley lines formed when she'd seen them near the gift shop in Grytviken. Nothing amiss stood out. She walked close enough to touch Rowana's arm. "Tell me how they appear to you."

The older Shifter twisted her mouth into a scowl. "It's not immediately obvious, but if you study the junctions where the lines bisect, there are notches in the corners. Like a hungry mouse decided to feed himself."

"Do you believe the lines are eroding?" Aura asked.

Rowana clasped her hands together so tightly, the knuckles whitened. "Yes. Worse than that, if we don't intervene, make them whole again somehow, I have no idea what will happen."

"We don't have a clue when the damage happened or over how extensive a period of time," Aura muttered. "It might have been a by-product of the Cataclysm."

"Sure," Rowana agreed. "Or it could have happened yesterday. No way of knowing, but I will keep a close eye on them now we know they've developed flaws."

"What exactly are they?" Viktor asked.

"The short answer," Ketha replied, "is ley lines are magical, mystical alignments. They've been around since the dawn of time. One school of thought believes they carry both negative and positive psychic energy. Where two or more lines converge, it paves the way for great power and energy to flourish. Sacred sites, places like Stonehenge, Glastonbury Tor, Sedona, and Machu Picchu sit at the convergence of several lines."

Daide made a snorting sound. "I always thought magical anything was so much fluff. But then I didn't believe in Vampires, either. Or anything beyond the world under my microscope."

Aura spoke up and hoped she didn't sound pedantic—or defensive. "Even without a shred of magic, you can detect a ley line by metaphysical means, like pendulums or dowsing rods."

"Yeah, well I didn't believe in them, either," Daide said.

"None of us did." Juan glanced at Rowana. "So the damage is where the lines converge?"

"Precisely, which is why it's so dangerous," she replied. "The places holding the most power are—or were—under systematic attack." She pursed her mouth into a harsh expression. "I suspect the process began after that perverted spell in Siberia ten years ago, so it's had a spot of time to establish itself."

"Is it spontaneous?" Juan asked. "Or part of a nefarious plan to create anarchy?"

"I have no idea." Aura opened her fisted hands, stretching fingers that had begun to hurt. At least she had a hook to hang her earlier feelings of impending doom on. She turned back to Ketha and jerked her chin at the whiteboard. "Any more ideas about your sketch?"

"Yes. One. Maybe the ley line problem is why everything from here up"—she pointed north from the center of her drawing—"fuzzed out. Probably what I saw in Wyoming during my earlier trance wasn't the least bit accurate."

"Why would the twelve of you see something different from one another?" Juan asked.

Aura shrugged. "We're all Shifters, but the gift manifests differently in each of us. It would be true of any Shifter. Our magic is similar in many respects, but unique in others."

"Aye," Zoe broke in. "'Tis why Ketha is a seer and Karin a healer. Some of us are more skilled with tarot than others. Beyond surface variations, we each work the four elements somewhat uniquely. For example, fire and air is my strongest blend."

"And water potentiates my spells," Ketha murmured. "Along with earth."

"When will we discover special talents—or if we have any?" Viktor asked.

"You beat me to the draw, *amigo*." Juan nodded at his friend.

"Those are all things we can work on when we begin our classes in Shifter magic," Aura said.

"We'll develop those sessions as a group," Ketha spoke up. "All of us."

Aura swallowed hard, remembering how she and Ketha had nearly come to blows over the same topic. "I can only speak for me, but I sense a negative undercurrent. We all seem edgy. It has to be more than a by-product of those miserable days crossing the Scotia Sea when I was hanging on by my fingernails."

"Aye. I feel it too," Zoe said. "My skill is as an empath. I see emotions as well as feel them. Everyone's aura—visual energy field—appears far more intense and multifaceted."

"Why didn't you say something?" Aura countered. "My bondmate is convinced the wickedness we faced earlier left a residue that's affecting us. Or at least me."

"It could be right. I kept quiet because we have enough problems, and I didn't wish to add to them," Zoe replied. "Besides, I wasn't certain if it was me being hypersensitive because of how ill I was during the crossing."

"Maybe we're reacting to emanations from the not-dead-yet Vamps," Viktor muttered.

"Or the demon in the church," Ketha suggested. "Churches have their own energy. Remember what Aura said about determining power points using tools available to those with zero magic?"

"Of course. What about the church?" Viktor asked.

"Most of them are built on places ley lines intersect," Ketha went on. "Clergy use tools at their disposal to determine the most auspicious place to build. You know that sense of…differentness? The alteration you sense when you enter a church? Well, it's a by-product of how successful the pastor or priest or whoever picked the particular spot was."

Ketha grabbed an eraser and cleared her depiction of the world. Once she had a clean surface, she drew a line down the center of the board. On one side she wrote, *Shifter Syllabus.* On the other, *Tasks in Grytviken.* She hesitated and then added, *Examine ley lines next to church* and *Vampires??* under the Tasks list.

Viktor strode to her side and hoisted himself up onto the broad, flat chart table. "Let's talk about those Vamps," he said. "It appears I'm the one with the strongest feelings about leaving them alone."

"What do you think will happen if we open their prison?" Juan trained his hazel eyes on Viktor.

"What do I think? Or what am I afraid of?" Without waiting for Juan to respond, he went on. "The edginess Aura and Zoe alluded to? It's had me firmly in its grip since I first got a whiff of Vampire when I was walking the beach road." He paused for a beat. "At first, I chalked it up to not being in control. You'd think I'd have gotten used to it, playing lackey to Raphael"—he snorted —"but I managed my antipathy by promising myself I'd kill him someday."

"What do you think now?" Juan asked. "Not about Raph, but about your uneasiness. And letting the Vamps out so we can kill them."

"Yeah, I never exactly answered you, did I?" Viktor's nostrils flared. "When you were insistent about taking care of them, my first concern was how the fuck I'd manage *Arkady* without you—"

"Why were you so certain I'd be killed?" Juan cut in and smiled crookedly. "You used to have more faith in me."

"I don't know. I've been trying to figure it out. I'm not usually quite so self-serving, either."

"Did you ask your raven?" Ketha raised one brow into a question mark.

Viktor shrugged. "Now, there's where the other list"—he angled his head toward the whiteboard—"would come in handy. Do we involve our bond animals at the front end of every problem?"

A chorus of yesses rang around the room, along with one aye

from Zoe. Aura smiled grimly as she remembered the months they'd spent in Ushuaia after they'd trounced the Cataclysm. Time which could have been spent teaching not only the four men here, but every single newly-minted Shifter about their magic. Even Raphael had taken the time to ensure his brand-new Vamps understood what it meant to be a Vampire.

Damn, but they'd been remiss. Part of her screamed they should return to Ushuaia immediately to correct their lack of foresight, but wicked powers were in ascendency. The Shifters left in Ushuaia would have to figure things out on their own. At least some of them would manage, and it was too late to worry about the others. Icy heat still tingling the length of her back was a sure sign she was on the right track: they had to focus all their energies on making sure they remained alive.

Once they'd killed its vessel, the fucking demon had run straight back to Hell for reinforcements. Whatever showed up next would do its damnedest to interrupt their planned exploration to discover what was left of the world.

"Aura." Ketha snapped her fingers under Aura's nose.

She started. "Sorry. What?"

"I asked if any of this ties in with a particular prophecy," Juan said. "Perhaps an end-of-the-world one." Concern pinched the corners of his eyes into a phalanx of lines.

"I haven't looked." Her voice came out flat and strained. "Sorry. Didn't mean to be so abrupt. I was kicking myself for not having the foresight to push lessons in Shifter magic to the front end. It's not just you four. A lot of new Shifters live in Ushuaia."

"And they don't have anyone to teach them," Karin said.

"Och." Zoe set her lips in a tight line. "Sure and it's obvious now. Why didn't any of us think of it then? Two months elapsed before we left the city. We were busy, but we could have prioritized…" She shook her head.

"We can't go backward." Aura kept her tone brisk. "How long will this storm last?" she asked Juan.

The snow and sleet battering the glass had been joined by hail. When she peered through the combination, she couldn't see Grytviken at all.

"My guess, and absent satellite weather feeds it's not more than that, is two days. Why?"

She took a measured breath and blew it out. "We have to return to the church. We ran out of there so fast, we probably missed a bunch of clues."

"Clues to what?" Ketha asked.

"The evil doing its damnedest to drive a wedge between us. The deeper we sink into feeling annoyed, irritated, and exasperated with each other, the less chance we'll figure out what's really going on." She paused for a beat. "It's what's driving Viktor's certainty that taking on the Vamps in stasis is wrong. Something wants them to remain right where they are."

"How can you be certain?" Juan asked.

Aura turned her hands palms up. "Intuition. Hunch. Instinct. Those things drive my magic. I could search for a prophecy, but there's not much point."

"How do you sort it out?" Juan asked.

"Sort what out?" Aura looked at him. The earnest expression on his face melted a place deep inside her.

"What's real and what's fueled by something trying to control you?"

"It's a big question," she replied. "One that fits in with knowing more about your Shifter side. We don't really need all of us right now. I suggest pairing up with one of the women and spending the next little while working on the blank column on the whiteboard: Shifter Syllabus."

"Good idea," Ketha seconded. "This isn't like Calculus 101 where we need to follow the exact same path for each man. I'll work with Viktor." She beckoned, and he walked to the far side of the bridge with her.

"Are you comfortable working with me?" Aura asked Juan.

He smiled broadly. "We already agreed, didn't we?"

Recco angled his gaze at Zoe. "Will you teach me?"

Color washed across Zoe's delicate cheekbones. "Certainly. How about if we settle in the dining room? Plenty of space down there."

"Guess that leaves me." Daide stood straight, as if he invited closer inspection.

Karin walked to his side. "If you'll have me, I believe we'd work well together, given our mutual medical backgrounds."

A relieved smile lit his face, and Aura understood he'd been worried no one would want him because of the dissension between him and his bond animal. "Want to join Recco and Zoe in the dining room?"

"Of course." Karin turned and led the way out of the bridge with Daide, Recco, and Zoe behind her.

Aura turned to Juan. "Where would you like to settle?"

"The bar on Deck Four? It has space to move around."

"Perfect." She set a course for the nearest staircase—the ship was riddled with them—and walked down two decks and along a corridor to the well-appointed bar. Couches lined three of four walls with small tables bolted to the floor. When she'd first boarded *Arkady*, she'd wondered why all the furniture was attached to something. Not anymore.

A chuckle escaped her.

"I'd like in on the joke," Juan said as they made their way to a couch. He waited until she was settled to sit near her but left a respectable amount of space between them.

"Nothing important. Musings about things unique to ships. Like the furniture being bolted down."

He muffled something like an amused-sounding snort. "If they weren't, they would have fallen on a passenger, who would have proceeded to sue us."

"Yes. I get it now." Aura turned to him. "That's not why we're here, though. Is your mountain cat front and center? It needs to be part of what happens next."

Juan shut his eyes for a moment. When he opened them, he said, "Yes. And it sounds excited. I'm guessing it's been waiting for this ever since it hooked up with me."

"It has. We go to school to learn about our Shifter magic. An extra class once a week at night that begins after we formally bond and continues until we're done with high school."

Juan's eyes widened. "Really? There's that much to learn? How will I ever hope to absorb so much in the short time we have?"

A rush of warmth raced through her. His humility was quite a counterpoint to the competence she'd seen him demonstrate. Men like him were often resistant to admitting they didn't know something. They'd done their time as apprentices and weren't anxious to revert to a novice role.

"What are you thinking?"

"Why would you ask?" she countered. Heat splashed her cheeks. She figured she was blushing and cursed her fair skin.

"Your mind felt busy to me. Sorry. I wasn't trying to be intrusive."

"It's all right. One of the things we'll do is mind-link so our animals are actively included." She tilted her head and made a decision. There shouldn't be secrets between them. "I respect your willingness to learn."

He raked curved fingers through his hair and met her direct gaze. "The sea keeps you humble. Sailors who are convinced they know everything end up at the bottom of the ocean." He exhaled audibly. "I've known lots of them. It's provided strong incentive to keep an open mind."

The more he said, the better she liked him, but Aura pushed the personal aside, burying it deep, and held out a hand. "This will be easier if we're touching."

He closed his fingers around hers, and she reveled in their strength and warmth.

Focus! she chided herself.

"Close your eyes. Join your mind to mine. My cat is already chattering away to yours. Can you hear them?"

He shut his eyes and leaned back against the cushions. "Now that you mention it, I can."

"Good. Your reward once this lesson is over is we can shift and chase each other around the ship. Cats love a good game of chase."

He tightened his grip on her fingers, and the fluttery feeling behind her breastbone turned into a torrent of longing. She buried that too, and damned fast before it leaked out and embarrassed her.

"Your cat has a story," she said. "Have you ever asked it to tell you about its life?"

"No." A chagrined expression crossed Juan's face. "I owe it a major apology. Again."

Aura shut her earth eyes and readied herself for a rare treat. She knew her bond animal's story, but she'd never heard any of the other animals recount their beginnings. "Encourage it," she urged. "I'm ready for it to begin."

Deep within her, her cat purred its encouragement.

10

A CAT'S TALE

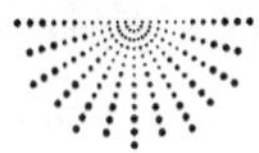

JUAN LOVED the feel of Aura's skin against his. Her nearness made him yearn for more. For her arms around him and the touch of her mouth against his. Her scent intensified, maybe because they were mind-linked. She smelled of candle wax and old leather and jasmine, comforting and stimulating by turns.

"It seems I'm forever apologizing," he told his cat. "I skipped over the same basic courtesy I'd extend to any new acquaintance, and we're so much more than mere acquaintances. Please. Tell me about you. I want to know everything you're willing to share."

"Apology welcomed and accepted," the cat replied. *"You should have asked if Aura and her bond animal could be part of what is normally a private conversation betwixt bond animal and Shifter, but I forgive you because you do not know our customs. Not yet, anyway."*

"Can they be part of what comes next?" Juan asked and held tighter to Aura's hand. If his cat said no, he'd have to let go of her. He didn't want to, but he wouldn't risk any further missteps where his cat was concerned.

A riffling sound that might have been feline laughter rolled through his mind. *"Of course. Her cat already knows everything there is to know about me. You must agree to one thing, though, before we begin."*

"Anything," Juan replied, delighted Aura could remain.

"You may not reveal what I tell you to anyone. Our histories are private."

"I won't," Juan said.

"Neither will I," Aura cut in without being asked.

"Thank you for that," Juan's cat said. *"I didn't wish to offend you by insisting, but nor could I have begun without your assent."*

"I know," she replied.

The cat purred, soft and rich and low. It soothed Juan, made progress healing the mutilated places from his years as a Vampire. He hadn't fully appreciated how much self-respect he'd traded to keep on living, and the truth of it shamed him.

Yeah, and if I'd known, I'd have somehow found the strength to refuse Raphael's wrist.

"Let the past lie," the cat instructed. *"Nothing was ever accomplished chewing over old bones."*

"I respectfully disagree." Juan spoke slowly and deliberately. "Those who ignore their mistakes are doomed to repeat them."

"You may not be a historian," Aura murmured, "but that's a variation of a very famous quote from George Santayana."

"Quiet. Both of you," Juan's cat commanded. *"Do not interrupt until I am finished."*

Juan leaned closer to Aura. The gesture was spontaneous, and he breathed her in hungrily. He held awareness of her thoughts, his own, and his bond animal's. Aura's mind was warm, welcoming. He couldn't sense her cat, but it had to be there. The experience was rather akin to watching different movies on triple screens. He smiled wryly at his backward foray into the life he'd left behind.

No more movies, probably. Not new ones, anyway. No more Internet or television or radio or modern conveniences. If Earth recovered, it would be a long, slow, painful process. Hopefully, mankind would pay more attention to potential consequences as people rebuilt.

"Focus on me," the cat intoned, its words mingling with a growl.

Juan did, knowing better than to give voice to the questions spilling through his mind. Did the cat require his energy, now they were bonded? Was it a mutual state of affairs, where he was stronger for having the cat's essence to draw from, but the cat needed him as well?

Aura squeezed his hand lightly. He took it as a yes to both questions.

"I was not one of the first Shifters," the cat began. *"The ones who opened our world to those insistent mages who refused to take no for an answer. Yet I didn't come far behind them. What it means, the way you calculate time, is I have lived thousands of years. Over that span of time, I have bonded with only two others before now.*

"Why, you might ask," the cat went on.

"The answer is simple. A human's need had to be great for me to take on the responsibility of bonding with them. While some bond animals welcomed the messiness and disarray and unpredictability of bondmates, I did not."

A sharp, riffling growl punctuated its words.

"My first bonded one was Jeanne d'Arc. When the bond sang to me, it was too alluring to resist. She had power, that one. True power that could have done so much good in this world. Instead, she ignored my warnings."

The cat hesitated, still growling. *"No. She did worse than ignore me. She repudiated the true source of her power, insisting its roots lay in the evil, evil church. Jeanne viewed Shifter magic as blasphemous, but I, fool that I was, was certain I could change her mind.*

"You must know history," the cat continued. *"Not only did I fail to alter her headlong rush to her own doom, but the selfsame church that sent her to her death canonized her in 1920."*

Juan opened his mouth to say it was scarcely the cat's fault, but he remembered its instructions to remain silent.

How many other historical figures had been Shifters? Or Vampires for that matter? Or other iterations of magical beings? It reminded him of a television series he'd watched voraciously until the network canceled it. The world drawn by *Grimm's* creators depicted a layered reality marked by secret magical strata coexisting with human reality, except none of the humans knew about it.

"My next bondmate," the cat went on, *"was Albert Einstein. The world needed the knowledge locked inside his head. He skirted madness his entire life. Not unlike Jeanne, he saw me as a manifestation of his unbalanced mind, but he listened to me, and we established an uneasy détente."*

"Wasn't his son mentally ill?" Aura asked, adding quickly. "Sorry. I didn't mean to interrupt."

"His second son," the cat corrected her. *"Madness such as Einstein carried runs in families. At least I did more good with him than with Jeanne. I first suggested—and then insisted—he not return to Germany in the early 1930s. The Nazis stripped him of his professorship, confiscated his home, and burned his books. Even after all that, he was reluctant to leave Europe behind. In his last years, he welcomed me. Even took my form so we could run."*

The cat paused. Maybe it was thinking.

"You view the bond from the human side of things," the cat went on. *"You never consider it from the animal's perspective. We do our best, but in the end you make your own choices. I couldn't save Jeanne from her folly. I had better luck with Albert, perhaps because he was a different personality. Neither ever acknowledged being a Shifter, though. I never understood how Albert came to terms with becoming a mountain lion and running through forested glades in my body. Once he was human again, it was like those episodes never existed."*

Juan wanted to ask why the cat purposefully chose such hard cases, but then he realized it was the way the cat viewed him.

"I lay low through the Cataclysm," the cat went on. *"You should know I was one of the animals wishing to close our world off from the*

human one permanently. I was outvoted. Enough of my kin were bonded —and they loved their mated ones—that they overruled the few of us counseling a return to our insular status."

"I am so glad we got past that little wrinkle," Aura's cat spoke up, but didn't open its mind to Juan.

"You got your way," Juan's cat snarled. *"It's wise not to gloat."*

Aura's cat hissed.

Juan's hissed back but then said, *"I was encouraged when your group succeeded against the Cataclysm. Once that happened, I set my cynicism aside and lent my efforts to rebuilding what had been lost. It turns out Aura's cat's contingent was correct. I'd given in to my baser instincts, the ones devoted to preservation of my kin no matter the cost. It was an error on my part."*

"Why were you so certain we'd lose against the Cataclysm?" Juan asked over a choking sense of outrage. The cat had said not to speak, but Juan was furious—and disappointed by its lack of faith.

"Because a third of you were Vampires." Derision rang through the cat's mind voice. *"Vampires. Abominations. You should have died before subjecting yourself to such humiliation."*

"You know that," Juan said, "but we didn't. Not really. I never believed they existed. Faced with the reality, it was hard to—"

"Spare me," the cat broke in acidly. *"Given the same choice today, what would you do?"*

"I'd let Raphael bleed to death before I'd drink one drop of his blood. Being dead trumps being a Vampire any day. Every day." Juan ground his teeth together. "Earlier, you said there wasn't any point in chewing over the bones of the past. Did you change your mind?"

"I like you. You have spirit. It's why I offered to bond with you."

"You didn't answer my question," Juan said, not willing to let himself be diverted.

The cat snarled; the sensation spread through Juan's chest

before it replied. *"I didn't change my mind, but I needed to know if you'd learned from those years as a Vampire minion."*

Aura tightened her fingers around his. He picked up thoughts tumbling through her mind. Disgust for Raphael and his ilk. Anger at his cat. Pride for the answer he'd given.

Juan pulled on their joined hands and drew her against him. He wanted her to be proud of him. Ketha may have fallen in love with Viktor while he was still a Vampire, but Juan wanted to come to Aura clean of evil taint.

"The thing about being bondmates," Juan's cat went on, *"is it's a lot like being married. A good marriage, that is. There are no secrets. You need to see me for what I am and love and respect me for those things. Not for what you'd like me to be."*

"I need you to believe in my side of the bond too," Juan said, tightlipped.

"If I didn't, I'd never have offered to bond with you." The cat didn't sound the least bit cowed. *"You're strong and capable and, for once, I've linked myself to someone who won't disavow my existence. Those first two experiences taught me a lot. I can't change anyone. Not even someone linked to me through the Shifter bond."*

The cat fell silent. Aura pulled away from Juan's clumsy embrace. "While we have the animals front and center, I'd like to take a closer look at the ley lines."

Juan shut his earth eyes, and a psychic view spread before him. He hadn't paid attention to it while his cat was talking. "Are you done with what you wanted me to know?" he asked his cat.

"I appreciate you asking, and yes, I am. Did you find it helpful?"

Juan nodded. "Very. Before right now, I knew less than nothing about you, other than you were irritated because I hadn't made more of an effort to immerse myself in Shifter magic."

"Do you understand why?"

"Yes. It's much clearer to me. But knowledge has to be a two-way street. You claim to know everything about me, yet you didn't realize how much I hated being a Vampire. That means it's also important for me to tell you things and not assume you can glean everything from trips through my mind."

"You shielded your hatred for Vampires," the cat pointed out. *"To make certain the one who made you didn't realize the depth of your antipathy."*

"Very true. I was also force-fed *Vampire 101*. It made me somewhat less enthusiastic about volunteering for more lessons in anything supernatural. That was a mistake on my part," Juan hurried on. "One I've begun to make up for."

Aura's mouth twisted into half a smile. She glowed like a fey creature in his psychic view. "Ley lines?" she urged.

"By all means," Juan's cat replied.

"Tell me what we're searching for." Juan focused his attention on shimmery lines cutting through the ship's bar. He supposed they'd always been there, but the evidence of a magical world layered beneath the one he'd always assumed was absolute still surprised him.

"Examine the places the lines intersect," Aura instructed. "There are two spots in this room. One high above the bar and the other over by the bank of windows."

The lines pulsed as he stared at them, alternating between shimmery white and pale gold. "Are they alive in some way?"

"Of course," Aura replied. "It's how we determine magic is active in the world. Ley lines both carry and are fueled by its power. Look there." She pointed to the high spot.

Juan got off the couch and walked until he stood right beneath the glistening cords. When he altered his view, even walking behind the bar to see the node from behind, he noticed a spot that wasn't as bright. "Is that it?" He stabbed his index finger at where the flaw floated above his head.

Aura walked to his side. "Yes. It's one of them. And the largest. Look over here." She wrapped a hand around his arm and pulled him farther to one side.

Once he knew what to look for, he saw a second damaged place, and a third. "They're subtle," he said.

"Yes, they are," she countered, "but I bet they've been growing for years."

As he watched, light flared around the smallest defect. When it died down, the spot had fixed itself. He sucked in a surprised breath. "The ley lines are self-repairing?"

"To a point," Aura said. "When the damage reaches the extent of the stain you saw first, I don't believe it's fixable."

Juan thought back to Rowana's statement. She'd said, *"if we don't intervene, make them whole again somehow, I have no idea what will happen."*

Juan held a hand out, and Aura clasped it. "I'm guessing this is something you've never had to deal with before."

"It's true." Her expression turned grim. "Those years in Ushuaia when we were hanging on by a thread, never enough to eat and the air and water becoming more and more poisonous, no one was worried about how healthy the ley lines were. Hell, we didn't think we'd escape the Cataclysm."

"It's too bad no one was keeping an eye on them," he muttered.

"Indeed. I see that now. If we had, we'd have some idea how much more damage they've sustained—and when it began."

"My assumption is the Cataclysm is responsible." He shrugged. "Kind of like bad magic doing its damnedest to stamp out good magic."

"Ask your cat," she suggested.

"I was about to step in," Juan's cat said, *"but I appreciate your confidence in my wisdom."*

Boots pelting down the corridor outside the bar made Juan's head snap toward the door. The view through his third eye broke apart, and he blinked, forcing his normal vision to take over faster.

"Whatever happened, it must be serious," Aura muttered and pulled her fingers out of his as she turned to face the doorway.

Recco burst through. "Come quick. Something's happening in Grytviken."

"What? When we left the bridge, you couldn't even see it," Juan sputtered.

Recco tossed his hands skyward. "I have no fucking idea. But the whole skyline turned black. Ketha says we have to get in a raft immediately, so we can go there and cast some kind of counter spell."

"Makes sense," Aura said. "These things get out of control really, really fast. If we tarry, not much point in leaving at all, but if the darkness grows too much, it could swallow the ship."

"What darkness?"

Aura directed pained green eyes on him. "We opened a portal into Hell—or the demon did when we cast it out of the priest's body. My best guess is he's returned with reinforcements. And he's out for blood." Pushing past Juan, she took off at a run.

"Get moving," Juan's cat exhorted. *"I don't want to miss this."*

Juan elbowed Recco. "We need to follow her." He raced out of the bar, heading for the nearest staircase.

"Welcoming power takes some getting used to," Recco said from behind him. "My wolf didn't like it one bit when I detoured to get you. Told me we could use telepathy and be done with things."

Juan didn't waste breath replying. He reached the stairs and took them three at a whack. When he stormed into the bridge, competing conversations rang from all sides. A quick glance out the windows stopped him dead in his tracks. Breath whooshed from him. Beyond the storm that had been raging when he left, everything had turned black. Not gray, like the normal backdrop of an Antarctic storm, but black.

"Shit!" he muttered. "Is the Cataclysm back?"

"No," his cat answered, *"but what's out there isn't any better."*

"Do you know what it is?" Juan pressed.

"I do." The cat didn't sound the least bit pleased. *"It's the same demon horde that drove Jeanne to her death."*

"How can you know it's the same?" Juan asked, following his question with, "Never mind."

"Demons are immortal." A jagged growl followed the cat's words.

"We have to go now," Ketha screamed at Viktor.

"No. It's too dangerous." He gripped her arm. "I'll pull anchor and set sail into the storm before I let you go to Grytviken."

Ketha hauled a hand back but stopped shy of slapping him. She skinned her lips back from her teeth. "I understand you love me and want to protect me, but you do not get to make decisions for me. I will welcome you if you choose to come with us, but we have to leave now. Every second we delay, that thing out there"— she waved an arm in the direction of the windows—"gathers momentum."

Juan bolted across the room to where Viktor stood. He recognized the closed-off expression on his friend's face. *"Amigo."* He planted himself dead center in front of Viktor, displacing Ketha.

"You too?" Viktor shifted furious eyes to Juan.

"Afraid so. I'll man one Zodiac. You take the other. We'll split everyone between the two boats. Either things will work out and we'll come back. Or not. What if that darkness spawns another Cataclysm, and we did nothing to stop it?"

"Who are we protecting?" Viktor's words were lined with bitterness.

Juan leaned close. "Ourselves. While we're ashore, we'll take care of those Vamps too."

Viktor shifted his gaze to Ketha. "Would you really have hit me?"

She shook her head sadly. "No. But I'd have figured out the contraption to launch the rafts with or without your help."

Something altered in Viktor's expression. Juan thought he saw the outline of a raven flutter in the air. "Is everyone game?" Viktor didn't raise his voice. He didn't have to since the side conversations had died away to nothing once Ketha began screaming.

The first yes came from Aura, but it was followed by a chorus of assents.

"One of you lower the gangway," Viktor said in a clipped voice. "Juan and I will float the rafts. Get the iron blade and both rifles and as much ammo as you can lay your hands on. Layer up. Be sure to wear your life vests. Bottom of the gangway in ten minutes."

Viktor bolted out of the bridge with Juan hard on his heels. "What changed your mind?" Juan asked as they ran.

"Ketha. And my raven. Both convinced me we didn't have a choice."

They reached the Zodiac launch deck and worked together to turn the first raft over, centering it in the crane's webbing.

"But you wish it were otherwise," Juan said.

"Of course I do." Viktor swung to face him. "I have a wife. I want to keep her safe. Is that so hard to understand? Your boat's ready to lower."

Juan gripped Viktor's forearm. "We'll get through this."

"I wish I had your confidence."

Juan squeezed harder. "Something Ketha said before we took on the Cataclysm was we had to believe we'd prevail. Goddammit, Vik. Alter your attitude. This isn't about you losing a power struggle. It's about all of us making it through so we can fight another day."

"You're right." Viktor set his jaw in a tight line. "I'll pull my head out of my ass. Now get out of here."

Juan leapt nimbly into the Zodiac and grasped the webbing to stabilize the raft as Viktor lowered it onto the water. Waves slapped *Arkady's* hull, and Juan readied himself to fire the engine. It would be a rough ride across the harbor to the beach hiding within the unnatural blackness.

11

HELL'S GATEWAY

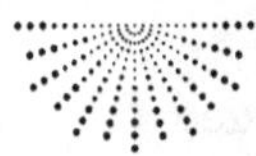

AURA GRIPPED the rope running along the top of the Zodiac's pontoons as the small craft careened toward shore. Wind howled; hail and sleet felt like shrapnel when they connected with her body. The raft hit the waves head-on, slapping each one with a sound like a gunshot. They had one rifle and the iron saber with them. As soon as they left *Arkady's* shadow, water splashed over the pontoons, threatening to fill the raft.

Juan sat in the stern, guiding them by some sixth sense because he sure couldn't see much. For one heart-stopping moment, she hoped to hell he wasn't in the grip of fell forces pushing them out to sea with all the finesse of a wayward Siren. She switched to her psychic view; relief burned hot when she saw the old whaling community bearing down on them.

Have faith in him, she lectured herself.

"And his cat," her bondmate added dryly.

"Sorry," she told her cat. *"I'm not thinking straight."*

"Better correct that. We'll be in the thick of things soon."

"We'll land in a minute or two," Juan said, his words almost swallowed by the shrieking wind. "Has anyone figured out what we're facing? My cat says it's a demon horde but didn't provide any further details."

Aura clamped her jaws together so hard, her teeth ached. She'd been so busy worrying about Juan—and being scared to her bones —she hadn't focused on what their enemy was. Hopefully, the others in the raft hadn't been quite so remiss.

"Your bondmate is right about it being demons," Rowana said.

"A lot of them," Karin added.

"So that's what feels so foul," Recco muttered.

"Beneath it all, I sense Vamps," Juan said. "Is it possible the demons freed the batch beneath the barracks?"

"Anything is possible, but it doesn't seem likely. No love lost between Vamps and demons," Aura muttered. She pulled the tattered edges of her sanity together. Never mind it wasn't fair they had to fight again so soon after facing the Cataclysm and the demon in the church. Never mind they didn't have an organized plan this time. How could they? They couldn't sense their enemy from where *Arkady* rocked on her anchor chain.

Excuses.

Bullshit excuses.

Anger bubbled from her guts, and Aura grabbed it with both hands. She needed its energy, had to move beyond the fear miring her in crippling inertia. Besides Karin and Rowana, Tessa, Moira, and Zoe were in her raft, along with Recco and Juan. Everyone else was with Viktor.

Sand scraped the bottom of the raft, and Juan leapt over the pontoon, hanging onto the anchor rope. "Get out," he ordered tersely. "Watch the waves. Time them. It's too cold to risk your boots filling up with water." He tied off the craft, piling rocks over the knotted rope end.

Soon they stood huddled in a tight circle on a rocky beach. The drone of the second Zodiac's engine grew louder, but the surrounding gloom reduced her vision to a few feet.

"We need a plan," Aura shouted to make herself heard. "Does anyone have one?"

"The unmaking spell to break the demons' hold?" Zoe suggested. "It was the only one I could think of that would make a clean break betwixt the underworld and here."

Aura did some quick calculations. "It will take all twelve of us women, but it's a damned good idea."

"How about if you and I go Vampire hunting?" Recco directed his words at Juan and shouldered the iron blade.

"Wait until Viktor's boat lands," Juan said. "If the women are all required for the spell Zoe mentioned to work, then the four of us men will take on the Vampires. There's the other Zodiac." He ran into the surf, water sloshing around his knee-high boots, and caught the rope Viktor tossed him.

Aura shifted from foot to foot, waiting for the other raft to disgorge its occupants. It was bitterly cold. She had layers of clothing on, topped by waterproof outer garments, but the wind bit right through all of it. She directed a ribbon of magic to her feet, in hopes of them not turning into useless blocks of frozen flesh.

The air felt thick, heavy, filled with death and rot. She kept her mind shuttered so she wouldn't fall prey to the same anxiety that had filled her when she'd been certain Juan was headed the wrong way. Whatever evil surrounded South Georgia Island sapped the spirit. If she opened herself at all, the urge to run as fast and far as she could from the rock-studded stretch of shore was overwhelming.

It didn't matter one whit nowhere safe existed.

The occupants of the second Zodiac trudged ashore. Aura trotted to Ketha on feet she couldn't feel. "Unmaking spell?"

"As good as any other." Ketha sounded rattled. "We need to begin now. Before this thing closes in even more and paralyzes us."

Viktor wrapped his arms around Ketha. "Be careful." His

words were a combination of threat and entreaty. "The men and I are going after the Vamps."

"You be careful too," Ketha said. "I love you."

A ghost of a smile flitted across his face, red and raw from the cold. "Love you too, darling." Turning, he took off through the gloom with Juan, Recco, Daide, and the weapons.

Aura considered running after them to request one of the rifles, but the gun part didn't matter. Not really. What they faced wasn't amenable to something as prosaic as bullets, whether they included silver powder or not. She wasted a few seconds wishing she'd hugged Juan and told him to guard himself, but his cat was more than competent. If anyone could pull Juan through this, it was his bondmate.

"*Good call,*" her cat spoke up.

"Gather close." Ketha gestured to all of them, and they formed a tight circle. "This will take less magic if we can cut some of the distance between us and the church."

"How do you know it's the epicenter?" Tessa asked.

"I don't," Ketha snapped, even surlier than usual. "But it's as good a guess as any. It's where we drove the demon to ground."

"So we'll angle toward the church until it takes so much magic to move forward, it turns into a crapshoot," Aura said and shook her head. "My words didn't come out right. We move forward until we hit a balance point where it takes equivalent amounts of magic to project the destruction spell versus plowing through evil."

"I understood well enough." Karin touched her arm. "Be sure to save some power to ward yourselves," the older woman exhorted. "Whatever's out there saps the will, and soon enough it will understand we're intent on its destruction."

"I'm certain it already does and is gearing up to throw more shit our way. Form three lines of four," Ketha said, followed by, "Let's go."

Aura brought up the rear in the last line with Karin, Moira, and Tessa. She alternated her psychic view with her earth eyes. The problem with her third eye was it saw all manner of impossible things flying—or lumbering—toward them. Gryphons. Furies. Man-sized bats and even a dragon. Despite the freezing temperatures, the stench of rot filled her nostrils with every breath she took. How the fuck could she be smelling roadkill. Dead things left to putrefy beneath a tropical sun. Human bodies with flesh rotting off the bones and glazed, empty eye sockets—

"Enough!" Her cat screeched from the sidelines.

"No kidding," she muttered and funneled more power into her wards. It helped sort illusion from reality, but not by much.

Karin made a gagging noise from next to her. "Jesus, but that's rank," she complained.

"Those things flying at us—" Tessa shouted.

"Aren't real," Karin spoke firmly, using her best no-nonsense doctor voice.

"How do you know?" Moira's eyes had become bottomless, dark pools, and she trained them on Karin. "If we opened Hell's gates, those things definitely could have escaped."

The rows in front of them ground to a halt, and Aura nearly pitched up against Rowana's back. "Why are we stopping?"

Rowana turned. "We must have hit the balance point you described earlier." Her voice was thin, strained.

Aura risked a view through her third eye. They'd passed the gift shop and post office, so the church wasn't much farther. The women formed two circles with eight in the outer ring and four inside.

Aura was part of the inner ring, and she held out her mitt-covered fingers to Ketha and Rowana. Karin stood with them as well. Aura understood this deployment. They were the oldest, the most powerful magically, and they'd carry the brunt of the spell. The task of the outer circle was to make certain nothing interrupted their casting. She sent a quick prayer to the goddess to watch over Juan and the men, and then she cleared her mind of everything but the task in front of them.

Ketha began to chant in her clear, pure soprano. Karin picked up the incantation, followed by Rowana. When they fell silent for the space of three heartbeats, Aura wove the strands that would cause evil to implode. Wings brushed her face. The foul odor intensified. It hit her so hard, bile splashed the back of her throat, but she swallowed it back and kept right on reciting her part. She could vomit later—if there was a later.

She needed her third eye for this casting. Had to see if what she was doing was working, or if she had to alter some of the elements. Ketha wielded earth, her strongest suit. Rowana channeled water, and Karin air. Aura threaded those three elements plus fire into an ever-changing panoply meant to confound the wickedness escaped from Hell. If they could get some traction, their next move would be to blow up the gateway. Once the demon spawn were trapped, much of their power would dissipate.

She hoped.

But that part was a long way off. Not in real time, but in magical reckoning.

Breath rattled in her lungs, and liquid sluiced down her face. She thought it was tears from the cold until some dripped into her mouth, and she understood she was bleeding. Christ! Had one of the Furies or Gryphons or things she had no name for cut her face? She was so cold, it could have happened without accompanying pain to alert her.

Her spell faltered, and she gave herself a sharp mental slap. Cuts, bruises, even broken bones, were nothing. If they failed, they'd all die here. The hell-spawned horde knew they were engaged in an all-out, to-the-death war, and they were fighting back.

Wind intensified, howling around them. The temperature, already impossibly cold, dropped another twenty degrees. Her teeth chattered, and an insidious lethargy—by-product of the intense cold—weakened her.

A trickle of heat, counterpart to the chill, began deep in her belly. Her cat was doing its damnedest to help, and she loved her bondmate beyond measure. It wasn't giving up; neither would she. Shock waves rolled through her. Until the idea about giving up intruded, she'd had no inkling how close she was to wrapping her arms around herself and sinking into a heap on the frozen dirt beneath her feet.

She took stock of their spell. Karin stumbled with fatigue where she stood, and Aura threaded an arm around her. "Steady," she said. "Not much more, and we'll have it."

"Thanks. I was fading." The old wolf Shifter was panting, and white showed around her bloodshot copper eyes.

A quick glance at Ketha and Rowana told her they were at least holding their own. "What we're doing isn't working fast enough," she shouted. "I'm done titrating my power. Give this everything you've got."

"But how will we kill those abominations after we close the gateway?" Rowana asked.

"If this works, everything will implode together."

Aura was done talking. The others would either lend whatever they had in reserve. Or not. She fanned fire into a blazing inferno and fed it with air. Karin added still more air to the mix.

"Wait on earth and water," Aura cautioned Ketha and Rowana. "Let this part of the spell close the gateway. Once it's accomplished, you can drown or smother whatever's left on this side."

"We need to move closer," Tessa yelled from the outer circle.

"Do it," Moira shouted. "We'll guard the perimeter."

Aura pulled her casting back, holding it in abeyance but ready to deploy if anything wicked attacked outright. The group surged forward until they stood directly in front of the white clapboard church. The bell clanged violently, banging against the sides of its housing atop the structure.

Aura loosed her spell again, screaming the words. Her throat was raw from the wind and the cold and forcing words through it. Something she couldn't see fastened what felt like talons around her throat. An unseen hand stinking of death clamped over her mouth.

She grappled with whatever had decided she commanded the means of their unmaking. Heat streaked down her face, and she tasted more blood. Shrieks rose around her. Maybe from outraged Shifters. Maybe from demons fighting for their lives. Aura couldn't tell which.

Power bubbled in her belly, and she let it flow through her fingers. Fire shot from her fingertips, shredding her mitts, but unholy grunts suggested her magic had found its target. The choking sensation lessened, and the talons fell away.

"Now!" Ketha shrieked. "Outer circle too. Funnel fire and air right at the church."

Aura tried to peer through her third eye, but blackness spread everywhere. No ley lines. Nothing but unremitting darkness. Her earth eyes showed the same vista. Christ! Had her attacker blinded her?

"Which way for my magic?" she shouted. "I can't see."

Someone gripped her shoulders and turned her in a quarter circle. "Dead ahead," Karin said. To her credit, the doctor didn't start probing about why she couldn't see.

Aura focused fire and air and let them fly. Pressure built in the ether surrounding her, pushing until she couldn't get a full breath into her lungs. She reached for her cat and its magic but couldn't find either.

"Yes! Goddammit, now!" Ketha shrieked before Aura could fully process what her cat's absence meant.

An explosion pounded through her, battering her with shock waves. A second and third followed on its heels, accompanied by a dead, burnt smell. Compared with the stench of rot, it felt clean, and Aura dared to hope maybe this deserted whaling station wouldn't turn into their tomb.

"What's happening?" she shouted, not knowing whether to keep magic flowing or not.

"The church. Its walls are pulsating as if it's going to blow apart any moment," Karin said.

"Do we need to get down?"

"I don't think so. I might be wrong, but I believe our power is doing battle with evil within its walls. We don't like to acknowledge it," the wolf Shifter went on, "but churches harbor power too. Power that stands against evil. I believe it's helping us."

"So moving closer was smart?"

"It appears so. What's wrong with your eyes?" The healer part of Karin finally bounded into the breach.

"I have no idea."

One more excruciatingly loud blast rocked Aura. It would have knocked her to her knees, but Karin grabbed her arm.

"Cut your power," Ketha shouted. "We did it."

"Talk to me," Aura pleaded. "Did what? Is the gateway shut? What about Hell's minions?"

Ketha closed on her and gripped her shoulder. "Your plan worked. We gave it everything, and the darkness is fading. To give credit where it's due, the church focused our efforts. Without it as a crucible, we might not have succeeded." She took a breath. "Jesus. Your face—"

"None of that," Karin cut in.

"None of what?" Aura screeched around the thick, sore places in her throat. "I can't see, but what else is wrong?"

"You look like you went ten rounds with a gorilla," Ketha said, ignoring Karin's warning. "Your face is all cut up."

"So's mine," Tessa said. "Zoe's too. Sharp shit was flying through the air. Did some of it damage Aura's eyes?"

Aura started to shiver. Nerves. An adrenaline overload. Relief they'd come through unscathed. Or had they? "Did everyone make it?" she asked, and sucked in a tight breath.

"More or less," Tessa said. "Moira's arm is broken. Several of us have deep cuts on our faces. Would have been worse except for all these layers of clothes."

Karin latched an arm through Aura's. "Come on. I'm taking you inside the church so I can assess your eyes."

"Good idea," Ketha said. "It will still be cold, but at least we'll be out of the wind."

Karin herded Aura to the left. "Too bad you can't see," she muttered. "A dead Gryphon is ahead, except the flesh is smoking off its bones."

"Makes sense," Aura said through chattering teeth. "Nothing from any of the other worlds can remain here without magic to power it. We severed the gateway."

"Yes, dearie. Having those abominations here in any form defies one of the many laws of physics, which means they won't be here long. Watch the steps. There are four of them. Hard left and head straight through the door."

The scents of rot and brimstone battled with incense, candles, and old leather as Aura walked inside the church that had lent its particular brand of power to help them.

"I feel like I should thank this building," Aura muttered.

"Meh," Karin replied. "If the priest was still in residence, he'd consider us abominations, not unlike the batch we ousted. Face this way." Karin closed her hands around either side of Aura's head, holding it steady. She was still numb from cold or the contact would have hurt if her skin was as abraded as Ketha had suggested.

"Is it only your earth eyes?" Karin asked.

"It's everything," Aura said. "I can't see shit with my third eye, either."

"Heh! There's a piece of good news."

Aura waited, but Karin didn't elaborate on her comment. The

sounds of footsteps surrounded her as the other women crowded into the church.

"I could use a spot of help," Karin called.

"I'm here." Ketha trotted over.

"Drop your warding," Karin instructed Aura. "All of it, and then lie on the floor. One of those bastards, maybe the dragon, did its damnedest to disable your magical center. Have you heard from your cat lately?"

Aura shook her head. "Not since the explosions."

"I see the blocked place," Ketha said. "What do we do about it?"

"Jesus!" Aura complained. "I'm right here. What blocked place? Where is it? Talk to me. Not about me."

Karin ignored her and focused her words at Ketha. "Open your magic so I can borrow from it. Once we're joined, hold steady until I say we're done."

"What are you going to do?" Aura fought panic.

"Correct the problem, what else?" Karin said with more than a touch of asperity. "Focus on your breathing. I'll have this fixed up in a jiffy. Might hurt, though. Do not move. No matter what."

A blast of white-hot pain shot through the dead center of Aura's forehead. She screamed but held still. She'd known Karin her whole life and trusted her.

A yowl came from deep inside her. *"Yes!"* her bondmate screeched. *"I'm back. The barrier between our magics fell. Thank every god and goddess that ever watched out for our kind."*

Aura wanted to tell Karin her cat was back, but *don't move* meant just that. Talking required movement.

"We're done here, Ketha," Karin murmured. "I'm relieved you still had some magic left for me to leverage."

"Me too," Ketha replied. "When you asked, I wasn't certain."

A cool palm settled over Aura's forehead. "You did very well, dear," Karin said in her best doctor voice. "I heard your bond animal, so I believe we were successful. Open your earth eyes first."

Aura swallowed around the tender spots in her throat and opened her eyes. The empty nave shimmered before coming into focus. Tears spilled over, and she reached for Karin. "Thank you."

"Don't mention it." She pulled Aura into a sit. "Your psychic view will return as your magic replenishes itself."

"Can you tell me what happened?" Aura asked.

"The non-technical answer is one of the hell horde drove a wedge into your magical center, which is in the same region as your visual cortex. So it effectively cut you off from your bond-mate and blinded you at the same time."

Aura swiped at her wet cheeks, and her fingers came away bloody. "Am I crying blood?"

"Nope. It's all the abrasions on your face. We'll attend to them later. The cold will keep the bleeding to a minimum."

"I'm worried about the men," Ketha said. "I'm heading toward the barracks."

"Not by yourself, you're not," Aura countered.

Ketha furled both brows. "Really? You probably should—"

"Stuff it." Aura rolled to her feet. "If you go, we all should. Not a good idea to split up."

"The gateway's closed," Ketha protested.

"That might be so," Aura shot back, "but there may be Vamps on the loose. In truth, there probably are, or the men would be back by now."

Zoe walked close. "I'm game."

Aura blanched at the sight of the other Shifter's lacerated face. "Aw, crap. Do I look like you?"

Zoe rolled her dark eyes. "Och. Worse."

"None of us will be in the running for a beauty pageant anytime soon," Tessa muttered.

"Sooner we get this over with," Ketha said, "the sooner we can return to *Arkady*." She trudged toward the church door.

Aura followed her through, and her eyes widened. Bodies lay crumpled as far as she could see. Maybe fifty. Maybe more. A collection of smoking, crumbling forms that would have made a Stephen King book tame.

"Shit," she muttered. "They look more menacing now than when they were attacking us."

Moira trooped past her. "See. Told you they were real, although this is one time I'd rather have been wrong."

"I feel like I should take inventory or something," Zoe muttered, "but it's my archaeologist side, and I'm ignoring it."

"Come on, people." Ketha clapped her hands together. Her mitts were as tattered as Aura's. "I asked my wolf for information, but it can't get through to the men's bond animals."

Aura stuffed her half-frozen hands in her pockets and stumbled after Ketha. Worry for Juan filled her. She had no idea how much time had passed, but it had to have been more than an hour. The men should have returned long since. How much time did it take to behead a few Vamps?

"Hold up," she called and ran back into the church. She grabbed the first reasonably portable crucifix she found and ran after the women. They didn't have the iron blade. Maybe the cross would buy them a moment or two, although it felt pretty paltry if they faced a passel of angry Vamps who'd recently emerged from stasis.

THE ONLY GOOD VAMP IS A
DEAD VAMP

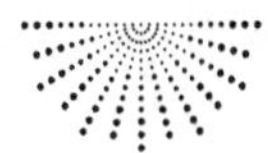

AN HOUR EARLIER

Juan missed the supernatural speed and strength he'd enjoyed as a Vampire. Granted, he'd traded it for something far better and cleaner with his Shifter bond, but he wasn't in cat form, running toward the barracks. Something about the darkness dragged at him. The cold too. He was used to polar regions, but the current chill was unnerving. It felt alive, ominous, hungry, as if it had targeted them. The bone-rattling sensation had to affect the other men as well, but no one said much as they loped through the gloom, dodging rocks and piles of bones.

Gathering his unfamiliar magic, Juan took a stab at assessing if the Vampire feel was growing stronger. Before he was done sampling from every angle, Viktor hissed, "Ssht. Wait."

Juan feinted sideways to avoid plowing into Viktor's back.

"Why'd we stop?" Recco kept his voice low, but he was close enough to hear even over the incessant roar of the wind that attacked from first one side and then another.

"Don't know," Juan muttered.

Recco had come to a halt on Juan's other side with Daide right behind him.

Juan twisted to face him. "This storm. Something's weird about it."

"Something's not right about all of this," Viktor growled. He had the saber lashed across his back. Juan held the ship's rifle in the crook of one elbow, and Daide had the old Remington from the barracks.

"The wind blows from the northwest across this island," Juan said. "The Allardyce Range protects this side." He hunched his shoulders against a particularly vicious blast of wind. "It's what I'm talking about, what I meant by *weird*. The wind just came from the south. Last gust was from the east."

"Jesus! Have you lost your mind, mate?" Viktor cinched his hood tighter. "I stopped because I sense Vamps moving our way. We need to find a defensible location and wait for them to find us. Not engage in a philosophical discussion about atypical weather patterns."

"Yeah. I felt those fuckers too, but I was waiting to be certain," Daide muttered.

"How the hell did they get loose?" Recco sounded spooked.

"How else?" Viktor asked sourly. "Demons must have opened their crypt."

Wind and weather were where Juan lived, elements he understood. Once Viktor gave voice to the obvious, he fought against a creeped-out sensation. Them against a few Vamps was one thing, but demons were a whole other level of threat. He narrowed his eyes, willing them to pierce the blackness shrouding them.

"Should we go back and help the women?" Juan kept his question quiet. No telling who might be listening.

"Pfft. They scarcely need our assistance," Viktor muttered. "Best thing we can do is our part, which is taking care of the Vampires."

Juan felt torn. He wanted to be both places. "Let's finish this off fast so we can tackle whatever's left of the demons."

"Psychic view," Juan's cat spoke up and fashioned the alteration.

Juan looked out at a gray world bisected by ley lines and determined they were about halfway between the last rickety building and the barracks. Going back wasn't wise because it meant turning their backs on the Vampires. He raked his gaze over the steep, inhospitable mountainside rising to their left. It wouldn't work, either, as a place to take a stand. They needed somewhere open and flat where they could fight.

"I'm going to assume those Vamps didn't lose their ungodly speed and coordination," Viktor said.

"They didn't," Recco replied. "For all I know, they could be worse. According to Raph, they'll be nastier, more aggressive—if it's even possible."

"Richard's farewell letter said there were five of them," Juan said still hunting for a spot that might offer them an advantage. "How about those boulders?" He jerked his chin at a spot about fifty feet behind them.

"What boulders?" Daide asked.

"I'm using my third eye," Juan explained. "Follow me." He broke into a shambling trot, moving faster since he could see obstacles before he tripped over them. He ducked behind a boulder that stood a good eight feet tall. A slightly smaller one sat off to its side.

"How about this?"

"Better than anything I came up with," Viktor acknowledged.

"I'm going to shift," Recco announced. "My wolf convinced me one of us needs to be in animal form. It also said all of you should use your third eye so you don't shoot us by mistake."

"Crap!" Daide muttered. "I'm not very good at the transition."

"None of us are," Juan said. "Ask your coyote to do it for you. If it understands how much you need it, maybe it won't be as put out with you."

"We made decent progress when Karin worked with me," Daide replied.

"Whatever you do, be quick about it," Viktor said. "I figure we have five minutes, tops. Probably less."

Daide nodded sharply and faced the boulder, splaying his mitts across it. Juan heard him muttering. *"Can you help?"* he asked his bond animal.

"In what way?"

"Tell, er suggest, to Daide's coyote this isn't the time to hold grudges. We need all of you."

His cat didn't reply, and Juan didn't push the issue. If he'd asked something of his bond animal that fell outside the acceptable realm, the cat didn't chide him for it.

Recco's clothing lay in a pile. He balanced his boots and a rock atop everything, so the wind wouldn't blow them into the restless ocean. "Fuck, it's cold," he managed through chattering teeth. Light flashed and shimmered, and a black-and-gray timber wolf formed where Recco had stood. It spread its jaws in the lupine equivalent of a grin, tongue lolling. The wolf nudged Daide's upper leg with its snout.

Daide dropped a gloved hand onto the wolf's head and stroked it. "All is well," he said. "My bond animal is on board, and I'll be careful with my bullets."

"Psychic view?" Recco's wolf demanded confirmation.

"Yes, brother."

The wolf faded toward the mountainside.

Juan got the ship's rifle ready and clicked off the safety. Daide did the same with the Remington. Viktor slid the saber from its makeshift scabbard. The reek of death and rot intensified as the Vamps drew closer. Juan's heart pounded against his ribs. This would be over fast. No point even trying to conceal themselves with magic. None of them were familiar enough with Shifter magic, and he didn't want to divert any of his power to finesse an awkward spell.

Vamps dealt in supernatural strength, stealth, and speed. Shifter magic was far more nuanced and multifaceted, but it also presumed someone had been a Shifter long enough to learn to use it, which counted the four of them out.

"I'll behead one or two of them," Viktor said. "Then I'll do my damnedest to get out of the way to give you clear shots at the others."

It wasn't much of a plan, but it was the best they were likely to come up with.

Juan balanced on the balls of his feet and moved the rifle to firing position. He was pleasantly surprised to find his third eye did dual duty as the night vision scope he didn't have. The Ruger Guide gun butting against his shoulder was designed to take down a polar bear, so it should at least slow a Vamp down.

He inhaled and wished he hadn't. The sulfur stench of hungry Vampire was overwhelming, and his gut cramped in protest. Rotten eggs raised to the millionth power.

"Ready," Viktor said in a tense voice. The wind, their constant, nagging companion, died to a brisk breeze, but Juan couldn't divert his attention to figure out what it meant. He hoped to hell Aura was safe, but he had more faith in her magic than his own.

As soon as we get out of this, magic hits the big time. I'll practice until my eyes bleed spells.

Daide swung the Remington to a shoulder, sighting down its barrel, and gave Juan and Viktor a thumbs-up sign before curving his right index finger around the trigger.

Five bodies shambled toward them, not moving at anything like normal Vamp speed. Juan ground his teeth. Were they as weak as they appeared? The lead Vamp tilted his head up, displaying a face where the flesh was eaten away. Bone showed through along his jawline on one side and around one eye socket, making him look like the ghoul he was. His hands were curved into bony claws. Any clothing he'd once had had rotted away years ago, and he was naked. As Juan watched, a clump of flesh peeled off one arm and splatted onto the ground.

The other four Vamps strode close behind, flanking the leader on both sides. They were in just as bad a shape, their bodies half-eaten away by rot. If he'd had time, Juan would have gloated. The bastards finally looked like what they were, any beauty they'd once held eroded by putrefaction and the passage of time.

Viktor shouted something in German and charged, sword raised and ready. One of the Vamps on the side bent and scooped something into a bony claw. "Watch out!" Juan shrieked, but the Vamp tossed a television-sized rock right in front of Viktor. He did his damnedest to avoid it, but it rolled. He tripped and sprawled into the dirt. At least, he still had hold of the saber.

With an outraged howl, Recco launched himself from the shadows and drove the lead Vamp to the ground, clawing and biting. The Vamp tried to shake the wolf off. When that didn't work, it flipped over and settled its skeletal fingers around the wolf's neck.

A rifle blast at close quarters pounded Juan, deafening him, followed by one more. Daide had shot two of the Vamps. The one who'd sabotaged Viktor's forward drive and the one right next to him. The silver-and iron-laced bullets did their work. Spreading holes in the middle of the Vamps' chests caught fire. Stinking smoke made the stench worse.

Two down. Three to go.

Juan leapt to Viktor's side and wrenched the blade from his grasp. Circling around behind, he swung it hard sideways and beheaded the Vamp, choking the life out of the snarling, snapping wolf. Black blood spewed skyward, showering him and Recco with something that smelled like a cross between a charnel pit and a mass grave baking beneath an Amazon sun. How could the thing still have blood after all this time?

Juan's stomach revolted. He spat out a mouthful of vomit and hunted for the last two Vampires. The bastards hadn't been moving this fast before. Had their slow speed been a sham to lure him into a false sense of confidence?

Recco's wolf howled its thanks and shook itself from nose to tail tip.

Viktor lurched to his feet. "Goddammit! What a fucking nightmare."

"This gun is loud. My ears are still ringing. Can you walk?" Daide asked Viktor.

"Yeah. Twisted my ankle good, but I'll live. Grab the head."

"Why?" Juan stared at the Vampire's severed head, its eyes wide and staring.

"Ketha wanted tissue samples. Won't be anything left of the first two Vamps. They're still burning."

"What happened to the last two?" Daide asked, and scooped up the head, letting it dangle by its matted black hair. At least its eyes were shut. Dark, smoking holes, they'd been filled with madness.

"Good question." Juan stared into the grayness, seeking answers. As a reality check, he switched back to his earth eyes. "Hey! It's not black anymore."

"It's not," Daide agreed.

Viktor smiled grimly. "My money's on the women. I bet they had some success. We have to find those Vamps, though. Before they attack anyone else."

"Absolutely," Juan said. "But I suspect the women are more than a match for a couple of Vampires not firing on all cylinders."

"I'll track them," the wolf said and took off, its nose glued to the ground. *"Could one of you bring my clothes?"*

Juan bent and gathered the stack into his arms. It was awkward carrying it and the rifle. He arranged things so he could drop the clothing pile fast to free the Ruger for use.

Viktor grunted with pain, but he kept up. "I should have been more careful." His words sounded like they were coming from the bottom of a well.

"Eh, that's what everyone says when something goes wrong," Juan countered. "We underestimated them because it's what they wanted us to do. It's why they looked so slow and stumbling when they came at us."

Daide trotted behind them. "I can take some of those clothes."

"Nah. You've got the Vampire head. Plus, I don't want to stop to rearrange anything." A scuffle fifty yards away made Juan hasten his pace.

"Look over there," Daide yelled. "Recco's herding them into the water. Smart. Vamps hate water. The closer they are to it, the more it dilutes their power."

Juan dropped the clothes and shouldered the gun. "One of those is mine."

"But you won't kill it with that," Viktor protested.

"Maybe not, but I'll knock it into the surf. Then you can take care of it with the blade."

"Recco. Get back," Daide yelled.

Juan waited for a split second. As soon as he had a clean shot, he aimed right between the Vamp's eyes and fired. The blast made his ears hurt worse, but all the target practice he'd done in case a tour group was attacked by a polar bear finally found a practical use. He'd have chuckled, but he was too busy making certain the Vamp didn't rise from the surf washing over its limp form.

The other Vamp turned tail and tried to run, but proximity to water stymied his efforts. Since he was on a roll, Juan fired again. The back of the Vampire's skull blew away, turning into a cascade of bone, black blood, and grisly bits of flesh. The thing crumpled to its knees and pitched facedown into the frozen dirt.

Viktor limped forward, blade ready for action. The Vamp still in the water roared and shot to his feet. Ichor streamed down his face, coating everything with stinking black fluid. It rushed Viktor, but he stood his ground and swung the blade. Medieval iron sliced through bone and sinew with a ripping, tearing sound, and the Vamp's head rolled into the ocean. He was still screeching when his headless body toppled into the water. God only knew how.

Daide dropped the head and ran to the last Vamp who lay groaning on the ground twenty feet away. When he got close, he fired a shot directly into its back at heart level. The silver-and-iron-laced bullet formed the same expanding, fire-rimmed hole it had in the other two he'd shot.

Viktor bent forward and cleaned black blood off the blade with seawater.

Juan had covered half the distance to Viktor after the Vamp leapt to its feet. He ran the rest of the way to his friend and looped an arm around his back. "Lean on me, *amigo*."

"Thanks. Don't mind if I do. Ankle hurts like a bitch." Viktor shot a pained glance at Juan out of eyes the shade of raw emeralds.

The wolf loped past them to where Juan had dropped Recco's clothes. The air developed a familiar glistening aspect, and Recco took shape, naked, shivering, and hauling on clothes as fast as he could sort through the pile.

"I'd have helped you," Daide said.

"By the time you figured out what was what, I'd have succumbed to hypothermia. Nice trophy." Recco pointed at the head and sat on the frozen dirt. He dragged on socks and boots, pulling his waterproof pants down over the tops of them. Rolling to his feet, he grinned. "I admit I had my doubts when my wolf said we were shifting, but it must be a seer like Ketha. It was fun to fight in my bondmate's body."

"Maybe the seer part is a wolf trait." Daide grinned back. "My bond animal forgave me. I'm so grateful and relieved, I could kiss it."

"There you are!" Ketha called, and footsteps pounded toward them. She launched herself at Viktor, and he yelped. "What? You're hurt. Where? Let Karin take a peek."

"Fine. I'm fine. It's only my ankle. It can wait until we're back aboard *Arkady*. Don't fuss over me. Look over where Daide is. He got you something to give all your new lab equipment some exercise."

"Oooh." Ketha let go of Viktor and trotted to where Daide stood, the head once again dangling from his closed fist. "It's not every day a girl gets a dead Vampire head. Thank you."

Daide mock bowed. "Any time, ma'am. Service is my middle name."

Ketha burst out laughing and mock slugged him in the shoulder.

The women formed a circle around them, questions flying fast and furious.

Juan held up a hand. "We can trade war stories once we're back on the ship. The unnatural cold receded, but it's still damned chilly. Don't know about the rest of you, but I'm up for a hot shower, hot coffee, whiskey, and dinner. Not necessarily in that order."

Aura walked to Juan's side. "The Vamps?"

"Well and truly dead. All five of them."

"I'm glad." Her nostrils flared. "As soon as we obliterated the gateway, we came as fast as we could." She pressed her mouth into a tight line. "If we'd been on top of things, we'd have closed the portal when we were here earlier. None of us thought of it."

Before he could say something soothing, she hurried on. "We've grown soft. Our ancestors never would have made such a stupid mistake."

He muffled a snort but didn't mute quite all of it.

"I didn't mean to be funny." She screwed her mouth into a disapproving moue.

"Your ancestors—mine too—made a whole lot of mistakes. People didn't live very long a few hundred years back. Except Vampires, maybe, and they don't count."

"Oho! If Raphael could only hear you now." Aura rolled her eyes.

Juan took her arm and followed the others making their way back to where they'd beached the rafts. "If he could, he'd know his indoctrination failed miserably." Juan shook his head. "The only question I have is why anyone would welcome the transition to Vampire."

"Two potent reasons. The alternative is death. Plus, some people get off on power."

"Sure. I get it. Neither Vik nor I were strong enough to resist, but that was then. Knowing what we do now, I'm positive we'd choose death over being turned."

"What was different inside you after you fed from Raph?"

Juan thought about her question. "I was tethered to Raphael. I felt the bond or the link here." He patted his belly. "At first, it nagged and burned. After a while, it settled out, but I never escaped from feeling him inside me. It disgusted me, but I couldn't do anything about it."

Outraged yells came from the beach where they'd left the rafts. Juan broke into a run; Aura paced him. When they got there, Daide was slogging through the surf, hauling the anchor rope of one of the rafts. The other one bobbed twenty-five yards out.

"It's okay," Juan told Aura. "We'll use this one to round up the other raft."

"Someone didn't plan on us leaving." Her voice held a deadly edge. "Probably one of the demonic host."

"My take too, since the Vamps came from the opposite direction and wouldn't willingly approach water. It appears the anchor rope for the one Daide has tangled in underwater wreckage close to shore. Lucky for us."

"No shit. Otherwise, it would have been an unpleasant swim."

He swung toward her and held her face between his hands for several moments. "The important part, Aura, is they didn't win. Whether it was demons or Vampires, they didn't succeed. Not this time."

"Not ever," she ground out.

Viktor piled into the raft and fired the engine. "Come on, mate." He gestured at Daide. "Get in and at least pour the seawater out of your boots. Wool socks and neoprene mean you won't get frostbite. Seven more of you get in too. Once we reach the other raft, I'll bring it back to pick everyone else up."

Juan helped Aura into the raft with Viktor and Daide, and then he jumped in and made his way to where Viktor sat on a pontoon in the stern. "I'll take care of the other raft."

"But—"

"Uh-uh. See you back on *Arkady*. Let Karin fix your ankle."

Karin, Tessa, and Ketha joined them, and they motored to where the other Zodiac bobbed on the surf. The sea had settled since their inward journey, and Juan bounded into the empty raft, hauling the anchor rope after him. The engine sputtered and then caught, and he headed back to pick up the small group remaining on shore.

He'd never view Grytviken in quite the same way after today. It was far more than a sleepy, deserted whaling station and Shackleton's final resting place. Juan made a wry face. Shackleton had always been one of his heroes, and now he'd had a chance to prove his own mettle.

Not that his years at sea hadn't been a testing ground, but the stakes had grown much higher since the Cataclysm ran their other ship aground. The idea of earning his own chops was heady, and he turned his attention inward to his mountain cat.

"We've got this," he told his bond animal.

"If you master your magic, we've got this," his cat corrected him. *"You made me a promise."*

"It's one I intend to keep." Juan tossed the anchor rope to Recco and waited while everyone climbed into the raft.

"Last train tonight," he joked once they were underway.

He got a few smiles, but no one laughed.

"It's all right," Recco said. "No need to coddle us. It's not like we coughed up fifty thousand bucks for an Antarctic tour."

Juan's expression turned sober. "Old habits do die hard, and entertaining passengers is a comfort zone for me. Be sure to kick my ass if I sound too cheerful."

Zoe snorted. "Sure and I'm an expert at it. Mostly I've kicked my own, but I'm more than willing to practice on someone else."

"You're on." Juan swung the raft around to line it up with the gangway. He was cold and weary, and he stank of Vampire, but they'd won. It was all that mattered.

"We won today's battle." His cat's tone was solemn. *"The war has just begun."*

Juan wanted to pin his bondmate down, ask it to clarify what it meant, but he didn't have the energy. Clearing his mind of everything, he tied the raft to two cleats and steadied it while everyone filed up the gangway.

13

LOVE'S NOT ON THE MENU

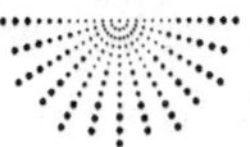

Aura stood in the shower in her cabin and let hot water pummel her. She didn't realize how chilled down she'd gotten until the pins-and-needles sensation of blood returning to her frozen toes and fingers made them ache all over again. She could have stood there until the water turned cold—if it ever did. The ship was fully self-contained with generators and desalinization backup in case they ran their fresh water tanks dry.

It was easier to let her thoughts drift than to relive the last few hours. She'd never spent any time on ocean-going vessels before, and the fact *Arkady* could sail from the tip of South America all the way to shipyards in Germany without stopping to refuel or resupply surprised her. The ship truly had everything needed not only to survive, but to be reasonably comfortable.

She flipped the taps off and reached outside the soaking shower curtain to snag a towel. Midway through combing out her hair, a knock sounded on her door.

"Yes?" Aura called, expecting one of the women.

"We have an early dinner underway," Juan called through the door. "I'm letting everyone know. Dining room in half an hour."

She set the comb down and slid a robe around herself, belting it securely. Each of the cabins had come with two thick robes made of white terrycloth with the ship's logo embroidered over a chest pocket. They'd been full of dust, but a tour through the ship's laundry made them good as new.

Without digging too deeply into her motivations, Aura crossed the cabin and pulled her door open. "Do you have a minute?"

Uncertainty crossed his defined cheekbones and squared-off chin, but then he smiled. "Sure. You were my last stop." Wet, blond hair had been combed back from his high forehead, and it began to curl where it streamed down his shoulders. Black stretchy pants hung off his slim hips, and a long-sleeved green shirt was topped by a black down vest. He still wore his knee-high Wellington boots.

She moved over and gestured him inside. "Take the chair," she said and perched on the edge of one of two bunks. "How come you always wear those boots?"

Juan shrugged. "They're warm and comfortable, but practical too. I never know when I might have to launch a raft or take part in a rescue. This way, all I have to do is layer my insulated jacket and waterproofs over what I have on."

"Kind of like a uniform, where you always dress the same?"

"Exactly. My working garb for shipboard life. Between *Arkady* and *Gavrill*, I lived on a boat 90 percent of the time—before my stint as a Vampire in Ushuaia." He moved to the chair and sank into it. "Nice to be clean," he said, "although when I breathe deep, I still smell Vampire."

"Might be from the head Daide rounded up for Ketha."

"Nah. It's from being drenched in Vampire blood. About the head, though. I'm glad Viktor remembered because it was the last thing on my mind. I'm interested to see what differences Ketha finds between its DNA and mine—or one of the other men's."

Aura closed her teeth over her lower lip, thinking. Retreating to academic mode, she said, "Too many variables."

"What do you mean?" Juan latched onto her face with his warm hazel eyes. Damn but he was a striking man.

"A huge unknown is what changes Vamp DNA experiences when those fuckers sink into stasis. It would be a miracle if Ketha could to do a direct compare and contrast. She'll have your DNA —except none of you are Vampires anymore—and DNA from Vamps that haven't had anything to eat for years. I walked over and examined that one in the shallows…"

She swallowed back revulsion. "The skin was sloughing off its bones. How the hell could something so decomposed still be alive in any form?"

"I wondered the same thing, but they weren't just alive. They were still sly, capable of reasoning." The smile faded from Juan's face. "Maybe Ketha will have some way of teasing out which alterations came from stasis."

"Maybe so. She was a talented researcher. She's modest, but she had more invitations to speak at conferences than she had time to attend them all. Her first love was teaching, and she was determined to not end up in a lab full-time."

"How about you?" Juan asked.

"How about me, what?"

"Were you more of a researcher, or did you enjoy your students? I know you're a historian, but what era did you specialize in?" He narrowed his eyes slightly. "Before you answer me, was there a reason you asked me if I had time to talk?"

Heat rose from the open neck of her robe and suffused her cheeks. Too late to send magic to defuse her blush. "No special reason. I enjoy talking with you."

He dragged the chair next to the bed and dropped a hand onto her thigh. "I like talking with you too."

His nearness skewered her with desire, and heat from his fingers traveled up her leg. Her belly tightened with awareness of how much she wanted to drag him onto the narrow bunk with her.

"Now there's a good idea." Her cat's voice was droll—and totally unexpected. It had never had boo to say about the occasional lover she took into her bed back in Wyoming.

Juan stroked her leg through her robe. Wherever he touched, his fingers ignited desire and need. Before it took over and turned her into a puddle of mush, she slithered out from beneath his hand.

"Did I do something wrong?" He laced his fingers together in his lap but didn't move his chair back to its spot next to the small desk.

She licked suddenly dry lips. "No. Not at all. I, um— That is, you..." She hooded her eyes. With him this close, she couldn't think straight.

"It's all right. I didn't mean to put you on the spot. I still want to hear more about you and history and teaching and research, but I need to get moving. Recco and Daide were working on dinner, and I promised I'd help."

Disappointment vied with relief. If he left, she wouldn't have to figure out what to do about an overwhelming urge to fasten her mouth over his. "I'll throw on some clothes and meet you in the galley."

"Great. We can always use extra labor—and opinions." He stood. "See you down there soon." His tone was casual, lacking the intensity that had marked his earlier words.

Aura watched him cross the cabin and let himself out the door. Her body vibrated with unslaked lust. She wanted Juan. Wanted to wrap her arms and legs around his tall, lean form and draw him into the secret place deep inside herself, but they didn't know one another very well.

"You're thinking with your modern brain." Her cat was back. Or, more likely, it had never left.

Aura stood and draped her robe over the hook where it lived. She rummaged through the closet for clothing purloined from the ship's stock and Grytviken's gift shop and dressed quickly. Thick dark sweatpants, woolen socks, and a thin ivory silk top covered by a fuzzy, patterned long-sleeved light jacket.

"Say more," she urged her bondmate.

"The secret to a successful pairing is being alike," the cat said. *"So you'll understand one another."*

"Alike as in, both Shifters?" She pressed for clarity.

"Yes, but there's more. You fought the Cataclysm together. You worked side by side to rebuild Ushuaia. There's not much left of the world. You two are survivors." The cat purred, contented, rich, and low. *"What more do you need?"*

Aura didn't reply, but the modern brain her cat had complained about buzzed with concepts like knowing each other better and sexual compatibility and well-matched intellects. Beyond those things, there were only sixteen of them aboard the ship. She couldn't afford to make a mistake that might impact everyone's ability to work as a tight-knit team. What if she and Juan embarked on a relationship and it went south? Would some people take her side and some Juan's? The more she thought about it, the more reluctant she was to pursue her attraction to the handsome Argentinian.

The purr turned into a growl. *"You get to know someone after you join your life to theirs. Anyone can figure sex out. You have better than a decade of formal education. He doesn't, but while you were lost in books and dreams, he was gathering a practical knowledge set you lack—"*

"Enough." Aura smothered a wry smile. "This isn't fair. You know me inside and out. It's as if I have a metaphorical husband already."

"Nothing like a spot of practice to prepare you for the real thing." The cat sounded smug.

Aura stuffed her feet into a pair of low shearling boots and walked out into the corridor. Karin's door opened, and the doctor let herself into the hallway. Dark circles etched beneath her eyes, and her luxuriant, white hair was freshly washed. It hung to her waist, and she shoved it behind her shoulders.

"You look trashed," Aura said.

Karin regarded her out of shrewd, copper eyes. "Thanks. I blew through scads of magic between healing you, fixing Viktor's ankle, and fighting demons. I have every right to appear *trashed*."

"It wasn't a criticism." Aura looped an arm around the older woman's shoulders. "I never got a chance to thank you for saving my vision—and my connection with my bondmate. How's Vik's ankle?"

"Not broken, but he tweaked some tendons and ligaments. Those can be worse than a break. I got his raven on board. Between Shifter magic and an Ace wrap, he'll be fine soon."

"Were you on your way to dinner?" Aura asked. They'd reached the next deck down from their cabins.

"Yeah. Originally, I'd thought to stop by the makeshift lab Ketha's setting up on the other side of this deck—the place where the crew used to bunk. But I'm tired. I won't be much help until I've eaten and slept."

Ketha hurried toward them from a side corridor. The distinct reek of Vampire clung to her. "Am I late for dinner?"

Karin wrinkled her nose. "No, but go up and shower and change clothes or you'll put everyone else off their feed."

Ketha rolled her eyes. "Damn it. My nose didn't exactly adapt, but I washed up and thought I'd eradicated the worst of it. Back soon." She vaulted up the stairs.

"I promised I'd help with dinner preparations," Aura told Karin. "Why don't you settle in? Food should be up very soon."

"There's a lot we need to talk about—" Karin began.

"Yup. My thoughts were tripping over each other when I stood in the shower, but all those things can wait until after dinner. Or even tomorrow. Besides, it requires all of us. Not just you and me."

"I suppose you're right. Hurry along. I'd offer to help, but the galley's none too large." Karin walked into the dining room.

Aura squeezed her arm and turned hard left through the

swinging galley doors. Juan, Recco, and Daide had an assembly line set up. Several dishes appeared ready to serve.

"Since I missed the cooking part, can I take those to the tables?" she asked.

"Sure." Juan barely glanced at her. Had her earlier withdrawal killed his interest?

If it did, she told herself, *he didn't care very much at all.*

Except maybe about getting laid.

She picked up two serving dishes and shouldered her way back through the swinging doors. Once she set them on tables, she returned for more. Good-looking men like Juan and Viktor probably had their pick of rich women on their many polar junkets. She wondered idly how many Juan had lured to his bed. The more she thought about it as she stocked the tables with food, the more certain she was it had been a close to perfect setup. Lots of sex with zero push for commitment.

After all, none of their passengers would have wanted to turn their lives upside down by living on a rustic cruise ship. The whole scenario pissed her off until she remembered the odd graduate student who'd found his way into her bed. None of those dalliances had ever been planned. They just happened, but she'd cut them off at their roots immediately afterward. Not only was it contrary to faculty standards of conduct, all the men had been much younger than her.

Babies, actually. And she'd never have been able to disclose what she really was. For the most part, Shifters mated with other Shifters. End of story.

She poked her head back into the kitchen, surprised to find the food preparation table empty. "Is there more?" She glanced Juan's way but avoided eye contact.

"No." He knitted his brows together. "I told you as much, last trip through. Sit down and eat before it all gets cold."

Aura turned and left the galley. He clearly wasn't interested in talking with her. Hell, he'd all but shooed her out of the kitchen.

And the expression on his face… It suggested she was brain damaged.

Anger simmered, but she instructed herself to move past it. Better for her to find out about his Lothario tendencies now, than after they'd made love.

She slid into a chair at an unoccupied table. The solitude wouldn't last, but maybe she'd have it to herself long enough to quell her tumbling thoughts. Her appetite had deserted her, but she piled food onto her plate anyway, chewing and swallowing mechanically. She was halfway through a beef and rice casserole, canned corn, and fresh biscuits when Ketha and Viktor joined her.

"Looks great!" Viktor dug into the community dishes, filling his plate.

Ketha did the same. For a while, they ate in silence, and Aura began to breathe easier. Maybe she'd escape the dining room before one of her sisters noticed her inner confusion.

"I almost hate to bring it up"—Viktor glanced at his wife—"but have you made any progress on the Vamp DNA?"

"Barely had time to get started. So, yes and no."

He looked askance at her, and she rolled her eyes.

Aura had been readying excuses to leave the dining room, but she wanted to hear what Ketha had to say.

"What I really need," Ketha muttered, "is a sample from a Vampire not in stasis. I could use a normal human for comparison too, but it's not likely to happen." She took a measured breath. "Even with the stuff we took from the biochem lab in the barracks, I'm still missing a lot of items. I can treat cellular matter with ethanol and extract DNA from there, but I could use far more sophisticated test equipment than a microscope."

"Did you find differences?" Viktor persisted.

"Yes. Lots of them. The question is the etiology of those differences. I have no idea what your profile showed before you turned from human to Vamp to Shifter. Surely, it's bound to have had some effect on every cell in your body. Likewise, it's not as if there's a textbook lying around that profiles Vampire physiology. So I don't have anything to compare my results with."

Aura thought back to her lessons on Shifter physiology. They'd been part of the special Shifter school she'd attended one night a week for years.

Juan strode to the front of the room. His hair had dried, and it framed his face in soft waves. Aura tangled her hands in her lap. She had to come to grips with the fact she'd never run her fingers through his glorious hair. Never crush her mouth down on his. Too many risks, and their survival still hung by a ragged edge. Eventually, they'd run out of supplies. If they couldn't find more, they'd be in the same dilemma they'd faced in Ushuaia.

Juan clanged a knife against his glass to get everyone's attention. "I ate my dinner on the bridge," he said, "because I wanted to cast some weather projections. I figure the storm will dog us for maybe one more day, but then we need to get moving."

Viktor pushed to his feet and limped over to join Juan. "I'd like to spend tomorrow learning as much as I can about Shifter magic." His gaze roved about the room. "Does it work for you gals, since you'll be our teachers?"

Rowana got to her feet. "We'll help all we can, but developing your magic will take time. It's not going to happen overnight."

"We know, but we'll prioritize it whenever we can." Juan sent a winning smile Rowana's way, and a jealous barb stabbed Aura right through the heart.

She looked away, maintaining a neutral expression until she feared her face would crack. She was being ridiculous. Reacting like a teenaged fool, not a woman in her forties.

"Before you all head off to bed," Viktor said, "I wanted to go over our choices of where we go next. We could head southwest to the Palmer Peninsula. It hosts more research stations. We may find survivors. No promises what they might be, though."

"If we don't go there," Ketha spoke up, "what's next? Back to Argentina?"

"It's one choice," Viktor said. "Or Chile. Punta Arenas is fairly close. Other options are Australia or New Zealand. When we shared Ketha's vision, we found life in Buenos Aires. My guess is most large cities will be much the same. There is a downside, though."

"Which is?" Karin asked. She didn't appear quite as beaten down as she had before dinner.

"Piracy," Juan replied. "Ships like *Arkady* have always been hot items because of how long they can remain on the open seas. Our other ship was boarded once, but Viktor persuaded the brigands to leave."

Viktor snorted. "Persuasion is one word to describe it, but that incident was more like a display of brute force. I showed them the business end of the Ruger and told them they had one minute to clear my deck. Guess they believed me because they swarmed over the side as if I'd already begun shooting."

"You believe we're safer limiting ourselves to places that have always been underpopulated," Karin said.

"Yes, at least for a while, but we all have an equal say in this," Viktor replied.

"This isn't a decision for us to make tonight." Juan's expression turned serious, and it made him even more appealing.

"I brought it up now because I want everyone to think about it," Viktor concurred. "We don't have to pick a firm destination until the storm blows itself out and we're ready to pull anchor."

He made his way back to their table and picked up his fork, clearly intent on finishing his supper.

"I'll bid you good night," Aura said. "It's been a difficult day." She picked up her plate and utensils, added Ketha's to the stack, and carried everything into the galley so she could wash them.

She was standing over the sink when Juan joined her, balancing a stack of dirty dishes. "Want some help?" he asked.

She kept her gaze firmly focused on the sink. If she looked at him, she'd soften, and it was a bad idea. "I'm okay," she said. "Go ahead and put them there." She pointed to the sink with soapy water in it.

"Aura..." he began.

She shook her head. "It's all right. Leave the dishes and go. We're all too wiped out to do much more than fall on our faces tonight. Spend what energy you have left getting to know your cat better."

He dropped a hand over hers. "It's exactly what I've been doing. And why I'm here. My cat says—"

The plate she'd been washing clattered into the sink and broke. Aura spun to face him. "Don't. Just go, please."

"But I don't understand. What did I do?"

"It's not you. It's me. We're not a good idea. Please, just leave." She wanted to punch him, but she also wanted to throw herself into his arms. The combination made her insides churn with indecision. Thank the goddess her cat had the good sense to lie low.

"As you will." Juan looked as if he wanted to say something more, but he turned and strode out of the kitchen, his tread heavy and purposeful.

It was the right thing to do, she told herself as she picked shards of crockery out of the sink and chucked them into a garbage can.

Only problem was she didn't believe it, and a part of her felt like she'd killed something wonderful before it even had a chance to get started.

14

CHANCES AND CHANGES

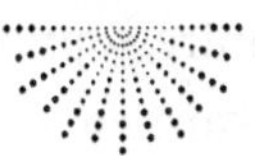

JUAN TOSSED AND TURNED. He'd spent the day working with Aura on mastering a rudimentary set of magical skills. She hadn't wanted to pair up with him. He'd seen it in the stiff set of her shoulders and her averted gaze, but their bond animals had been quite clear regarding their wishes. He'd done enough to piss off his cat, and he hadn't wanted to alienate it further by refusing to partner with Aura when the cat pushed him in that direction.

His cock throbbed hotly between his legs. Lusting after Aura hadn't made the day any easier. Why wouldn't she talk to him? Tell him why she was giving him the cold shoulder treatment. He'd been encouraged when she invited him into her cabin the afternoon before, but she'd edged away like a skittish colt as soon as he touched her. He sucked in a deep breath, but it was a mistake. Her scent clung to the clothing he'd worn all day. Candle wax, old leather, and jasmine. His cock jerked against his belly. He closed a hand around it and stroked himself a time or two, but that wasn't what he wanted.

Bringing himself off was a stopgap. Nothing more. It wouldn't make a dent in the lust spilling through him.

He swung to a sit, planting his feet on the floor. Sex had been a simple proposition for years. He'd never lacked willing partners aboard his ships. Many of their passengers were older, single women who welcomed a romp—or two. He'd taken care not to become attached to any of them, but none of the women exerted much pressure, either.

They'd guessed he'd never leave the sea, and none of them saw living on a boat as a viable lifestyle. A wry snort blew past his lips. Once he'd become a Vampire, opportunities for sex had been plentiful, but he'd never warmed to any of the female Vamps. Raping humans who were frightened to their bones wasn't his style, either. He stared at the hard-on jutting from his body amazed he was still capable of producing one after a ten-year hiatus.

Juan stood and paced back and forth in his small cabin, mostly to move blood somewhere besides his penis. He had to relax enough to sleep. They'd leave the protected harbor guarding Grytviken tomorrow morning, and he had to be at the top of his game. He understood the dynamics of keeping them on course, but until now he'd had the advantage of satellite feedback to inform his navigational choices.

"I managed to get us to South Georgia," he muttered. It would have been easy enough to miss such a small island in the midst of the riotous South Atlantic, but he'd been here hundreds of times.

"You did well today." His cat popped up from nowhere, but its appearance didn't surprise Juan as much this time.

He plopped into the room's only chair and sat in front of a desk crowded with nautical charts. "Why doesn't Aura like me?" Juan winced and hastily added, "Never mind. Not an appropriate question."

"She sees more than you think," the cat replied enigmatically.

"What's that supposed to mean?"

"Whatever you want it to."

Juan tried a different angle. "Fine. Why did you tell me to pursue her?"

"Because she's the right mate for you."

"Not if she doesn't agree with your assessment, she's not. Besides, we're miles away from signing on to anything permanent."

A long, hissing growl filled Juan's chest, stretching his mouth in unusual ways as it emerged. Rather than fight the sensation, he used a technique he'd learned today and embraced his bond animal's display of emotion.

"Permanent hasn't been part of your life plan," the cat observed after it was done growling.

Excuses marched through Juan's mind. Before he could sort through them and pick the best one, the cat was gone. Another trick he'd learned today was tapping into the spot in his magical center where the cat resided. Its absence left an obvious void.

Only obvious once I knew where to look.

At least his erection had subsided. Before it returned to torment him, he grabbed a pen and wrote *Permanent hasn't been part of my life plan* on a scrap of paper.

Juan stared at it and drew a vertical line beneath the sentence. On the right side, he listed *Arkady, Gavrill,* navigation, improving navigational skillset, learning Antarctic and Arctic history. All those items were relatively permanent. They'd been part of his life forever. So had his friendship with Viktor.

He set the pen down and picked it back up. What was the point of this exercise if he weren't honest with himself? With a great deal of reluctance, he added seduction schemes to his list. On the other side—the place to memorialize transient or nonexistent matters—he wrote girlfriend, children, family. During his trance-induced visit to Buenos Aires, his lack of communication with his blood kin had stung. They weren't much for letter-writing, but he could have sent emails, whether they replied or not.

Yeah. Could have, but didn't.

He dragged a hand down his face. He was a competent navigator. Was the rest of his life a wasteland? Worse, had he designed it to make absolutely certain nothing got in the way of his love affair with boats and the sea?

Juan winced at the truth in his thoughts. Most of the old-time seafarers and explorers had wives back in Europe. Wives who accepted being alone for months and years at a time. The world had changed—a lot.

He'd made choices as a much younger man. Ones that had fit for him then.

He placed the pen in its usual place, lay back down in his bunk, and pulled a blanket over himself. Was the main reason he wanted to pursue Aura because she was here, on his ship? Because he liked her, and she was convenient? Those two variables—proximity and a level of attraction that lent sparks to lovemaking—had been key elements in his earlier choices of partners.

He didn't have to search for an answer. Aura was different. She made him feel things no other woman had. Before, he hadn't cared if a prospect turned him down. When it happened, he'd moved on to the next likely candidate. Not this time. He'd never wasted as much as ten seconds considering any of the other Shifters. Or any of the human women who'd emerged from hiding once Ushuaia was clear of Vampires. Many of them had been young and attractive, but they didn't call to his soul like Aura.

"Now all you have to do is convince her." His bond animal was back.

"How do you do that?" Juan sputtered. "Shit! You sneak around like a bloody ghost."

"Over time, you'll come to trust I'll be here when you need me."

Juan felt like snarling at his bondmate. He'd asked it a question and received a sanctimonious speech.

"Time to focus on action, not shortcomings—yours or mine."

"Damn it!" Juan made a fist and brought it down on his mattress. "I was never one of those kids who wanted an imaginary friend, let alone an external manifestation of my conscience."

"I am not imaginary."

"Poor choice of words."

"I'll overlook it. This time. Are you going to get up and go talk with her, or not?"

Juan didn't realize it was exactly what he was considering until the cat shaped his jumbled emotions into words. He was on his feet again before he could talk himself out of a middle-of-the-night trek down to Deck Three. He still had his trousers and socks on, and he pulled the shirt that still smelled like Aura over his head. From long habit, he started to stuff his feet into his boots, but they'd only get in the way.

Way of what?

I'm going to her room to talk with her. Talk. Nothing else.

He donned a pair of scuffed slippers. His cock began to thicken again, almost as if it felt the need to remind him of its existence. He told it to stand down. He needed a clear head. Input from his unruly appendage would only cloud matters. Juan slid out the door. The tang of sex floated in the corridor. Not surprising since Viktor and Ketha's cabin sat catty-corner across the hall from his.

Juan smiled. He'd never taken Viktor for the marrying type, either, but he seemed deliriously satisfied with Ketha. Juan was happy for his old friend. The addition of a wife had altered things between them, though, and Juan missed the deep, wide-ranging conversations they used to have. He hurried down stairwells, not giving much thought to where he was going. He knew *Arkady* inside and out. Sometimes he even stalked through its branching corridors in his dreams.

All too soon, he stood a few feet from Aura's door. What if she were asleep? Probably better not to waken her. His smile faded. What the fuck had he been thinking? It was pushing one in the morning. He sorted out a slender thread of magic and urged it through the door to determine if she was still up. If he'd been smart about things, he could have done the same thing from farther away. Maybe not as far as his cabin, but surely from the end of the corridor—

Her door fell open; light streamed into the dark corridor. Blonde hair tumbled over her shoulders to waist level in sleep-tousled curls, but her green eyes were very much awake. The same robe she'd worn earlier was tightly belted about her waist, and her feet were bare. Her expression broke his heart. Tight, guarded, but laced with heat.

She wanted him, but she didn't trust him.

Apologies for disturbing her rushed to the fore, right along with assurances he'd die before doing anything to hurt her. Rather than voicing any of them, he surged forward and wrapped his arms around her. Right before he crushed his mouth over hers. For glorious moments, she returned his embrace, and a combination of muscle, sinew, and curves pressed the length of his body. Every dream he'd ever had came true at the same time, bombarding him with sensation. She felt right nestled in the curve of his arms, like she'd been born to be there. Her nipples hardened where they pressed against his chest, and she threw her arms around him, nails digging into his back.

He bit and sucked her lips, and she opened her mouth to his tongue. His cock roared back to life, pressing into her belly. He slid his hands down the curvature of her spine until he cupped her high, tight ass in his fingers and pulled her against his erection. Sharp, sweet, and urgent, desire swept everything else from his mind. His breathing quickened, and his heart hammered against his chest.

She inhaled his tongue, sparring with it as she straddled one of his legs. The heat from her core seared his thigh, and he pressed upward to make better contact with her sensitive flesh. As quickly as she'd thrown herself into his offered embrace, Aura pulled away, moving a few steps back. Spots of color splotched both cheeks, and she was breathing fast.

"Sorry." She glanced away. "I, er we, shouldn't have done that."

Juan stared stupidly at the space between their bodies. A space she'd occupied seconds before. He grappled with a tongue that didn't want to cooperate enough to form words. "I only wanted to talk."

She grinned crookedly. "Yeah. Exactly what it looked like from my end when you grabbed me."

The corners of his mouth twitched. "You grabbed back."

"So I did." She angled her gaze over one shoulder at her bed. It was as disheveled as his, as if sleep had eluded her as well.

Juan spread his arms in invitation. "Feel like a nightcap? I make a mean Irish coffee."

After a slight hesitation, she bent to slide on a pair of tattered sheepskin slippers and then laced her fingers with his. "Sure. If it's heavy on whiskey and light on caffeine."

He walked by her side, fingers still entwined, one floor up to the bar. She perched on one of the upholstered couches beneath the windows while he mixed drinks. Lots of sugar. Lots of powdered cream. Lots of whiskey and a splash of instant coffee with water to hold it all together.

Juan made his way to a chair opposite where she sat, afraid if he settled next to her, the temptation to touch her would be overwhelming. He'd already established once he got his hands on her body, he was a lost soul.

"Mmmm, this is good." She took another appreciative sip.

Juan sampled his drink. "One day, we'll run out of everything, so we may as well enjoy it while it lasts."

She met his gaze over the rim of her mug. "That's kind of a metaphor for life."

He hadn't meant for it to be, but it was as good a lead-in as he was likely to get. He swallowed hard. Time for truth. "My plan— as much of one as I had—was I wanted to talk with you. Honest up, as it were."

Aura opened her mouth, but he shook his head. "Let me get through what I have to say. Most of what you believe about me is true. The sea has always been my first love. I avoided entanglements that would have challenged how I chose to live my life. How it played out in reality was I had a series of flings with women who never asked for anything beyond my body or my company at dinner."

His face grew warm, and he took another slug of the whiskey-laced coffee. "Doesn't exactly make me a man-whore, but I wasn't far from it, either. Viktor and I, we were the original close-knit dudes. We had our ships and each other and women to warm our beds from time to time. I'd be lying if I told you I longed for more. At the time, I didn't. I had everything I needed to make me happy."

"What changed?" She focused soft, liquid eyes on his face, and he felt her magic probe his mind.

He sent a pointed glance her way. "What didn't? I almost died in a shipwreck when the Cataclysm hit. I blamed myself for the forty-odd passengers and crew we lost. So did Vik, but before we got too far down the road where we argued about who'd fucked up worse, him or me, Raphael shanghaied us."

"Kind of a game-changer," she murmured and drained her mug, setting it on a nearby table.

"Ya think?" Juan shook his head. "I don't have to describe those years in Ushuaia. You lived them right along with me, but they were probably worse for me."

"Because you'd been turned into something you hated?"

"Exactly. And I couldn't complain. Couldn't let anyone know how being a Vampire undermined my will to live and made me yearn for a way out." He inhaled sharply. "One of the downsides to Vampirism is anything shy of beheading—or silver bullets—won't do you in. If I'd known ingesting silver powder and iron would do it, I'd have hunted some down. I came within an angstrom of asking Vik to end me, but I didn't want to put him in that position."

"Would he have done it?"

"I believe so. But we'd have gotten into an argument because he didn't ask first. See, I knew how much he hated being a Vampire. I played my cards much closer to the chest. For one thing, I didn't have Vik's cozy relationship with Raphael, so I was certain I wouldn't have Vik's latitude with the old bastard."

"What did Viktor do to ingratiate himself with Raphael?" Aura walked to the bar to mix herself another mug. "Want me to freshen yours up?" she asked.

"Nah. Just bring the whiskey back with you. To answer your question about Vik. He did nothing. I have no idea why Raph glommed onto him beyond maybe his quiet competence. Most of the men Raphael turned were a collection of losers, thugs, and fools."

Juan waited until Aura had returned to her spot on the couch. "I didn't plan to talk about Vampires, except in passing. What I wanted to tell you is you're different. I don't view you the same way I looked at..." He stumbled over how to word things.

Aura placed the Irish whiskey on a table and picked up the slack. "The other women you took to bed?" she suggested, a sly glint in her eye.

"Uh, yeah. Them. It's a shitty thing to admit, but none of those trysts ever meant anything to me."

"What about the women?" Aura's steady gaze never left his face.

"I was someone to pass the time with. Women are a wise lot. They knew they'd lose in a head-to-head contest with the sea. And maybe it was a self-sorting process at the front end."

"Do you mean they didn't want lasting emotional commitments, either?"

He nodded, not feeling very good about himself. He'd been honest with his partners. Never offered more than he had to give, but his self-indulgent shallowness made him cringe. It wasn't the man he wanted to be.

He set his drink down and moved to sit next to her. "I haven't painted a very pretty picture, but I'm not the same man anymore."

He angled his body so he could cup the side of her face in one hand. "You haven't been far from my thoughts from the day I first laid eyes on you. I'd like to give what I feel for you a chance to develop."

She leaned into his touch. "That was a pretty big speech."

"For a fellow who barely finished secondary school before he ran off to sea?"

"I didn't mean it the way it came out." She closed her teeth over her lower lip. "Do you want to know what my cat told me?" Without waiting for him to answer, she forged ahead. "It told me that while I was lost in books and dreams, you were gathering a practical knowledge set I lack."

Quiet pleasure filled Juan, radiating outward from his belly. "Your cat likes me."

Aura nodded. "Indeed, it does."

"Good, because mine likes you too. It told me you were the only mate for me."

Aura smiled softly. It transformed her lovely face into something so beautiful, his heart cracked open. "Beyond my cat liking you," she went on, "I do too. I fought against it because I saw all the things you just told me. In the life I left, you would have been labeled a commitment-phobe."

She ran her tongue over her lips and looked away. "The hard truth is, I was too. Not for the same reasons, but the end result was the same. The odd student warmed my bed, but I was very selective and only picked men who wouldn't give me any trouble when I told them we were done."

Surprise rocked him. "None of you ever mentioned husbands or boyfriends," he spoke slowly, thinking about the dozen Shifter women, "but I figured it was because you kept your personal lives to yourselves."

"We never mentioned them," Aura said, "because none of us were connected on more than a superficial level with anyone. Shifters marry other Shifters. Think of the problems hooking up with a human. They'd never keep your secret, no matter how good their intentions were. Once humans found out about us, we'd have been as screwed as the Vamps were, with their retreat to a shadowy existence. Doing things our way, we got the best of both worlds. Normal lives plus our animals to run with and Shifter magic to deploy when we needed something extra."

"No wonder Raphael was so fucking cheerful," Juan muttered through clenched teeth.

"Yeah. He could finally be out in the open again," Aura agreed. Leaning toward Juan, she kissed him quick and hard, letting go before he could gather her close. "I want to get to know you better, but I have a caveat."

"Anything."

"We do this the old-fashioned way. Spend time with one another. Keep sharing our histories. Work together as a couple. Once we're very sure we've got the stuff to go the distance, then we can make love."

He chuckled. "If I design a bundling board down the center of a bunk, can we sleep in the same bed?"

She tossed her head back and laughed. "Oh hell, no. I'd be over the board in a trice. You saw how weak I was back in my cabin."

Happiness and hope speared him. Aura was going to give them a chance. He drew her to her feet and held her against him before letting go. "You won't be sorry. I promise."

She rolled her eyes. "Maybe you will be. I'm not a very good sailor, and we'll be back in open water tomorrow."

He took the whiskey bottle back to the bar and slid it into a slot where wooden framing meant it wouldn't fall on the floor and shatter when the water grew rough. "Want me to walk you to your cabin?"

She slid her fingers beneath his elbow and picked up her mug with her other hand. "That would be lovely. Then you should get some sleep."

"You too."

He didn't want to sleep. He felt light and buoyant, as if even flight weren't beyond him. He kissed her lightly at her door and ran up three decks. Rather than going into his cabin, he entered the glassed-in bridge and stared out into the velvet of an Antarctic night. Constellations formed patterns in the blackness.

Daide sat at the helm, keeping watch, and he nodded at Juan. "Is everything all right?"

"More than all right, *amigo*."

Juan walked slowly to his cabin. He reached inward and found his cat, quiet and watchful. "Aren't you going to say I told you so?"

"Why would I? Go to sleep. I'll watch over you."

Moved beyond words by his bondmate's offer, Juan lay on his bunk and pulled the blanket over himself. He'd been a loner all his life, but he wasn't anymore. His choices from here on in would be dictated by what was best for everyone, not only for him. He vowed to meet the challenge with grace and honor.

No matter how hard it was, he'd make it work. Aura was worth it. So was the cat he was just getting to know.

15

WARNINGS

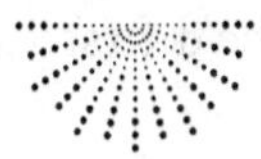

Aura flexed her fingers and glanced up from pages of closely spaced script. They'd been at sea for the last three days. The water had been rough, but nothing like their transit of the Scotia Sea. After a few queasy hours the first morning, a combination of magic and maybe the pills Karin passed out had done the trick. The nausea departed, and once it was gone, it hadn't bothered her again. Juan reassured her he'd seen the same thing happen many times, but she hadn't believed him until another day had passed.

She closed her teeth over her lower lip. Wanting not to be a total loss as a sailing partner might have been a driving force too. The sea was Juan's life. It would be a major disappointment for him if she couldn't tolerate living aboard a ship. Or spent all her time curled up in her bunk, trying not to puke.

She read through the last couple of pages, making annotations a few places. She'd been remiss not writing down her account of how they'd fought the Cataclysm earlier. Because of her history background, she'd been a natural to end up with the task of tracking prophecies for her Shifter pack. The fourth unfinished prophecy had played itself out while they fought the Cataclysm,

183

but if no one memorialized what happened, it would remain unfinished in the Shifter archives.

Back in her old life, she'd have committed the pages to electronic format and added them to a master scroll carefully maintained by generations of Shifters. The scroll resided in an underground vault on the grounds of a mansion east of Portland, Oregon. She recalled the arguments that had flown back and forth across the Atlantic when she'd first suggested moving it so she'd have better access.

It only made sense to keep the scroll in the UK if the Shifter in charge of preserving it lived there. She'd finally won, but bitter feelings still lingered. Or they had. Who knew if anyone remained alive to contest the location of their living history?

Or if she'd ever return to add her account of the fourth prophecy to their archives.

After a brief tap on her door, it opened, and Ketha stood framed in the doorway. "Mind if I come in?" A black wool top covered her to hip level, and a pair of thick navy sweats clung to her legs.

Aura crooked two fingers her way. "Not at all. I was finishing up memorializing how the fourth unfinished prophecy turned out. Guess there are only six unfinished ones left now."

"Maybe. Others might have rolled through to their conclusions over the decade we've been out of touch with the rest of the world."

Ketha shut the door behind her and crossed the room to perch on the bunk that ran beneath the cabin's porthole. She splayed her fingers in front of her, and a thin line formed between her eyebrows. "By the way, congratulations."

"On what?" Aura cast a sidelong glance Ketha's way.

"Juan. What else? You two are so well matched, it's positively inspiring."

"Hang onto the congrats until he and I have a wee bit more than a couple of days under our belts."

"Nah. It'll stick. He told Viktor you were the only woman for him." Ketha made a snorting sound. "Juan must have been as big a womanizer as Vik. From the stories I've heard, it's hard to tell whether those two were running a polar cruise line or a dating service."

Aura snickered. "Ashley Madison á la shipboard romance?"

"Wasn't that the online service encouraging married people cheat on their spouses?" Ketha asked.

"Yup." Rather than twisting like a pretzel in her chair, Aura turned it to face the other woman. "Asking me about Juan isn't why you're here. What is? Everything all right between you and Viktor?"

Ketha scraped her golden gaze up off the floor and skewered Aura with it. "Vik and I are fine. I wish everything else was so easy. We'll sight land again soon. I felt blindsided by how bad things were in Grytviken, so I got out my glass. Sort of as an exercise, so we could be better prepared."

Aura propped an elbow on the arm of her chair and settled her chin into an open hand. "And?" she prodded.

Breath whistled through Ketha's teeth. "Aw geez. Where do I begin?"

"If it's going to be that bad, maybe we don't want to stop there." Aura hunted through her memory. "South Shetland Islands, wasn't it?"

"Our destination is a Polish research station. Arctowski. It's on King George Island at the northeast end of the South Shetlands."

Aura grabbed a fresh sheet of paper and sketched out the map as she remembered it. "Was it here?" She turned the page so Ketha could see it.

"More or less. Anyway, the geography isn't important."

Aura dragged her chair close enough to touch Ketha's knee. "What'd you see, sweetie? And what did Viktor say?"

Ketha screwed her face into a grimace. "Haven't told him yet. I might be overreacting. My visions aren't always exact depictions of the future, plus I'm still spun out over how fast things spiraled out of control in Grytviken. I keep dreaming we missed a spot, and the gateway didn't close like we believed."

"Do you really think demons took over after we left?"

"I have no idea what my dreams signify." Ketha turned her hands palms up. "Maybe nothing at all beyond my own paranoia. I haven't wanted to move the lens closer. It's not as if we're going back there."

"We might someday. You haven't told me very much yet. Only that you're worried."

"Let me start at the beginning. Hang onto your questions until I'm done." Ketha drew her scrying tool from a deep pocket. Oblong glass, it was about eight inches across and framed with antique metal. Placing a palm over its surface, she shut her eyes, murmuring, "The glass will keep me on track."

Aura waited. She cleared her mind so no negativity would intrude on Ketha's concentration.

"We dropped anchor in a bay, protected like the one at Grytviken. A long, low row of bright-yellow structures was scattered along the shore, and an old lighthouse sat atop a point. I was encouraged nothing like the Cataclysm stood in our way." She exhaled noisily. "Guess I've been expecting to run into a malevolent barrier ever since we left Ushuaia."

Aura laid a hand over Ketha's to encourage her to go on. The glass rippled beneath their fingers, but Aura didn't try to see anything. The mirror probably wouldn't reveal images to anyone but its owner.

"We dropped the gangway," Ketha went on. "Launched rafts. By the time we were headed to shore, about twenty people piled out of the yellow boxcar things."

"People? Not Vampires or Shifters?" Aura snapped her mouth shut. She wasn't supposed to ask questions. "Sorry."

"It's okay. Shocked me too. It's not as if we didn't leave humans in Ushuaia, but I wasn't expecting anyone, let alone a crowd."

Ketha shook her head. "They were happy, smiling. Delighted to see us. After we greeted each other on the shoreline, they invited us in and fed us tea and dried meat. Not much. They were apologetic, said they were rationing everything. They'd managed to kill seals and seabirds. Without them, they'd have starved."

Ketha opened troubled eyes, pinched at their corners, and focused on Aura. "All of a sudden, this dark cloud descended and settled over everybody. No one seemed to notice it. People went right on chattering away, sharing their stories. At first, I thought it was an artifact—leftover negative vibes from goddess only knew where—but the black part grew denser, heavier. I couldn't make excuses for it, and it threatened horrible consequences if we didn't get out of there."

"Well? What happened, then?" Aura asked after Ketha fell silent for several moments.

"My vision shattered. Happens sometimes when whatever powers them believes I've seen enough to shape a decision."

"Mmph. Are you certain nothing magical lurked in the shadows? Maybe Vamps who had those humans in thrall or something?"

"Yeah. I'm at least half-certain. It was one of the first things I hunted for when I culled back through the sending."

"Is it bad enough we shouldn't land there?" Aura regarded her friend.

"I wish I knew. I don't want to overreact, or we'll end up at sea forever. Probably every potential port will have something wrong with it—if I examine it through my third eye."

"Yes, but you don't want to underreact, either. You have to tell everyone what you told me. We'll kick it around and decide what to do."

"There's another argument for landing there," Ketha said. "If those are truly humans, they can provide me with comparative tissue and serum markers. It might make interpreting what I found with the Vampire head easier."

Aura made a face. "Ewww. I suppose you still have it."

"You bet. In a deepfreeze, which is why it's not stinking up the ship."

"What did you discover so far?"

Ketha shrugged. "None of the men have biologic markers I found in the Vampires—"

Aura sat straighter. "Back up. Are the men all the same? Within the parameters you'd apply to any two samples from the same species."

"I don't think so, but Karin disagrees." The words were flat, uncompromising.

"Any idea why you're looking at the same data but drawing different conclusions?"

"No to that question as well. No matter how I argue it, Karin's not as convinced as I am."

"About what?"

"She believes our findings are probably an artifact of normal intraspecies variation."

"Maybe she's right. It's not as if the four men aboard are anywhere close to normal. Changing from human to Vamp to Shifter must have altered a whole lot. Beyond that, Recco and Daide have indigenous genetic material. Juan is probably descended from the Spaniards who settled in South America. Viktor is from Germany."

"I understand those things." Ketha tucked her legs beneath her. "We're starting with three distinct genetic patterns. Each of them probably reacted differently to their stint as Vampires. And then, each heeded the call from a different type of bond animal when they became Shifters."

Aura laced her fingers together. "Exactly. Not a bad guess for a historian. Never have mucked around in a lab with dead things—"

"You make it sound so attractive." Ketha sent a pointed look skittering Aura's way.

"Call a spade a spade, I always say. Where I was going with my line of logic was you have too many uncontrolled variables to float any conclusions that mean zip squat."

Ketha made a sour face. "Same thing Karin said."

"See? There you have it. Two against one. What precisely were you hoping to pin down?"

"I had three questions," Ketha replied, back in researcher mode. "The first was whether Vampirism left lasting changes. The second was if the Shifter adaptations were an overlay or if they wiped out anything Vampirism might have left."

"You said three."

"Um, yeah." Ketha raked a hand through her hair. "I wanted to know if having once been a Vampire, the men would be more susceptible to being turned a second time."

Understanding filled Aura. "You're worried about Viktor."

"Of course. Why wouldn't you have the same fears about Juan?" Ketha's tone was brittle, defensive.

Aura chewed on her lower lip. "Probably because I don't believe you'll find what you're hunting for in a laboratory. The choice to drink from a Vampire who's just finished draining you is psychological. Juan told me he'd die before he'd let another Vampire turn him. He meant it. He had no idea how bad it would be."

"Viktor's said the same thing, but how much choice did they truly have?"

"Let's hope we never find out. Ketha."

"What?" The wolf Shifter met Aura's direct stare.

"The lab is your comfort zone. Sharing your life with a man isn't. Believe me, I've been grappling with the same fears. Sometimes I want Juan more than I can fathom, more than I want to breathe, but the next moment I'm so full of anxiety and what-ifs, I want to run the other way."

Ketha blew out a breath, and then one more. "I suppose you're right. And I'm not certain how we got so far afield. I need to alert everyone not to let their guard down when we land at the research station. Hey!" Her eyes lit up. "Maybe they'll have some of the chemicals and other materials I'm missing."

"And maybe they'll volunteer samples for your agar plates or petri dishes or whatever you've got cooking in that lab of yours."

"You could visit." Ketha got to her feet.

"No thanks. I avoided the hard sciences for a reason."

Ketha quirked a brow. "Yeah, because you suck at math."

"Go ahead. Blow my cover." Aura laughed.

The public-address system crackled. "Land ho," Viktor cried.

"Seals and albatrosses off the bow," Juan added, sounding happy and excited.

"Son of a bitch!" Viktor was back. "There are people here."

"Come on." Aura hopped out of her chair. "They'll need help setting the anchor."

Ketha stood, but her face wore a troubled expression. "We shouldn't be here until tomorrow," she muttered. "Not according to my glass."

Aura gave her friend a quick hug. "Maybe the rest of your vision wasn't quite right, either."

"If I understood where my visions originated, I'd have a better answer for you." Ketha jerked her chin toward the door. "We may as well head up to the bridge. I'll know once I get a peek outside if it's the same place."

"Try my porthole."

"I already did. It faces out to sea."

Aura grabbed a jacket from off a hook next to the door and stuffed her feet into the knee-high waterproof boots she'd appropriated from the ship's stock.

"Good idea." Ketha glanced at her slippers. "I'll layer up and meet you on the bridge."

Aura latched curved fingers around Ketha's arm. "I know it goes against the grain, but try not to worry. We've made it this far. Maybe the goddess wants us to be out here. Earth isn't going to repair itself."

"Ain't it the truth. Thanks for the pep talk. The part about rela-tionships was right on. My chronic independence is nipping at my heels. Viktor is the best man in the world. Sweet and kind and strong." A soft smile spread across Ketha's face. "But I still have this bitchy voice predicting gloom and doom and reminding me I never needed anyone before."

"Tell it to pound sand."

Ketha grinned and pulled the door open. Aura followed her through and climbed the three decks to the bridge. Everyone but her and Ketha was already there staring through the windows at a scene right out of Ketha's vision. The lighthouse sat off to one side, and a collection of yellow prefab buildings dotted the beach.

"Look!" Rowana pointed. "People. Just like Viktor said."

"Wonder if they're human?" Recco yanked on one of two doors leading to the open deck beyond the bridge and stood staring at the small settlement.

Juan moved to her side. His face had lit with pleasure when she walked onto the bridge. "Did you finish your work memorial-izing the fourth prophecy?"

"Yes." She wanted to talk about Ketha's concerns, but it wasn't her place.

Something in her voice must have alerted Juan because he leaned closer. "Is something wrong?" His deep voice was full of concern.

"Um, maybe. Wait until Ketha gets here. This one's her baby."

"So long as you're all right." Juan settled a protective hand over hers. Firm, warm, solid. She could get used to him fussing over her.

"Hey! They're on their way out to us." Zoe slapped the glass. A single, patched Zodiac with four people aboard was indeed motoring across the cove.

Ketha swarmed into the bridge and loped to where Zoe stood next to the windows. "I don't get it," she said. "This has to be the right place. How many spots have yellow buildings and a light-house? But them coming aboard wasn't in my vision."

Viktor frowned. "Vision? What vision?" he demanded. "Hurry. No time for titrated versions. They'll be at the gangway very soon."

"They met us on the beach," Ketha replied.

"Who are *they*?" Rowana narrowed her dark eyes to slits.

"Humans, I think."

"What's the problem with that?" Daide asked.

"Aye, so long as they're not Vampires, we should be fine," Zoe said.

Ketha turned to face everyone. "I'll be brief. I scryed the future and saw this place. We went ashore. Everything seemed fine for a while, but then darkness closed in, and my vision broke into pieces."

"Which means what?" Viktor's question had sharp edges.

"I don't know," Ketha answered. She squared her shoulders. "I need samples from them—assuming they're human and not being driven by something we don't yet know about."

"Do Vampires keep minions they haven't turned?" Aura glanced from Juan to Viktor to Daide. Recco was still outside or she'd have included him in her query.

"I don't think so," Juan said. "At least Raphael sure didn't operate that way. There were humans he turned into food, humans he turned into new Vamps, and prisoners while he made up his mind which we'd end up."

"I know those things," Aura said. "But was his practice wide-spread or unique to his need to control everything?"

"Vampires eat, spit, shit, and breathe control." Juan twisted his mouth into a scowl.

"People." Viktor raised his voice. "We don't have time for this. I'm going outside to greet those folk as ship's captain and see what they want. Unless they give me a very good reason not to, I'll lower the gangway."

"We'll all go," Juan said. "I'll be there as soon as I've dropped anchor."

Aura ran out of the bridge and caught up with him. "Need help?"

"No, but your company is always welcome." He hurried toward the broad foredeck and the anchor apparatus. "Did Ketha see anything she didn't tell us about?"

"No. Not really. This might be fine. Maybe we have to go ashore to activate whatever spurs the darkness she sensed. Or maybe it wasn't real at all."

"Darkness, eh?" Juan held a door open for her and trotted to the anchor housing, fiddling with controls. The screech of heavy chain grinding against itself pounded against her ears. "What? Like demons again?"

"Doesn't work that way." Aura shouted to make herself heard.

"There. Done here." Juan looped a hand beneath her arm and drew her a few feet away from the noisy, clanking chain. "Doesn't work what way?"

"Ketha was worried because of our experience in Grytviken, so when she went into her vision state, she was already somewhat on edge. It may have colored what she found. Although, she did describe this settlement to a T. I'm not sure about anything, other than we should watch ourselves."

"What precisely are we watching for?" His expression grew worried, and he frowned. "Maybe you should stay in your cabin."

Aura wrapped her arms around him. "Don't go all Neanderthal on me. If something turns to shit, we're stronger with all our magic front and center. Plus, why would you think I'd be comfortable sending you out to face danger without me?"

He grinned crookedly; it added a boyish allure to his defined cheekbones and squared-off chin. "I don't get to play Sir Galahad?"

"He went out with the Middle Ages. Come on. I want to meet

whoever was so excited—or appalled—by our arrival they felt the need to seize the initiative and motor out to meet us."

"I bet we're the very first ship they've seen since the Cataclysm hit," Juan muttered. "That alone would get anyone moving."

Aura followed Juan around the corner and down the walkway running beneath Deck Three's cabins. Her porthole was the one on the far end. Juan had a cool head, and he projected quiet strength. It was hard to believe anything bad could happen with him standing by, but that was a dangerous road. He'd been suckered by a Master Vampire. All the men had, which meant they were far from invincible.

She and her sister Shifters had guessed wrong about the Cataclysm. They'd ignored the slender window right after it happened, a span of days that might have allowed them to leave Ushuaia.

Yeah, we were waiting for something more auspicious. Except, it never happened.

"Your mind is busy," Juan observed.

"We're stronger with all of us in the same place," she repeated, not wanting to go into how each of them had failed because they'd miscalculated.

She sent her magic ahead, hunting for wrong spots, places the warp and weft of the ether was off. It would be easier to examine ley lines, but she should have thought of it sooner. When she deployed her third eye, her other senses weren't as sharp.

The gangway creaked as Viktor lowered it to water level, but Aura had completed her scan. Nothing set off her internal alarms, and she breathed a little easier. Maybe Ketha's anxiety had contaminated her trance state.

When she peered over the edge, the raft had already tied off to cleats, and its occupants had their eye on the slowly descending gangway. The roar of a second Zodiac drew her attention, and she saw another raft on its way from the pier. This one held two additional occupants.

"What the hell?" Juan turned to her. "Those rafts can hold twelve. Fourteen in a pinch. Why didn't the first batch wait?"

The gangway clanked into place, and the raft's four occupants hustled up it. The first, a man in his fifties with silvery hair and dark, frantic eyes said, "Who is your captain?" in a voice with a heavy Eastern European accent. He was dressed in poorly tanned seal skins stinking of rancid fat. Even his boots appeared to have been made from seal hide, and they laced to below his knees.

"Me." Viktor stepped forward.

The man bowed formally, but straightened fast. "I request sanctuary for myself and my companions. You must raise the ladder and leave this place."

Meanwhile two women and one more man had crested the gangway. They all looked like refugees with tattered clothing and deeply lined, grimy faces. Aura guessed fuel to heat water for bathing was in short supply.

"Who's in the other Zodiac?" Juan asked.

"I—I can't reveal anything," the first man replied. "Please. You must do as I say. We will answer all your questions once we are safely away from here."

Aura scanned the newcomers with magic. They seemed human, but when she looked a second time, traces of a subterranean shadow teased her. Were they shrouding magical underpinnings? She couldn't tell. The harder she tried, the more elusive the undernote became.

"Why are you so frightened?" she asked the man who'd exhorted them to leave. "You've been living in the settlement with whoever is in the other raft."

The man didn't answer, and one of the women stifled a low, terrified moan.

The other Zodiac had almost reached them. Its driver was yelling something, but Aura couldn't hear him over the roar of the raft's outboard engine. Viktor hit the button to draw the gangway out of the water.

"Thank you." The man who'd requested aid gripped Viktor's arm, but he shook him off.

"I only did it to give us time to sort things out. The International Association of Antarctica Tour Operators requires me to offer aid to polar settlements in need."

Juan sent an incredulous look arrowing right at Viktor. "Maybe ten years ago, *amigo*, but—"

Viktor waved him to silence. "Talk," he ordered the man who'd begged them to leave. "Nothing extra. Focus on bare-bones facts."

Meanwhile, the second raft circled below. "You must let us aboard," the driver shouted. A parka shrouded him from the top of his head to hip level. His English carried a hint of a Spanish accent, so not everyone at the Polish research station was from Eastern Europe.

"You're in grave danger," the second man on the raft yelled.

Aura peered over the side and then at the four men and women standing in a tight circle at the top of the gangway and opened her Shifter magic. Only one of these factions was telling the truth. How hard could it be to figure out which one?

16

MONSTERS ON THE LOOSE

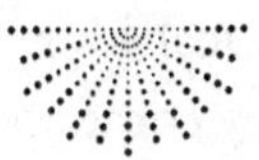

Juan played the pros and cons of lowering the gangway one more time. At least if they had all six people aboard, they could listen to what each group had to say. He caught Viktor's eye. "We need everyone in one place. Shouting over the railing is ridiculous and counterproductive."

"Please," one of the women spoke up. She had a thick Eastern European accent exactly like the man and could have been anywhere from thirty to fifty. Matted black hair hung around her face, and her dark eyes were smoky holes in her grimy face. Her lips trembled. That kind of emotion couldn't be faked.

Or could it?

"You have to say more." Aura reached for the woman, but she shied away.

"Are we the first ship you've seen since the Cataclysm?" Viktor asked.

The man who'd begged for asylum appeared surprised. "The thing that held us prisoner has a name?"

Juan ignored his question. "How many are on this base? Is Boris still in charge?"

"No. He's dead," the man replied. "We number twenty-three. How do you know about Arctowski?"

"We sailed these waters for years," Viktor said.

The men in the raft had disappeared from view, clearly hunting for another way aboard. Juan jerked his head toward the boat's port side. "Bet they find the rope ladder. I'll return once I have them in tow."

"Nooooo!" The man in sealskins clawed at Viktor. "We must leave now. Right now. If they come aboard, all will be lost."

Viktor stared him down. "You will let go of me immediately, or I will order you off my boat. Are we clear? You claimed there are twenty-three of you. I count six. What happens to the other seventeen if I sail away from here?"

The man dropped his hands to his sides. Something flashed from his eyes. It might have been defiance, but Juan had other priorities. He took off at a run for the other side of *Arkady*.

Aura followed him. "This seems very odd," she said. "I can't exactly put my finger on it, but none of those four feel quite right to me."

"How about the ones in the second raft?" Juan asked.

"Can't tell."

Juan glanced over the side. Sure enough, the raft was heading straight for where the emergency rope ladder dangled over the side. He could reach it first, yank it beyond their reach, but was that the best course of action?

Aura saved him the trouble, sprinting ahead until she reached the handles designed to draw the heavy rope farther up the ship's side. "We might want them aboard," she said, "but I thought of something that might determine what's going on. I asked my cat, but it hasn't answered—yet."

Juan gave the pulley system another couple of turns. He regarded Aura. "Beyond demons, Vampires, and Shifters, what other manner of magical creatures are out there?"

"You're smart. It's one of the many things I like about you.

That's almost the same question I asked my cat. More specifically, I wanted to know if it sensed something odd about the four folk standing over on the starboard side." She pressed her lips together. "Shifter history includes other forms of magic, but not in any depth, which was why I didn't know much about Vamps."

The men in the Zodiac were yelling, but Juan tuned them out.

"What did you ask your bondmate?" Juan pressed.

"Back at the beginning, when mages first breached the borders of the animals' world, some animals disagreed so vehemently they left. What I don't know is where they went, or if they ever returned."

"Are you thinking there might be a second type of Shifter out there?"

Aura shook her head. "Not exactly. Our bond animals are powerful. Their magic is strong. You'll appreciate it as you spend more time with your cat. Even if they didn't choose to ally themselves with human mages, they might have gone another route."

Juan thought about it, shuffling possibilities. "They didn't bond with Vampires."

"No, they didn't, but there are other possibilities. You'd asked about magical beings. A small subset of humans holds magic. Only a bare handful of them become Shifters. Some are Druids. Some Freemasons. Some run cults. Some are witches—"

"Drop the ladder," blasted from below.

Juan glanced over the edge. Both men had shoved their hoods back. One was dark, the other fair. Tangled hair caught in a brisk breeze. Juan narrowed his eyes, peering more closely at the dark-haired man. "Boris D'Costa?"

"But the other fellow said Boris was dead," Aura protested. "Or were there two with that name?"

"No. Only one that I know of," Juan replied.

One of the men in the raft shielded his eyes against the glare of daylight bouncing off the surf. "I'm Boris D'Costa. Who are you? I can't see."

Juan bit back a surprised grunt. The dark-haired man's identity had been a guess on his part. The Boris he'd known was always impeccably turned out—by research station standards. The fellow in the boat was gaunt and dressed in tattered rags with a ratty beard spilling down his chest. Juan searched for a question only the real Boris would know and asked, "What did you and I do last time *Arkady* was in port here?"

The man's lean, whiskered face broke into a smile. "*Arkady.* Of course. I was so excited to see a ship—any ship—I didn't bother checking which one it was. Juan, right? Juan Torres?"

"What did we do?" Juan pressed.

"Played poker." Boris grinned up at him. "You lost, but you kept right on hoping. Must've been dawn before you gave up."

Juan chuckled. "You cheated. I still haven't figured out how."

"I'm dropping the ladder," Aura said. She made a funnel around her mouth. "Why'd the other man say you were dead?"

Boris's pleasant expression shattered, replaced by grim determination. He tied off the raft to a metal stanchion, grasped the rope ladder, and hauled himself up it, hand over hand. The fair-haired man followed.

"You didn't answer me," Aura said as soon as Boris tossed a leg over the rail and landed lightly on the deck.

"He wants me to be dead. Then no one will know about the evil haunting him and his ilk."

"That doesn't sound like you. You never had a superstitious bone in your body," Juan said, followed by, "This is Aura Mackenzie."

Boris shook her hand but angled his words at Juan. "Ten years is a long time, *amigo.* Things change."

"Who are you?" Juan asked the other man.

"Ted Rogers," he drawled in pure Brooklynese and held out a hand. Juan shook it. "Shit, but I'm glad to see your ship. I figured we were all going to die here. We've been out of ammo for a year, and those seals are smart bastards. Tough to kill them with knives."

"And they bite back," Juan said.

"We discovered as much," Ted said. "Seal bites get infected like nobody's business."

"Why are there still seals here, and not on South Georgia?" Aura asked.

"There aren't many left," Ted said. "Leopard seals had a big breeding ground in the center of the island, but it's thinned out to almost nothing."

"This island is close to the Antarctic continent," Juan said. "Only about seventy miles. Seals probably swam across the channel."

"Not if the sea was in as bad a shape as it was around Ushuaia," Aura muttered.

"Mmph. Not going to solve that problem. We need to get back to where the others are," Juan directed.

"Not a good idea," Boris said. "There's something wrong with Stephan and his followers. Weird, wicked wrong."

Aura leveled her gaze at him. "Weird wrong, how?"

An uncomfortable expression rippled across Boris's stark cheekbones and bearded chin.

Juan snapped his fingers beneath the other man's nose. "I don't care how bad whatever this is creeps you out. Spill it."

Ted cleared his throat. "Ten of us weren't here before the monstrosity closed in and trapped us. Only good thing about the force field—or whatever it was—was it herded seals onto shore. We ended up with a pile of fish the same way, and a couple of beached whales. Good thing we were proactive curing the meat, otherwise—"

"Focus." Juan made his tone harsh.

"Yeah. Sorry. I'm rambling." Ted raked fingers through his windblown tangles.

Boris glanced at Ted. "Maybe a couple weeks after the mother of all storms left an eerie barrier around King George Island, Stephan and nine others marched out of nowhere. Said they came from the other side of the island, except it's not that big."

"Lots of countries have research stations here," Ted cut in. "Russia, Argentina, Brazil, China, Korea, to name a few, so their appearance didn't seem strange."

"Not at first," Boris said, "but when we got a free moment to question them, some pretended they didn't speak any language I'd understand, which is bullshit since I speak Russian, Chinese, Spanish, German, English, and about ten others."

"Stephan was evasive as hell," Ted agreed. "Didn't seem to know anything about the other research installations, but when we asked if he'd been on a ship that foundered, first he said no. Then he said yes—"

Outraged shrieks sounded from the far side of the ship. Juan grabbed Aura and ran hard for the group he'd left behind. If anything happened to any of them because of the freaks they'd let aboard, he'd rip Stephan and the others to shreds with his bare hands.

"Claws," his cat snarled.

"Ha! You're back. Do you know what we face?"

"Abominations. I wasn't certain until just now, but they only look like men. They're not what they appear."

"Did you hear my bondmate?" he asked Aura who ran next to him.

"Yes, but I have no idea what it means, and my cat still hasn't answered me."

Juan skidded around a corner. Shock hit him in the guts, but he kept on running. Four creatures out of a nightmare hissed, spit, snarled, and screeched while the Shifters fought back. Blood sizzled where it contacted the deck, stripping paint from the concrete. Scraps of clothing that had apparently ripped when the four faux humans altered form blew everywhere.

Boris and Ted came to a stop right behind Juan. "Yeah. This.

Welcome to my world," Boris muttered.

Viktor was locked in combat with something like a cross between a dinosaur and a bat. At least twice Viktor's size, it had thick silver scales the size of dinner plates. Two pairs of red eyes were placed laterally on either side of a pig-like snout. Its mouth was open, displaying triple rows of razor-sharp teeth with disgusting bits of flesh trapped between them. Midback, wings slanted outward, except they weren't big enough to lift something that heavy off the ground.

Ketha launched herself onto the thing's back. The air around her thickened and glistened. Amid staunch ripping, her clothing tore, and her wolf formed, closing its jaws around the monster's neck.

"What kills them?" Juan shouted to Boris.

"Not bullets."

"We don't know," Ted said.

Recco flew into the fray, clutching the iron blade. "Ketha!" he screeched. "Jump down."

The wolf let go, and Recco leapt into the place she'd been, blade swinging. It hesitated when it came in contact with the brute's scaled neck. Zoe chanted like a madwoman, and the blade glowed with bright-white light. The magical charge, or whatever she'd done, brightened still more, and the blade sliced cleanly through hide, bone, and everything else in between.

The abomination's head flew from its body and over the railing, landing in the water with a splat. Water boiled around it, turning red-black. The headless torso spewed hideous-smelling black blood before it lost form, becoming an amorphous mass of jelly-like protoplasm running across the deck with Recco in the middle wiping gunk off his face and head.

"Thanks." Viktor was breathing hard. Ketha ran to him, nuzzling his side with her snout. He dropped a hand on her furred head. "Love you, darling, but we're not done yet."

"Jesus Christ and all his bloody saints." Boris fell back, gape-mouthed.

"You're exactly like them," Ted's blue eyes rounded until white showed all around them. He backed away from the tableau, horror streaming from him in dark waves.

"We are nothing like them," Aura snapped. "And you're not going anywhere. You will remain until this is over."

Light flashed from her fingers, and Ted and Boris froze mid-step.

"What'd you do to them?" Juan asked.

"Snared them with magic. Last thing we want is for them to run back to the settlement and sound the alarm. We'll end up with torches and pitchforks aimed our way."

"God but you're gorgeous when you're—"

"Fighting for my life." She smiled wryly. "Three to go."

"More like nine," Juan said. "According to Boris, ten of those fuckers showed up, which means six are still back at the base."

"Three? Eight? Who cares? We'll get it done. They dabbled in magic they had no right to. Or maybe something is behind this controlling them. Regardless, death is too good for them."

Juan surveyed the battle. Recco had beheaded a hundred-pound Gila monster with the head of a sea serpent. It had the same nauseating red tissue bits stuck in its teeth. Shit! Had this bunch fed recently? If so, from what? Not dried seal meat, that was for sure.

The other two monstrosities, a seal body with a shark's head and a pterodactyl with a long, sharp beak and an eight-foot wing-span, seemed to have given up after their companions were killed. The pterodactyl spread its wings, likely intent on leaving. With a wild shriek, Rowana shifted to her eagle form and met the thing in midair, her beak aiming for its eyes. Viktor shifted too, and his raven joined the fray.

While the seal stared upward, mouth hanging open with what might have been apprehension, Daide grabbed the blade and came around behind, neatly beheading it. More black blood joined what flowed freely across the deck. Juan reached for the head, intent on chucking it into the ocean, but Ketha raced to him, growling, hackles at half-mast.

"She wants it for her lab," Aura said.

Juan hunkered to Ketha's level. "I'm cleaning this deck. If you want to hang onto any of this shit"—he waved an arm wide—"for souvenirs or experiments, you have five minutes."

"Hold up on the cleaning project. We're not done." Aura angled her gaze skyward where Rowana and Viktor were chivvying the pterodactyl back toward the boat.

"Daide!" Juan yelled.

"Yeah?" He trotted over, blade dangling from one clenched fist. His dark eyes shone with fascination. "As horrible as this is, I want to know how these cross-mutations happened."

"Ketha wants lab samples. She almost bit my hand off."

"Not even close." Ketha was human again, naked and shivering. "I'll be back as soon as I'm dressed. Do not even think about jettisoning so much as one lock of hair into the ocean."

"I'll watch over your stash," Aura told her. "Go before your lips turn blue."

Ketha pulled open a door and ran inside the ship.

Juan sucked in a tight breath and nudged Daide. "Never saw anything like this in vet school, eh?"

"You'd be right about that." Daide glanced up. "Here they come. Give me room to maneuver."

"Watch out for Rowana and Vik," Aura cautioned.

Daide kept his gaze trained on the tumbling display above. He raised the sword, keeping it poised for action. The raven closed from one side, the eagle from the other. They divebombed the dinosaur, putting out its eyes. Shrieking, sightless, the pterodactyl fell like a stone.

Daide sliced through its neck with the iron saber before it

even hit the deck. Scales clattered, and the body burst into the same jell, sticking to Juan's booted feet.

He smiled grimly. He'd been of two minds about even bringing the blade with them when they left Ushuaia, but Viktor was convinced they might need it. Lucky one of them was thinking ahead. Juan had wanted to leave everything about being a Vampire in Ushuaia. Boris—or was it Ted—had said bullets wouldn't kill the unnatural animal forms. Driving a knife through scales would have been far harder than beheading them. Plus, it might not have worked, either. Maybe the silver-and-iron imbued bullets would have made some headway.

Viktor and Rowana landed on the bloody deck. The air took on a glistening aspect, and they stood naked, surveying the globs of black gel interspersed with streaks of red.

"Damn. My eagle loves fighting." Rowana shook silver hair over her shoulders to cover her breasts. Her dark eyes held a satisfied aspect. "Be back once I'm dressed." She pushed the nearest door open and walked through it.

Viktor jerked his chin toward Ted and Boris. "What happened to those two?"

"They came from the second raft," Juan replied. "They weren't any happier about us, once we began shifting, than they were about Stephan and his cronies."

Viktor took a few steps closer and narrowed his eyes. "Boris? Is that you?"

"Aura froze them with magic once they freaked. He can't answer you," Juan replied.

"Fascinating. I'm going to throw something on, and then—"

Juan flapped his hands at Viktor. "Go. I'll get rolling on cleanup. I'd have begun already, but your wife threatened me with bodily harm if I disturbed so much as a single cell of what's left of those bastards."

"Sounds like the woman I love." Viktor made a noise between a grunt and a laugh. He sorted through protoplasm and clothing scraps, coming up with three pairs of Wellingtons: his, Ketha's, and Rowana's.

"We'll douse them with seawater," Recco said. "Daide and I will collect samples too."

Viktor nodded and trotted up one of the flights of external stairs.

Aura joined Juan. "I'm about to release Boris and Ted. Hope they'll listen to reason."

"Would magic help?" Juan picked his way around the worst of the debris littering the deck to where Boris and Ted stood.

"Probably, but it's not allowed. Once a mortal discovers what we are, we have to tell them the truth." Aura spoke a few words in Gaelic.

Boris shook his head as if he'd been asleep. "What the fuck happened?" he muttered, his gaze canting from side to side. When it settled on Juan and Aura, his face twisted into a horrified expression. "Shit. Aw, shit. I remember. Ted." He shook the man swaying on his feet next to him. "Wake up, goddammit. We have to get out of here."

"What? Why? I'm tired." Ted trained bleary eyes at a distant point on the horizon.

Aura stepped between them. "I apologize for holding you against your will with magic, but I had no choice."

"Are we prisoners?" Boris balled his hands into fists. "Christ, Juan. We grew up in the same rathole of a neighborhood in BA."

"Right you are, *amigo*." Juan nodded once, sharply. "Which is one more reason you need to listen to what the lady here has to say."

"We don't have to listen to anything," Ted said, sounding marginally more with it. "You're like Stephan. He and his sick, twisted family have been eating the rest of us. They cull one or two and hang onto them for months, leaving just enough to keep them alive."

"Interesting. It explains what was clinging to their teeth." Juan shrugged.

"That's all you can muster?" Boris rounded on him. "A shrug?"

Juan grabbed the other man's shoulders and shook him. "*Si, amigo.* Like you said earlier, ten years is a long time. Things change. I spent most of those years as a Vampire, so you'll excuse me if I don't fall all over myself at the specter of eerie, weird, or impossible."

"Listen to me." Aura gazed from Boris to Ted. "I'm a mountain cat Shifter. Every woman on this ship is some type of Shifter, but we're the authorized variety. The ones who bonded properly—"

"As if there's a proper way to turn into an abomination." Ted sneered.

"I am not an abomination. Neither are any of my sisters. Our brand of magic is ancient. It's stood the test of time. Our animals are noble, pure. True bond animals take the mettle of a human before agreeing to link with them. Stephan and his brood failed that test."

She took a measured breath. "My guess, and it's only a guess because I'll never know, is Stephan wanted to be a Shifter. The perverted energy from the Cataclysm provided the substrate he was missing to spin his weak, ineffectual power into an animal form. Because he lacked a true bond animal, the thing he turned into was a product of his twisted imagination.

"Once he figured out how to shift, he talked a bunch of others into trying it. I bet many of them died. When you dabble in things not meant for you, bad things happen."

Karin joined them. "It's an interesting theory, but what's left on this deck argues for another explanation. Once we killed those creatures, they gave up any semblance of form. If they'd been Shifters, they'd have reverted to their human bodies in death."

"Good point." Aura nodded, her expression somber. "Beyond where they came from, the other thing I'm curious about is why they hustled out to *Arkady.*"

"And told us we had to pull anchor and head for the open sea immediately," Juan added.

"They probably planned to add you to their menu," Ted muttered. "Easy enough to turn the boat back around once the lot of you were imprisoned."

"I still don't get it," Juan said. "How could they have guessed we didn't have a full complement of crew and passengers?"

"Because nothing's been the same since the Cataclysm hit," Aura said. "They must have been desperate, and desperate men take chances."

"I'm sure they assumed once they took their"—Boris made a gagging noise—"other forms, everyone aboard would be frozen with fear."

"It worked for them at the base," Ted mumbled.

Boris straightened beneath Juan's hold. "You can let go. Did I hear you right? You were a Vampire?"

Juan lifted his hands from the other man's shoulders. "You heard right. It's a rather involved story, but I'm not a Vampire anymore."

Boris squeezed his eyes shut for a moment before zeroing in on Juan. "*Vaya por dios.*"

Juan wrapped one arm around Aura. "I'm a Shifter like her, now."

Boris flinched as if Juan had told him he'd signed on with a devil-worshipping cult, but he didn't say anything.

Juan thought about the discussion he'd had with his cat about Buenos Aires. His bond animal had been quite clear Juan's family would never understand. Boris's reaction hammered the point home.

Aura met his gaze with her clear, green eyes. Her calm acceptance centered him, and he turned back to Boris and Ted. "Stephan said there were twenty-three survivors at Arctowski. Did it include his band of freaks?"

Ted frowned. "Six of us managed to outwit them. We were

double that number, but Stephan and them killed the others. I have no idea where he got twenty-three."

"So four of you are back on the base?" Aura asked.

"Sort of. The others are in an ice cave thirty feet under the base. Something about it repelled the monsters. It was pure, blind luck Boris and I were aboveground when your ship arrived. We're in better shape than the others, and we were making a run to scavenge food."

"Do you know anything about the other research facilities scattered around this island?" Juan asked.

Boris nodded. He edged closer to Ted, and something about their postures suggested they were more than friends and colleagues. "We had radio contact until we ran too low on gasoline to waste what was left powering the generators."

"How long ago was that?" Aura asked.

"Maybe two years," Ted replied. "Back then, the only manned bases were the Argentine and German ones. The others were either empty to begin with, or everyone died. We were one of the best-stocked bases here. It's the only reason any of us are still alive."

"I need to oversee cleanup," Juan said, "but Aura can take you inside. We have hot water for showers. Clean clothes. Coffee. Whiskey."

Boris smiled. "You're making it damned hard to be afraid of you."

"I'm not being nice." Juan didn't smile back. "Once we have the ship set to rights, we're taking the rafts to Arctowski, and we're not leaving until every one of those imposters—the ones who leveraged and perverted Shifter magic when they had no right to —is dead."

"Don't jump to hasty conclusions." His cat was back. *"Evil lurks there, but I don't believe it has anything to do with Shifter ability gone bad."*

It was almost exactly what Karin had suggested, and Juan filed it away as fair warning they had to be prepared for anything. He focused his next words on Boris and Ted. "When we launch for Arctowski, you'll have to come along so we can locate your companions."

"Damn straight we will." Boris clacked his teeth together.

Aura herded them inside along with the beginnings of a lecture about Shifters' proud, powerful history.

By the time Juan returned to the battle site, it was 90 percent cleared of debris. Viktor sloshed another bucket of seawater across the painted concrete. It had blistered and scarred in places, but at least it was clean. Straightening, he gave the bucket to Juan. "A couple more of these, and we'll have it. I'd forgotten you and Boris were old mates."

"Hell, I nearly forgot myself. Until I laid eyes on him and even then, he was almost unrecognizable. Ketha get what she needed?"

"She and Recco and Daide and Karin were chattering like a flock of magpies." He rolled his eyes. "They're in the lab now doing whatever lab rats do to preserve biologic material. Damn, I could use a drink."

Juan elbowed him. "What? And miss the showdown on Arctowski?"

Viktor shook his head. "Is this what it's going to be like every single fucking place we drop anchor? Some hideous manifestation of evil waiting to pounce?"

Juan didn't waste breath answering, just trudged to a bilge outflow and turned the tap to fill his bucket.

17

LET ME GO

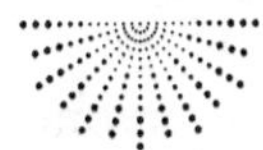

AURA CROUCHED in a Zodiac as it sped across the bay. Boris, Ted, Juan, Recco, Zoe, and Karin were in their boat. Since the rafts from Arctowski were already in the water, they'd used them rather than launching their own. Viktor, Ketha, Rowana, Daide, Tessa, Moira, and Becca were in the second raft right behind theirs.

"Thank you for helping us," Boris said.

"Yeah. Apologies for the meltdown," Ted added.

"Understandable," Recco said. "You should have heard Daide and me when the totality of Vampirism sank in. Before, we figured we'd be able to sidestep it, somehow."

A bitter laugh blew past Juan's lips. "Not the time to shamble through memory lane. As soon as we land, Boris and Ted will make a run for the ice cave and retrieve the four people hiding there."

"And then we'll take a raft and return to the ship," Boris said.

"Is there anything we can salvage from the base?" Karin asked.

"Like what?" Ted asked.

"Scientific instruments. Chemicals. This was a research station. Presumably, you studied something."

213

"Mostly geology and archaeology," Boris replied. "There's a decent microscope and years' worth of journals detailing our findings. We do have barrels of biodiesel, though."

Juan made a chopping motion with the hand not wrapped around the tiller. "We'll take the fuel. The rest isn't critical. Did you ever try to alter your generators to run on diesel?"

"Of course. It gummed up their carburetors," Ted replied. "We'd have needed bigger jets."

"Figures. Once we land, everyone but Boris and Ted remains together. Six of those perversions are left, and we only have one blade."

"Which is why I brought the Remington," Recco said. "Maybe the silver and iron bullets will kill them."

Aura turned to Boris. "What do the other creatures look like?"

"I don't know."

"What do you mean, you don't know?" Aura peered at him and wiped spray out of her face.

"They're different every time they show up."

"Yeah," Ted chimed in. "We'd never seen those particular beasts before today. The seal one was bizarre. So was the Gila monster with wings."

"The thing that caught my attention," Karin spoke up, "was what they turned into once they died. No bones. Only things left were clumps of unrelated DNA. I didn't have enough time to tease through it, but in the one sample I stained, I found genetic patterns from birds and fish. Nothing even remotely human."

"Does it mean they weren't human anymore?" Aura asked the doctor.

"Not sure they ever were. My guess is 'human' was one more form they wore." Karin creased her forehead into a mass of worried lines. "DNA is a nucleic acid. Once you loosen the links between the monomers, the four bases—adenine, thymine, guanine, and cytosine—become fluid. They can form anything, but getting them to hang onto any one shape for more than a short time requires a big energy output."

"What exactly are you getting at?" Juan asked and swung the boat around preparatory to landing on a rock-and-ice studded beach.

"Maybe they revert to puddles of goo in between." Karin turned her hands palms upward. "If we could capture one of them alive, it might go a significant way toward—"

"Forget it." Juan cut her off. "No fucking way am I letting one of those things on my ship."

Karin snorted. "Aha! The time-honored friction between practicality and science rears its head. We'd have beaten the Black Death in the 1600s, if the fuddy-duddy officials hadn't insisted on burning the bodies in mass graves."

"Fuddy-duddy, is it?" Juan cut the engine. "I'll do whatever it takes to keep my ship safe."

"Same thing the magistrates said about their cities and the plague." Karin made a sour face.

The second raft drew alongside them with Viktor at the helm, and both vessels scraped against the beach as they hit shallow water. Aura sent her magic zinging wide, but she hadn't picked up anything from Stephan and his three sidekicks. Maybe their twisted version of being a Shifter wasn't truly magic, or maybe it was so foreign, she lacked a place to pigeonhole it…

Neither explanation satisfied her. Juan and Viktor sloshed through surf, dragging the rafts by their anchor ropes. Aura tapped Zoe and Karin. "Why couldn't I sense something off about Stephan and those other three? I looked. They didn't feel quite right, but nothing alerted me about how bizarre they were. Or how dangerous."

"Aye, it's been troubling me as well," Zoe said.

"Breaking the interconnections in DNA is science, not magic," Karin said. "The perverse combinations that crop up only appear magical. It's why they didn't trip your radar."

"How in the goddess's name will we locate them absent magic?" Aura asked, but no one answered her.

Juan stood next to the rear of the raft, stabilizing it while everyone exited. He reached over and plucked the key from the engine, offering it to Boris.

"Nah. Better hide it. Maybe in the wooden box. If something happens to me, you won't be stuck with no way to flip the ignition."

"It'll be right here." Juan tucked the key in the ridge between a pontoon and a sidewall.

""After a while, Stephan's associates will surmise the boarding party isn't coming back, and one of two things will happen." Boris stopped next to Aura. "It will either drive them to attack or push them into hiding."

"Any chance they'd retreat to where they came from before they showed up at Arctowski?" Juan asked.

"Remember, we have no idea where that is," Ted said, "but it's possible."

"Nah. Not likely," Boris cut in. "Their food is here."

"Could they go into stasis like those Vamps on South Georgia?" Zoe spoke up.

"I doubt it," Karin said. "Without an ongoing energy source herding it, the unlinked DNA will become more and more disorganized and unruly. Won't take much time for it to devolve into the same bits and pieces scattered across *Arkady's* deck."

Viktor, Ketha, and the others joined them.

"We're off," Boris said. "Good hunting to you. Wish us luck."

"Hang on." Viktor grabbed Boris's arm. "Where exactly will you be? So we know where to search if the Zodiac is still here when we return."

Boris leaned close and spoke into Viktor's ear. Aura didn't bother to listen in.

"Can't thank you enough." Ted turned and hurried across the beach with Boris next to him. Both men peered anxiously about.

Aura scanned the empty beach. Up close, the yellow prefab buildings had serious structural defects. They'd been set on pier blocks to protect them from unusually high tides, but floors had fallen in, and windows were either boarded over or broken.

Wind scoured the open shoreline; cold and sere, it smelled like snow. What a desolate, lonely place. During the Antarctic winter, which lasted from April through August, darkness would be unremitting for at least two months.

"People actually volunteered to live here?" she muttered.

Juan nodded. "Yes. Maybe two or three hundred if you count all the settlements in this area. McMurdo is well over a thousand miles away, and it had maybe seventeen hundred residents. Then there was Scott base nearby. It—"

"We need a plan," Viktor broke in.

"So long as it entails remaining together, I'll support it," Juan said.

Aura did a nose count. Four men and eight women. The other four Shifters—two wolves, a mountain lion, and a bear—were guarding *Arkady*. "We're twelve," she ventured. "Maybe we should form two groups. We could cover more ground that way."

Juan shook his head. "Nope. We have three weapons, only one of which we're certain of. If the Remington has enough stopping power to be effective, then we could split up, but at the moment it's an unknown."

"May as well be methodical," Viktor said. "We'll begin with the closest building and work our way through them."

Aura spread magic around her. If even the slightest ping didn't feel right, she'd be all over it. They moved from building to building, traveling fast but making sure they weren't missing anything, either. Clearly, the yellow boxcars had come in sections on ships because they were all the same. Each core building was roughly fifteen feet square. Sometimes two or three had been cobbled together to make a larger structure.

"This was the main gathering place," Juan said and stepped into a building that appeared in better repair.

Aura glanced at a mudroom with boots still lining cubbies on two walls. Past the entry hall, a display case held a three-dimensional likeness of the Antarctic continent. Although she couldn't have articulated quite why, her sense of unease had grown with each dilapidated building, running deeper than the bleakness of deserted habitations. Ushuaia had been full of them, but they hadn't given her a good case of the heebie-jeebies like this place did.

"This whole settlement feels wrong." She trailed into a large room after Juan. Most of the windows were intact, but they held years of grit and grime and were impossible to see out of.

"Know what you mean," Ketha said. "It's probably ridiculous, but it seems as if someone is luring us right where they want us."

Her words struck a chord, one that curdled Aura's gut. She felt like someone had doubled up a fist and socked her in the stomach, but she was afraid if she sounded a general alarm, invisible trap doors would slam shut. She recalled Ketha's vision about how everything had fragmented after they arrived on the beach. Maybe the seer's prediction wasn't as far off as they'd assumed.

She made her way to Juan who'd moved through to yet one more room. This one held trestle tables and benches and had clearly been a dining hall. A door obviously led outside. She trotted toward it, twisted a very rusty dead bolt, and threw it open.

"Nothing in here," she said, cheerily. "Come on. I prefer the fresh air. Everything inside these boxcars smells musty."

Juan caught her up. Two of the four wooden steps had collapsed, so he jumped down like she had. "I have a lot of warm memories of meals in there." He crooked a thumb at the building with its peeling yellow paint.

Karin poked her head out the open door, took in the damaged steps, and said, "Eh, I can go around the other way."

Aura ran lightly to her. "No need," she said brightly. "Let me help you."

Karin leaned heavily on her. Once she stood on the frozen dirt, she frowned. "It's a relief to be out of that place. Nothing I can exactly put my finger on, but—"

Aura shook her head, and the other Shifter shut up fast.

"There you all are." Viktor jumped down and angled his head toward the open door, calling Ketha's name.

The sense of unease, which had begun as a trickle, turned into a torrent. Aura couldn't hold still any longer, so she grabbed Juan's arm—the one not busy balancing the Ruger. *We have to get everyone out of there.* She used telepathy, but it wouldn't fool whatever they stood against.

Ketha emerged through the door and leapt nimbly down the splintered boards.

A deep, crashing boom built in Aura's belly, gathering in intensity until she wasn't certain where it was coming from.

The smile on Ketha's face blew apart, and she screamed. "Get out, everyone. Break windows. Do what you have to, but get out now. This is exactly like the vision I had."

"Goddamn it!" Viktor shouted.

Ketha ran back toward the open door, but he grabbed her shoulders, holding onto her. "You are not going back inside."

Daide blasted through the door right before the entire structure ripped loose from its stanchions and began to spin. An out-of-control vortex, it formed a black cloud. Bits and pieces of it ripped off, and Aura ducked to avoid a club-sized chunk of wood. As bad as this was, it beat the hell out of her creeping certainty something had them in its gunsights.

She'd been right about that. Now they needed to figure out what it was. A chill wind stinking of death and rot with an overlay of ozone made her nose and lungs ache.

Daide picked himself up and limped toward them. "Fuck. What the hell is going on?"

"We'd all like to know." Viktor stared at his wife. "If you scryed something beyond what you've already told us, Ketha—"

"I didn't. Not really. I talked it through with Aura first, but—"

"Not how I run things." Viktor's voice was deadly quiet. "We play with all the cards on the table faceup. Not with factions who know things but keep them hidden."

"I'm telling you I did not hide anything." Ketha squared off against her husband, eyes on fire with annoyance.

"Stop it." Juan faced Viktor down. "Six of us are left inside whatever that building turned into. How do we get them out?"

Aura counted. Recco, Zoe, Tessa, Moira, Rowana, and Becca were missing.

"By all the bluidy, fecking saints, what is going on?" Zoe pelted toward them.

Aura hugged her. "Bad shit. An ill wind has it in for us. Where were you?"

"Had to pee."

"Your bladder saved you." Aura exhaled sharply. "Crap. Five of us are trapped in there."

Zoe raked her gaze across their small group. "Trapped? Recco and Rowana and Becca and Moire and Tessa?" At Aura's nod, Zoe made a fist and shook it at the rotating house. It looked like something out of the Baba Yaga myth, minus the chicken feet.

Aura switched to her psychic view, hoping for information. Maybe the vortex was an illusion they could punch through. Zoe gripped one of her hands and Ketha the other. Karin joined them, and the four women focused magic at the whirling, stinking menace. Aura had been born to wield magic, but until the Cataclysm trapped her in Ushuaia, her power had been more abstract than practical. Even the years in Ushuaia, she'd mostly snuck around, muffling her gift on the rare occasions she was out so as not to tip off a Vampire.

Ley lines formed, but instead of glistening golden ropes, they were dull and frayed. Was this an extension of the damage

Rowana had warned them about only a scant handful of days ago? How could it be so much worse here than in Grytviken?

Juan's energy closed from behind her, along with Viktor's and Daide's. "What can we do to help?"

"Join your magic to ours," Zoe answered. "Sure and we could use a boost."

Aura felt a jolt as the men latched onto both ends of their line. The view through her third eye shifted. Other ley lines blasted into place, appearing more like they should. She squeezed her earth eyes shut, not expecting it to alter her psychic view. The gesture was reflexive, something she did when she didn't believe what was laid out before her.

The new set of lines snapped into place, mocking her.

"Christ!" Ketha blurted. "Which ones are real?"

"These," Karin said.

Aura liked the answer so she didn't grill the other Shifter on why she was certain. Male energy potentiated female-driven magic. Synergistic, more than additive, perhaps it had kicked the door open to what was really there. A high, keening howl ripped through her. At first, she thought she might have screamed, but it came from outside herself.

The whirling boxcar began breaking apart, and the shrill ripping, tearing sound grew so loud her ears burned with white-hot agony. Debris careened through the air. A piece of wood two feet long, several inches wide, and studded with nails hurtled toward her. She met it with magic and it exploded a foot in front of her body, shooting upward as she'd planned.

All around her, the women blocked, dodged, and ducked. The air was so thick with wreckage, she couldn't see the men.

"Fall back," Juan screeched. "We have to put some distance between ourselves and the house."

"But our companions are in there," Karin protested. Light blasted from her fingertips, and a bowling-sized ball of mortar exploded, forming harmless dust.

"We can't help them if we're dead." Viktor dragged his end of the line back a few feet.

Aura couldn't stand her ground, launch defensive action against incoming crap, and fight the pull of their joined hands moving backward.

"Fall back." Viktor repeated Juan's order. "We'll regroup once we're beyond the worst of this." They moved back a step at a time, still joined together. The sea lapped around her feet before they were finally clear of the rubble piling up between them and where the joined boxcars had stood.

The grinding, tearing, shearing hadn't slowed one whit. It formed a hole in the ether. The ley lines shuddered, and Rowana came into view. The old Shifter's face was white with strain, and her lips were skinned back from her teeth. She had hold of a horizontal line and was using it to drag herself forward. Recco was behind her with the others lined up behind him.

"My God. Her hands," Karin gasped.

Aura stared at them and saw bone where flesh had been. Ley lines carried high voltage magic. It had stripped Rowana's hands to bone. Shifters healed fast, but fear for her friend filled Aura with dread.

"Focus all our power where she is. Help her break through," Aura screamed, but her ears were so trashed, all she heard was a gurgle as if she were yelling from the bottom of a well.

Magic formed a multihued arc shot with pure, brilliant white. Aura reached deep, giving it everything she had. Rowana was taking the brunt of the punishment. By the time the others dragged themselves forward, the power had eaten through Rowana's fingers and dissipated to some extent.

Pressure built around them until breathing hurt. Aura's lungs felt crushed, and something harsh pressed against her throat. "Push. Through. It." She gritted the words out.

All of a sudden, the compression released. Rowana flew through the air toward them, followed by Recco, Moira, Tessa, and Becca. They landed on rocks, dirt, and jagged rubble from the boxcar.

Karin launched herself at Rowana, healing energy shooting out in quick jabs. Blood gushed from Rowana's shredded hands, one of her legs was bent at an unnatural angle where she'd landed on a large rock, and she yowled with pain. Aura knelt on Rowana's other side. The woman's body was so broken, it was hard to know where to touch her.

"Help me," Karin said in a strained voice. She built a healing shroud around Rowana, chanting furiously.

Aura opened herself, so Karin could borrow strength from her magic.

Juan squatted next to Aura. "Will she—?"

Aura turned eyes that felt like sandpaper his way, and the rest of his question died unspoken. She'd only seen a healing shroud once before, and the Shifter had died. The last-ditch effort would drain Karin to her foundations, which was why she'd asked for help.

The others gathered close. "She was so brave," Recco said. "I wanted to take the lead, but she said I didn't have enough magic. Damn it. Do not let her die."

Karin didn't even glance up. Tears streaked her cheeks. "Goddammit, Ro. Try."

The eagle Shifter's dark eyes fluttered open. Cloudy at first, they cleared. "Let me go. I love you, Karin, but you're all that's holding me here. It's not only my hands, and you know it. No one can touch the lines and live, but it was our only way out of there."

Blood bubbled past her lips, staining her chin, and she fought to get more words out. "It's not what we thought. Those twisted shapeshifters are powered by a dark mage. Strongest bastard I've ever run across. He's who blew up the house. He..." More blood shot past her lips, and her words disappeared in a strangled gurgle.

"He planned to drain us," Becca said. "Not our blood, but our essence. Once he had it, he would have used us like he used the others to form warped perversions for his entertainment."

"Where is he now?" Viktor jumped to his feet and turned in a full circle, blade raised and ready.

"Even he needs to regroup," Moira said. "Ro's trick with the ley lines flattened him. He'd erected another set of lines to fool us, and she blew them out of the water."

Rowana's bloodstained mouth twisted in pain. "Hurts. Everything hurts. I'm dying. Let me go."

Tears sluiced down Aura's face. She bent over Rowana and gathered her into her arms, no longer worried about causing her further pain. "Safe travels, sister. We'll never forget you."

The warm honey of Karin's magic dissipated. While Aura held Rowana in her arms, an eagle formed in her mind's eye. The bird spread its dark wings and flew toward a brilliant horizon.

18

AS GREEN AS SHIFTERS COME

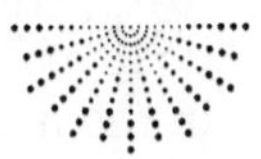

JUAN SAW the outline of an eagle take wing and understood Rowana was gone. He knelt next to Aura. "I'll take her now. We'll bury her at sea, far from this place."

Aura folded Rowana's broken body into his arms, and he got first to his knees and then to his feet.

"Did all of you know?" Recco gazed at the three women who'd been trapped with him and Rowana. When they nodded, he said, "Why didn't you tell me?"

"What good would it have done?" Becca asked, her voice vibrating with sorrow. "It was a sure death for all of us or certain death for one. Would you have taken her place?"

"Yes. I would have."

"You couldn't." Karin got heavily to her feet. "Rowana was right. You didn't have enough magic to absorb the ley line's energy. If you'd taken the lead, two of you would be dead now. Maybe three." She blew out a breath and scrubbed her hands across her wet cheeks, leaving bloody tracks. "We should leave this place. Before the mage recovers and seeks vengeance."

Juan plodded across the shore toward where they'd left the rafts. Both were still there.

225

Viktor ran to his side. "Christ. Can this day get any worse? I have to see what happened to Boris and Ted and the others."

"Where were they?" Juan asked, adding, "Good thing you had the foresight to find out before Boris left."

"Beneath the building that blew up, but it should make locating them easier."

Juan wasn't sure about Viktor's assessment. Rubble from the exploding building could have blocked egress from an underground lair. He laid Rowana in the nearest raft. "Take her back to the ship," he told Aura. "I'm going with Viktor."

Desperation vied with determination in Aura's red-rimmed eyes. "Not without me, you're not. What if you run into trouble?"

Juan opened his mouth to argue, but she shook her head. "Not up for discussion. I just lost a woman I loved like a mother. I am not losing anyone else today if I can help it."

Ketha stalked to where they stood. "I heard you. I'm going too."

Viktor's harsh expression softened when he regarded his wife. "Go back to the ship. Please."

Ketha shook her head. Her golden eyes turned to pools of molten pain. "This feels like my fault. I should have scryed our future earlier, made certain I understood the meaning of what formed in my glass."

"It wasn't as if we had a whole lot of time." Aura touched her friend's arm.

Ketha flinched, brushing her off. "If I'd started earlier, we would have."

"Ketha. Please." Viktor gestured toward the raft with Rowana's body.

"No." She grimaced, skinning her lips back from her teeth. "Ten years. For ten fucking years I managed to keep us all safe in the hellhole Ushuaia turned into. We've been gone for what? Less than a month, and Rowana is dead." Her face rippled with pain, and she scraped the heels of her hands down her face.

"I'm going with you," Karin announced. "You might need a doctor."

Recco stepped in front of her. "I can manage any emergency that comes up."

"But you don't understand how to weave medical treatment in with magic," Karin protested.

"Won't matter. Boris and Ted and them are human. You only use magic to treat Shifters, right?"

Karin straightened her back as if the motion cost her. "Yes, it's true. I'll prepare Rowana's body for our ritual ceremony to bid her farewell."

Juan gave the Ruger to Daide along with a handful of shells. "See the women back safely."

"I will. Who's coming with me?"

Before anyone could answer, Viktor said, "Juan, Aura, Ketha, Recco, and Zoe will remain. The rest of you return to the ship."

No one argued. Viktor pried a wooden box in the empty raft's stern open and looped coils of ratty-looking rope around his body. Motioning to the others to follow, he set a fast pace through piles of broken wood, shattered glass, and clumps of mortar.

Styrofoam insulation reminded Juan of macabre, blue snow as the wind moved it from one spot to another. He cast sidelong glances at Aura. Her expression was so harsh, it could have been carved in stone. He wanted to comfort her. Hell, he wished she'd returned on the raft with Karin, but he didn't have the right to tell her what to do. Viktor tried that approach with Ketha, and she'd told him to piss up a rope.

Something Viktor had said hit home. *Is this what it's going to be like every single fucking place we drop anchor? Some hideous manifestation of evil waiting to pounce?*

Juan ground his jaws together. Apparently, the answer was yes. The new normal was they couldn't let their guard down. Not ever. The Cataclysm had altered something elemental, made it easier for wickedness to rise to the top like curdled cream.

Viktor slowed, and Juan peered at stacks of wreckage. The bulk of the building had been where they were standing. "Here?" he asked.

Viktor narrowed his green eyes. "I have no idea. It all looks the same. I figured we'd find a hole in the ground, but it will take days to systematically move everything."

"I'm game." Recco didn't sound anything like his usual, easy-going self. His words were terse with a bitten-off aspect.

Ketha, Aura, and Zoe joined them. "We can narrow this down with magic," Aura said.

"Aye, if anything lives down there"—Zoe jerked her chin at the debris-strewn beach—"we'll find it."

"Can you sort out if it's the dark mage or someone human?" Viktor asked.

Aura screwed her face into a scowl. "Maybe. Depends how much power the mage has left to cloak himself with."

"We're wasting time. Let's scrap the conversation and search." Ketha extended her hands. Aura and Zoe grasped them, and the women began to chant in Gaelic.

The feel of their magic, clean and fragrant with their combined scents, was like a balm. Juan shielded himself from a warm complacency because it threatened to blunt his anguish over Rowana's death. He needed every sharp edge at his disposal.

"They're over here." Aura jumped a splintered boxcar panel, skirted more debris, and stood over a pile of lumber stacked at crazy angles.

"Alive?" Viktor grunted the word out.

"Barely, but I can't tell how many," Ketha replied.

"The energy feels human to me," Zoe added, "but the mage fooled us good when he lured us into that building."

Aura had already begun dragging the topmost slab of insulation-coated wood out of the way. Juan grabbed a corner and helped her heave it aside. The wind worsened, fighting them every step of the way as they rearranged wreckage. The sky darkened until it developed a bruised gunmetal cast. Snow began, whipping into bundles of ice crystals that stung when they hit his exposed skin.

They formed three groups of two, but even working as fast as they could, an hour passed before a small opening emerged.

Juan knelt and cupped his hands around his mouth. "Boris!"

A flurry of Spanish was followed by, "Thank God it's you. I had a pretty good idea what trapped us. What I didn't know was who was digging their way in. Hang on. I'll move the ladder."

Scraping noises wafted upward, and Juan motioned for Viktor and the others to make the hole big enough for someone to climb through. Because they had to work from the top down, another half hour dripped past before they'd cleared a space large enough to accommodate a person.

"I don't like this," Aura muttered.

"Yeah. It's taking too much time," Ketha said.

"Can you sense darkness?" Juan asked.

"Maybe," Zoe replied.

"I'm not sure, either," Aura said. "A nasty patina from the warped magic the sorcerer used to turn the building into a maelstrom is coating everything."

"We have to hurry." Ketha bent close to the opening. "Boris. Get your people moving now."

A wraith-thin brown-eyed blonde woman swathed in filthy rags emerged first. Her hands were patchy with frostbite. "I'm Diana," she said in a gravelly voice with an American inflection.

Juan pulled her through and shouted. "Come on," at whoever was climbing the ladder.

A man with a face like an overused roadmap dragged himself out next. His torso was covered by an ancient black down jacket with feathers escaping from multiple holes. He was panting like a steam engine that couldn't get enough fuel. Bald, he turned haggard brown eyes on them and rasped, "Sasha," with a Russian accent.

Ted stuck his head out. "James is dead. Nora is unconscious. I tried to carry her up the ladder, but I'm not strong enough. Neither is Boris. It's why we weren't faster."

"Are you certain James is dead?" Recco asked.

"Yeah." Ted's reply was terse, and Recco didn't demand details.

"Move over," Aura ordered and slithered through the opening.

Juan tried to grab her, but she was gone. Had she fallen? Thirty feet was a long way down. "Aura!" he cried.

"I'm okay. Used magic to cushion my fall."

Ted climbed through, moving like an old man. His face was streaked with dirt and grime, and his blue eyes were even more haunted than they'd been aboard *Arkady*.

Juan started down the hole, but Viktor yelled, "Stop. We can do more good from this end. I have rope. Aura didn't need to go down there."

"Toss it my way." Juan grabbed an undulating coil and wrapped one end around his waist to make a primitive belay. He dropped the end into the ice cave.

"Got it," Aura called, followed by, "Pull her out."

The rope tightened around Juan's waist. Viktor moved to his side, and between the two of them, they hauled the rope up. Recco stood next to them, ready to take over as soon as Nora was out.

Ashen faced, she hung in loops wrapped beneath her arms and tied across her back. Lank red hair fell around her, and she was barely breathing.

Recco gathered her into his arms, unlooping the rope and moving aside. Boris crested the ladder. Dried blood splotched his face, and his eyes held a horrified expression as if he'd traversed the backside of Hell. He scrambled out of the way and lurched unsteadily to his feet. Ted wrapped his arms around Boris, and the two men leaned into each other.

"Aura. Get out of there," Juan yelled.

"I'm bringing the other guy. No way am I leaving any raw material for that mage bastard to turn into fodder for his power."

A low, ominous booming began deep beneath their feet, followed by a tortured cry from Aura.

Juan clattered down the ladder, ignoring Viktor's shouts. Aura was at the bottom chanting furiously with an emaciated, dark-haired man clutched in her arms. Magic boiled around her in a sickly luminescence as the booming gathered intensity.

"You cannot call magic down here," Juan shouted. "It's waking the fucker up."

"How the hell could you possibly know?" Aura demanded. Her face twisted into a rictus of determination. "Shit. You're as green as Shifters come."

Her words stung. Did they reflect how she saw him? Stupid? Ineffectual? He shook off his hurt feelings. The only thing that mattered was getting her out of the cave. James—or whatever his name was—didn't matter.

"Let go of him. We have to get out or we'll be trapped here. Christ, woman! Do you want to die in this cave?"

Ice began to shatter around them, falling on their heads. It was uncannily similar to what had happened in the doomed boxcar. Pressure built around Juan, and he recognized the dark mage's twisted magic. He reached for the dead man. "I'll take him."

Aura nodded once, sharply, and hustled up the ladder. The earth shook around them, and ice broke off, hitting unnaturally high notes that made Juan's ears ache. He draped the man, who didn't weigh much more than a child, over his shoulders and started up the ladder. The gray daylight streaming through from the top was blotted out by something, but whoever stood guard over the hole pulled the blockage aside.

"Jesus, Juan. Get the fuck out of there," Viktor yelled in an anguished howl. "Things are turning to shit out here."

Juan reached the top. Someone dragged the corpse off his shoulders, and he heaved his body through what was left of the opening. His arm caught on a jagged piece of something, and it ripped through his jacket. Maybe his skin. He was too cold to tell.

The infernal booming kept right on pounding against him like a set of church bells on steroids.

Aura linked an arm through his. "Run! The ocean's gone mad."

Juan couldn't look at it. He had to watch where he put his feet, so he didn't end up sprawled over a stake, which might impale him. By the time he and Aura got to the Zodiac, everyone else was inside and the engine was revving. He ran through knee-high surf that sloshed into his boots with Aura by his side. She hurtled over a pontoon, and he followed her.

Juan was no sooner partway in the raft when Viktor gave it full throttle. Panting, Juan pushed to a sit and stared out at three-foot swells. The water had developed an eerie, rust-colored hue. Breath stuttered around a thick place in his throat.

"It looks like the Cataclysm," he ground out, and added, "I've never seen surf like this here. It's a bay for chrissakes."

The raft shuddered as it hit the waves head-on. Juan eyed the pontoons. Zodiacs were sturdy. They had multiple air chambers, which meant one or two could sustain a puncture and the raft wouldn't sink. But they were tippy bastards.

"At least we got him out." Aura smoothed dark hair back from the dead man's bony face. "How's Nora?" She glanced at Recco.

"In shock. Malnourished, but I believe she'll pull through."

"James was her son," Boris said. "He appears old, but he was only fourteen."

Juan tasted salt spray on his dry, split lips. What a hell of a way for a young man's life to end.

Viktor swung the raft to line it up with the gangway. Both the ladder and the raft bounced crazily. "You're going to have to time how you leave the raft." Viktor's words were devoid of inflection. He was back in ship's captain mode. "If you don't, you'll end up in the water, and it will be damned hard to rescue you."

"How do we time leaving?" Zoe asked. Her voice cracked on the last word.

"Do exactly what Viktor and I say," Juan replied. He helped

Viktor secure the raft to the cleats, but not too tight. Waves this high could snap the ropes or drag the raft out of the water and upend it. At Viktor's nod, he stood, grabbed the cage at the bottom of the gangway, and swung into it in one fluid motion. The ship bounced down a full four feet, and he stared at the raft's occupants.

Viktor was readying Recco, who still had Nora in his arms. As soon as the raft and gangway were close to level, Juan clasped Recco's outstretched arm and hauled him and Nora onto the platform. For one heart-stopping moment, all of them hovered over the hungry, red-tipped waves.

"Crap!" Recco gasped out the word.

"Never mind. Get moving up the gangway," Juan directed.

The next person off the raft was Ketha, and her exit was much smoother since both hands were free. One to grasp Juan's arm and the other to grab the cage around the bottom of the gangway.

One by one, everyone made the safety of Arkady until only Viktor and the corpse were left. "What do you want to do with him?" Juan shouted.

"Use the crane to drop the webbing," Viktor shouted back. He undid the rope holding the raft in place and turned the small, bobbing craft toward the crane's drop-off point. Waves crashed over the bow, dousing him.

Juan understood it would never work. There was no way to stabilize the raft sufficiently to drape the webbing around it and lift it out of the water. He started to yell at Viktor to come back when a series of waves hit the raft like a one-two punch and flipped it.

Juan crouched on the small platform, frantically scanning the waves for Viktor's tawny head. He readied the ring buoy, ready to toss it the second Viktor surfaced. A minute dripped past then another.

"Come on, *amigo.*" Juan stared at the waves, willing Viktor to appear. Diving in himself would be suicide. Then there'd be no one who could pilot the boat. Finally, Viktor's head broke the surface. Juan threw the buoy as hard as he could. Viktor latched his fingers around it.

"Pull," he shouted, spitting out seawater.

Juan scarcely needed instructions. He hauled on the rope against the drag of the water, but it wasn't working. He needed both arms to fight the waves, so he latched his feet around slats in the bottom of the gangway's platform and lay on his belly. Water sloshed across the platform, but he was already soaked. It felt as if he battled a giant, tugging the ring buoy toward the platform, but Viktor was finally close enough for Juan to grip his waterlogged jacket and haul him to safety.

Viktor spat more seawater. "You saved my life, mate. The ocean turned deadly. I couldn't figure out which way was up. If it hadn't been for my raven, I'd have kept right on swimming toward the bottom of the sea."

Juan untangled his feet and stood. He tied the ring buoy back in place. "Get moving and out of those soaked clothes." His voice was gruff to cover his relief. He'd been certain Viktor was dead.

"No more heroics for corpses," Viktor muttered and slogged up the gangway.

Juan cursed himself for not leaving James at the bottom of the ice cave. He'd promised Aura he'd take care of the dead teen, but she'd crested the ladder, and he could have done whatever he wanted. She saw him as inferior, anyway. It had been one of his fears, and she'd hammered nails into that coffin when she mocked his opinion.

Her words—*How the hell could you possibly know? Shit. You're as green as Shifters come*—rattled through his brain as he climbed the gangway and activated the electronics to lift it out of the water.

He wiped water out of his face. Every part of his body hurt. Good thing he'd found out what she really thought about him before he invested any more emotional effort in their relationship.

Aw fuck. Who am I kidding. I'm in love with her, and she just "dear-Johned" me.

A shiver started in his shoulders and ran the length of his body. Hypothermia was insidious. He needed a hot shower and hot coffee or soup far more than he needed to wallow in feeling sorry for himself.

An expert at clearing everything nonessential out of his mind, Juan picked up the pace as he headed for his cabin. Aura had been an enticing dream, but he'd be fine without her.

He was trashed, so it might have been his imagination, but he thought he heard his cat growl disapprovingly from the sidelines.

19

AN HONORABLE DEATH

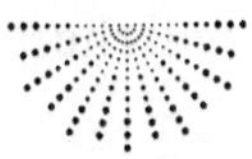

AURA GRABBED the edge of a table for balance. Arkady was underway again. Viktor and Juan hadn't lost any time pulling anchor and putting distance between themselves and King George Island. She and the other ten women were in the second dining room, a space they didn't ordinarily use because so few were aboard.

Rowana was laid out on a table. They'd washed her body, dressed her in her dark robes, and said their farewells. Aura's eyes felt hot and gritty. She hadn't cried since her friend begged them to let her go on the shore beyond the ruins of the Polish research station.

"We owe her the full court press," Ketha said. "My wolf wants to bid a formal farewell to her eagle and offer thanks to it for being a compassionate and loyal bondmate."

Amid murmurs from the other women, everyone started shucking their clothing. Aura pulled her jacket off her shoulders as she walked to Ketha's side. She still wasn't totally warm, but her mountain lion would fix that problem. "How are you doing?" she asked Ketha quietly.

The other Shifter turned toward her. "Viktor nearly drowned. Rowana is dead. How do you think I'm doing?"

"Sorry. Didn't mean to be intrusive." Aura sat on the carpeted floor and took off her boots.

Ketha squatted next to her and did the same thing. "Sorry. I'm as edgy as a scalded cat. You were being kind and thoughtful, and I was a bitch. I'll get over Viktor's near brush with death, but Rowana being gone will hurt for a long time, maybe forever."

"Know what you mean." Aura undid her storm pants and her inner trousers, sliding both down her legs.

All around her, the air kindled with Shifter magic, and a variety of animals took shape. Aura stripped off her woolen underwear and let the shift magic take her. In cat form, she padded to Rowana's body and laid her head on her friend and mentor's chest. A painful yowl rose from her cat, followed by howls and screeches from the other animals.

Rowana's eagle formed in the middle of a blaze of light and landed on her chest, displacing Aura's cat. The eagle bent its feathered head and laid it against Rowana's cheek, cooing softly.

The tears that had refused to come formed in Aura's cat's eyes; it blinked them aside. *"She had an honorable death,"* Aura's bondmate said. *"We cannot ask for more."*

Aura swallowed bitter knowledge. She could, indeed, ask for far more than that. She wanted Rowana's soft laughter and understated sense of humor. She wanted her friend's wisdom and compassion and the knowledge shining from her dark eyes.

Is this going to be our lives? she wondered. *Where we die off one by one, killed by some abomination that got a new lease on life because of the Cataclysm?*

By those standards, Rowana was lucky. Her tenure in this brave, new wasteland had been brief.

"Get hold of yourself," her cat spoke sternly.

If Aura had been human, she'd have nodded glumly. As things

stood, she remained silent and waited while all the animals bid farewell to Rowana and her eagle.

When everyone was done, the animals formed a circle. Rowana's eagle spread its wings but continued to stand on her chest. Its intense, avian gaze moved from one to the other of them.

"She was proud of all of you," the eagle said. *"She valued your courage and your determination and your friendship. Rowana may be gone, but you must not let her down. You must honor her belief in you."*

The air around the eagle grew impossibly bright, and the bird broke into motes of light as it left this plane for the animals' special world.

The brilliance faded, and Aura reached for her human body. They'd done all they could to pay tribute to Rowana, but a dull ache throbbed behind her breastbone. As she dressed, tears spilled down her cheeks. The eagle had spoken bravely, but Aura had no idea where she'd get the strength to go on.

Viktor walked into the room and gathered Ketha into a hug. "The ceremony was beautiful," he said. "I arrived about the same time as the eagle, but I didn't want to disturb you so I remained in the doorway."

"Did the sea settle enough to…bury her?" Ketha stumbled over the word bury.

Viktor nodded. "Once we left the cove, it improved, which is very unusual."

"Maybe in the world you understood, but in a world powered by magical factions fighting one another, it's not odd at all," Karin said, and then added, "After we passed beyond the area controlled by the sorcerer, things would have grown better."

Juan and Recco joined them, carrying a makeshift stretcher with cord threaded through it, and headed to the table where Rowana lay. "Is she ready?" Juan asked.

Aura nodded. While Rowana had moved beyond caring what came next, Aura would never be ready to commit her friend to the sea. She did her best to drag herself out of the funk she'd fallen into. Burial at sea was a clean end. It beat the hell out of leaving Rowana on that cursed island for the dark mage to tinker with.

Viktor let go of Ketha and helped the other men roll Rowana onto the litter. Aura joined them and secured her to lash points on the frame. "What happens once we get her on deck?" she asked.

"We cut the cords and offer her to the sea," Viktor said. "Normally, I'd say a prayer, but I believe you covered those bases. Nothing I could articulate would be as poignant as what I saw when your animals gathered around her body and her eagle." His voice cracked, ragged with emotion.

Juan grabbed a handle next to Rowana's shoulder. Recco took the other handle at the head end of the bier, and Viktor picked up both grips at the foot end. The men carried Rowana from the dining room. Everyone followed them up a flight of stairs and onto the large open deck one floor up.

Daide and Boris were there. So were Ted, Sasha, and Diana. Boris touched Aura's arm as she walked past. "I'm so sorry about your friend. If it weren't for us—"

"Rowana did the right thing," Aura cut him off. "It was how she lived."

"She had a brave heart," Boris went on. "And I am truly sorry for your loss."

"Thank you." Aura met his kind brown gaze.

Viktor and the other two men had laid the bier on the deck. Juan sliced through the cords and stood. He gazed from one woman to the next. "Which four of you will offer her to the sea?"

"I will." Aura stepped forward.

"As will I." Karin joined her.

"Me." Ketha squared her shoulders.

"Och, and I shall as well." Zoe marched to one of the bier's handles. Kneeling, she kissed Rowana's pale, withered cheek.

Something about the gesture smote Aura, and sobs spilled

through her. She stepped to one of the handles ready to do right by her friend.

Once all four of them were in place, they lifted the pallet to rail level and tilted it. Rowana's body sank into the gray-green waters. The pallet clattered when it landed on the deck, empty of its burden. Aura curled her fingers around the icy metal railing. Pain sliced through her, so raw and primal she feared it would rip her in two. No one could hurt this keenly and keep on living.

Arms closed around her from behind.

Juan murmured, "I'm sorry, Aura. Is there anything I can do?"

His words were so kind, they unhinged her further. She'd treated him like a high-handed bitch in the ice cave. All he'd been trying to do was ensure her safety, and she'd been wrapped up in being right and saving someone who was already dead. A corpse that had almost been the death of Viktor.

"You have nothing to be sorry for," she managed between gasping, choking sobs. Turning in his arms, she wrapped hers around him. "It's me who owes you a huge apology. I'm very sorry. No excuses. You didn't deserve what I said." A fresh spate of sobs obliterated her next words.

He stroked her hair and murmured wordless soothing endearments. They stood there so long, no one else was left on deck when she finally dragged her head away from Juan's chest.

"It's never easy," he said.

"What isn't?" Her words echoed, hollow and pained.

"Giving bodies to the sea. I've done it many times, and every single one has felt like I failed somehow."

She tilted her head back, welcoming the cold wind on her overheated face and swollen eyes. "We should go inside."

"We should," he agreed. "We could all use dinner, and we have to plot a course for where we go next."

Aura didn't want to go anywhere else new, but she was ashamed to admit it. It besmirched Rowana's eagle's faith in them. To avoid talking about it, she asked, "How's Nora doing?"

"Conscious, but weak. Distraught over her son's death, but it's to be expected." Juan led them to the closest door leading inside.

Aura's cabin wasn't far. "Mind if I stop and throw some cold water on my face?" she asked.

"Not at all. Would you welcome company, or would you rather I met you in the bar? It's where everyone's congregating to drink a toast to Rowana."

"Come on in." She pushed her door open and walked to the sink, sluicing water over her face.

Juan settled in the desk chair, watching her. "I've been trying to figure out the connection between the wicked wizard who took over King George Island and the Cataclysm."

Surprise rocked her, and she dried her face. "I'm not sure there is one." She turned to face Juan. "Shifters and Vamps created the Cataclysm when their spell went off the rails."

"Yeah. I understand that part." Juan angled his head to one side. "But once evil was loose in the world, I bet it strengthened every other damnable creature. Fed them, breathed life into them."

"I was thinking much the same thing in the dining room with Rowana and the others."

Juan sent an encouraging glance her way, so she went on. "We were all so focused on the Shifters' spell—the one interrupted by Vampires a decade ago—none of us dug much beyond the Cataclysm." She took a measured breath. "We assumed if we could pick up where the spell was interrupted, it would run to its conclusion and disrupt the Cataclysm."

"And redesign Vampires into Shifters along the way," Juan added.

"Exactly. What we weren't attentive to was the other fallout from having pure evil loose in the world for a protracted period of time. Ketha needs to consult her spell book. It might contain historical information that sheds light on our circumstances."

Juan smiled crookedly. "Spoken like the historian you are."

Aura shrugged. "If I learned anything, it's that history repeats itself. If we want to know what's likely to happen next, the best way to figure it out is to study what's gone before."

"How about prophecies? Do any of them—finished or not—address where we are now?"

"I don't know, but we need to explore every single avenue before we make any more mistakes."

Juan's expression turned solemn. "We were tricked, but it's no excuse. We were so busy searching for more of the unnatural beasts that attacked us on the ship, we missed what was right under our noses."

"Yeah. I felt stupid about our oversight too. Particularly when it turned out the whole goddamned thing was illusion. The humanoids weren't any more real than the animals they morphed into. The whole thing was like a perverted light show with a sorcerer manipulating puppet strings backstage and laughing his head off when we fell for his deception."

Juan stood and crossed the small space to stand in front of her. When he held out his arms, she walked into them and hugged him back. He felt good against her. Solid and warm and dependable. He cupped one side of her face in a calloused palm. "I'm going to kiss you, but then we're going upstairs to toast Ro and her eagle and wish them safe passage to the other side."

Aura drank him in. Banked fires smoldered in the depths of his hazel eyes. A woman could get lost in those eyes. She tilted her head, eager for the press of his lips, and he closed his mouth over hers. Beard stubble tickled. He tasted of salt spray, and her mouth came alive beneath his touch. He moved his hand to the back of her head and laced his fingers beneath her hair, holding her in place while he explored her mouth lazily, nibbling, sucking, biting, kissing.

Heat began in her belly, spreading in expanding circles, and she splayed her fingers across his back, drawing him as close as she could. Her breath quickened, and her nipples turned to exquisite points of sensation where they pressed against his chest.

He groaned, a decidedly male sound, and dragged his mouth from hers. "Upstairs," he said. His voice held a raspy edge, betraying his hunger for her. "If we don't leave now, we never will, and you'll kick yourself for missing the wake."

Aura untangled her arms from him and nodded. "You're right, of course. I want to be there while everyone tells stories about Rowana and shares their fondest memories."

He held out a hand, and she took it. Together, they made their way out of the cabin and down the hall. "Ketha told us about Viktor almost drowning," Aura said. "Must have given you a hell of a scare."

A shadow crossed his face, and the line of his jaw tightened. "I've never felt so conflicted. I wanted to go in after him when he didn't surface, but if I had and didn't make it, there'd have been no one who knew the first thing about how to move *Arkady* from Point A to Point B."

"Torn between love for your friend and duty toward the rest of us." She stopped on the fourth deck's landing and turned to gaze at him.

"That's about the size of it, but he's not the only one I love." Juan gripped her tighter. "I love you too, Aura. It came to me clear as day out there on the gangway's platform when I was fighting the sea for Viktor's life. Except I thought you and I had no chance." His mouth curved into the half smile she'd come to cherish, and she traced the line of his mouth with her fingertips.

"Thanks for not giving up on me."

"Never. I'll always be here for you."

She inhaled raggedly and pushed past her lifelong fear of letting anyone close enough to hurt her. "I'll always be here for you too."

He broke into a million-watt smile. "You've made me a very happy man."

Her gaze roved over the sculpted planes of his face. God, he was gorgeous. No man had a right to be so beautiful, but she'd had handsome men in her life before. The big difference was none of them had possessed Juan's glorious spirit.

"What? I can almost hear that brain of yours churning."

Heat rose to her face, but she held his gaze. "You are one beautiful man, but what I fell in love with is your spirit. It shines through your eyes, pure and decent and vibrant. Not that pain hasn't touched you, but you've found ways to keep on living and remain true to yourself."

His salt-stained, whiskered cheeks turned ruddy. "Try being a Vampire. It would push anyone to their limits."

"See? That's exactly what I mean."

A shout rose from the bar down the hall. Juan tugged on their laced fingers. "Come on. We're missing the healing part. The reason we hold wakes is so the survivors aren't immobilized by grief—or guilt."

Aura remembered the despondency shrouding her with misery as she stood at the rail and watched Rowana plunge into the sea. She rose up on tiptoe to kiss Juan's cheek, and then they covered the fifty feet between them and the large, well-appointed ship's bar.

"There you are!" rose in a chorus.

Ketha ran to them. "If you hadn't shown up soon"—she shook a finger beneath Aura's nose—"I'd have come hunting for you."

"Here you go." Viktor passed them shot glasses filled with what smelled like scotch.

"To Rowana," rang around them.

"To Rowana, closest thing I had to a mother." Aura clinked her glass against Juan's and drained it. The liquor burned a path through her mouth and throat, but it felt warm and comforting in her stomach.

Juan led the way to two empty seats beneath a window. Aura settled into one of them and gazed around the group. "Where's Recco?"

"He has the helm," Viktor said.

"It's not good to leave the ship on autopilot for extended periods," Juan added. "Not without satellite guidance."

Viktor rolled his eyes. "Hell, even when we had satellites, I still wanted eyes on instruments."

Ketha nudged Aura. "We all shared stories about Ro. It's your turn."

Aura got back on her feet. She didn't have to search for the memory she wanted to recount. "When I was about nineteen, I was in college, but I wasn't doing much studying. Mostly I'd take my cat form every night and run and hunt with a mixed Shifter pack. Come morning, I'd sleep, and then do it again the following evening. I'd hooked up with the equivalent of Shifter delinquents on the University of Washington campus. I was surprised how many of us were enrolled."

Juan offered her a full shot glass, and she took a sip. "I went home for Christmas break that year. I'd been home for maybe half an hour when Rowana stopped by, arms full of wrapped gifts and Christmas cheer and reeking of sugar and cinnamon from cookies and pies.

"She hauled ass up to my bedroom, snapped up a coat, and dragged me out of the house. Told me she had something to show me, but instead she drove to a deserted field and used magic to seal us into the car. She gave me hell. Told me I was headed down a nowhere road, a disappointment to her and everyone else who'd invested in my future."

Aura pressed her lips together, embarrassed, but determined to finish what she had to say. "I might have blown her off. I was young and full of hubris, but one thing she said got through. Apparently, my cat was within a hairsbreadth of breaking its bond with me. I thought it loved romping every night, but I'd read the signs all wrong."

Breath whistled through Aura's teeth. "At the end of her diatribe, Rowana hugged me. She told me she had faith in me to do the right thing, that all wasn't lost. Not yet, anyway. And then, she retracted her spell and told me I could leave if I wanted."

Ketha leaned closer. "I've never heard that story. What did you do?"

"After I got done crying?" Aura smiled softly. "I asked her to bring me back to her house, and we spent the next two days baking and practicing magic in human form. I'd spent so much time as a cat, mine had grown rusty.

"It was a turning point for me. I went back to school and prioritized why I was there. I've always loved her for putting out the effort. She didn't have to, and if my cat had severed our bond, it would have broken me."

Aura raised her glass. "Here's to Ro. I'll love her forever, and I'll never forget her selflessness or her generosity."

A chorus of "To Ro" and "To Rowana" circled the room as everyone clinked glasses and drank a toast.

Aura sat next to Juan and eyed the group. "If my story was new to Ketha, which of you told tales I didn't know about?"

Voices vied to be heard. Stories continued to flow as the group moved from the bar to the dining room where they turned out an impromptu meal. Recco returned, and Juan left to take his place at the helm, guiding the ship through the night.

The hurt places in Aura didn't feel quite so hopeless and dead.

Viktor strode to the front of the dining room. "Before we turn in for the night, we need to talk about where we go next. I've set a course for McMurdo. If anywhere on the Antarctic continent has humans left who haven't been tainted or turned by evil, it'll be there."

He stopped to take a measured breath. "Our experiences since we left Ushuaia haven't been great. One of my other rationales for choosing McMurdo is if it turns out to be another hotbed of evil, we can head due north for New Zealand's South Island. It's only about a five-day journey."

"What about returning to Ushuaia?" Karin asked. "At least we knew what we had there."

"I considered it," Viktor replied. "The reason we're having this conversation is because everyone gets a vote. If a majority of you want Ushuaia, it's where we'll go."

"Those are only two options," Boris spoke up. "McMurdo or Ushuaia. I can think of many more."

Viktor smiled. "So can I. The world really is one ocean, and we have the perfect tool to explore it."

Aura's attention wandered as the conversation plodded on. Everyone was tired, and most of them were half-drunk. "What will it cost us to put this decision off until tomorrow?" she asked.

"Nothing, assuming we continue on our current course," Viktor replied. "If we end up turning around, we've only lost double the distance we traveled in the wrong direction, which is roughly twelve nautical miles every hour."

"So twelve hours could cost us almost three hundred miles?" Aura asked, wanting to be sure she understood.

Viktor nodded and shrugged. "It sounds like a lot, but isn't. Not for a ship with a range measured in thousands of knots."

"I vote to table this," Recco said.

"Agreed," Karin said and added, "We'll think better after a few hours' sleep."

When a round robin of good nights began, Aura slipped out the door intent on joining Juan on the bridge. She was tired, but she wanted to tell him good night.

20

AFFAIR OF THE HEART

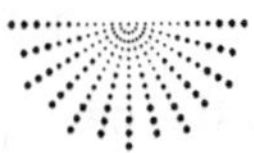

JUAN BALANCED ATOP A HIGH, three-legged stool behind the polished, mahogany wheel. The ship had a second command center down on Deck Two, but it was in an enclosed room where all he'd be staring at was a bank of instruments. He far preferred gazing out the windows at the dark velvet of an Antarctic night. For once, the sky was shot with stars, and he picked out familiar constellations.

From long habit, he revisited the day—every grueling aspect of it—in his mind. He'd done that for as many years as he could remember. The instant replay provided perspective and insight. It was how he'd survived at sea. And as a Vampire. Even though tragedy struck today, they'd picked up five new crew members. It put them four ahead of where they'd been. A good thing since *Arkady* was woefully shy of crew.

From now on, they'd bring radios. And everyone would wear life jackets, including himself and Viktor. If Viktor had one on, he would have bobbed to the surface. It wouldn't have been any easier reeling him in, but Juan could have avoided the tense, anxiety-ridden moments, staring at the restless water, willing his friend to appear.

In addition to a full complement of life preservers, the ship also had a stock of specialized coats with inflation devices built into them. Juan had no idea why he and Viktor had gotten out of the habit of wearing their Mustang flotation jackets, but their lapse had just come to a halt. They might not have passengers anymore, but it wasn't a reason to set basic safety aside. The jackets were bulky as hell, and weighed a ton after they got wet, but they worked.

Once he sorted through the hard parts of the day, he allowed himself to think about Aura. That aspect of things made up for a whole lot. The shell she wore like an armor shield had cracked, and she'd not only let him in, she'd welcomed him.

He caught a glimpse of his reflection in the windows surrounding the bridge, and he was grinning like a fool. He didn't even try to modulate his joy. Why should he? The impossible had happened. The woman he loved might not have said she loved him—not quite yet, anyway—but she'd told him she'd always be there for him. It was kind of the same thing.

He thought back to what she'd disclosed about herself when they'd had their first serious discussion in the bar. She'd held men at arm's length to preserve the secret she had a dual identity. Would any of them have believed her, even if she'd told them? Juan doubted it. If a woman had told him she could turn into a wolf or a bear or a bird, he'd have chalked her up as a mental case.

Off on a tangent, he marveled at the existence of a secondary world. It had been there all along, right under his nose. He'd listened when Raphael launched into his "Vampirism in Ten Easy Steps" lectures because he was still having a hell of a hard time believing Vampires existed. Let alone the other creatures Raphael mentioned in passing.

"Amazing level of denial," Juan muttered. "I was one, and I still didn't believe in them. Not for months." He grimaced as he recalled frantically drinking blood from a variety of animals, all the while telling himself he didn't really need it. That he could stop anytime. Shit! He'd sounded like a drug addict.

He checked his course indicators, an exercise he did every half hour. The seas were calm for this neck of the woods. Two-foot swells with the wind at less than ten knots. Weather didn't get much better in the Southern Ocean. He hoped to hell it held as they made a run for McMurdo. Conditions could change fast, and pack ice might force them into a major course correction. It wouldn't crush *Arkady* like it had Shackleton's *Endurance*, but it could trap them for months while they ran out of food and fuel. The net effect would be the same, except South Georgia Island— and so far, the Antarctic continent—were devoid of anyone who could offer them aid.

The door at the far end of the bridge popped open, admitting a smiling Aura. "Hey there."

Joy speared him, bright and shimmery with promise. "What a lovely surprise." He hopped off his stool and walked toward her. "Did dinner break up?"

"Yeah. It's been a difficult day. Everyone is sloshed and heading for bed."

Juan quirked a brow. "But not you?"

"I wanted to say good night." Her smile faltered. She offered him a tentative glance, eyes darting away as soon as they contacted his.

He swept her into a hug before she changed her mind and made a run for it. "I'm glad. I love the bridge at night, and having you here makes it ten times better." He tilted his upper body back so he could gaze at her.

A brilliant rose crept up from the open neck of her jacket until it stained her cheeks. "Are you, um, working all night?"

"Not much left of it," Juan replied. "But yes. Vik will relieve me at six."

A tiny vertical line formed between her eyebrows. "You won't get any sleep."

Evidence of her concern touched him. "It's okay. I'm used to it. A catnap or two, and I'll be right as rain."

She gazed up at him, and her full lips curved into a soft smile. "I've always wondered where that expression came from. Why is rain any righter than, say, sunshine or clouds or—"

He placed two fingers over her mouth. She flicked her tongue out and licked them. His reaction was instantaneous, like tossing a match onto a pile of dry wood shavings. Heat roared through him, and he crushed his mouth over hers. He may have fantasized making slow, passionate love to her, but his body would never cooperate with the slow part. Urgency spilled through him, and his cock thickened, rising in a column to press against her belly. She opened her mouth to him and twined her arms around his neck. The scents of old leather and candle wax and jasmine bloomed around them; he inhaled hungrily.

He plumbed her mouth with his tongue and forced his body to slow down. They had all the time in the world, and he'd be damned if he wouldn't savor the kiss. She had an amazing mouth, lips designed for kissing. She sucked on his tongue, and then she sparred with it. Little biting kisses alternated with deep, probing ones as they got to know one another. She tasted of the scotch they'd shared, and spices from the risotto dinner he'd finished on the bridge.

Her nipples felt like polished stones where they pressed against his chest. She moaned into his mouth and straddled one of his legs. Heat from her core seared his thigh, and her hips bucked against him. She tore her mouth from his, and her eyes glowed with delight.

"Tell me no one will bother us," she said breathlessly.

He smoothed hair back from her face. "No one will bother us. Everyone is asleep. Back in the day when we had twenty-five crew, there were always several of us in here. Not anymore."

His entire body vibrated with wanting her, but he didn't want to scare her off, either. "Why'd you ask?"

"What? About anyone coming in here?" Her lips were swollen from their kisses, and her cheeks tinted the shade of pink roses.

"Yes. Did you have something in mind?" He held his breath. His cock beat like an ancillary heart where it was jammed against her lower body.

She drew her tongue over her lower lip and snaked a hand between their bodies, curving it around his erection. A low, purring growl rose, filling his chest. It fit his mood exactly. Hungry male cat intent on marking his mate.

Instead of answering with words, she let go of him long enough to unzip his jacket and pull it off his shoulders, tossing it over a chair. Once it was out of the way, she ran her fingers beneath his stretchy black underwear top. The touch of her fingertips against his bare skin, teasing his nipples, drove him half-mad with lust, but his cock wanted more contact too. The simple pressure of fabric stretched across its sensitive head was almost enough to make him come.

His nipples turned into points of liquid heat as she flicked her nails over them. "Much more of that, and you'll end up spread-eagled across the chart table." He took advantage of her not being smushed against him to cup her breasts through her layers of clothing.

"Chart table, huh? It's a nice, flat surface. Maybe a wee bit hard. How well does it work?" She sent a coquettish look his way.

"I have no idea. Viktor may have had sex in here once or twice, but I never did."

"Good," she said, her tone low, fierce. "I want how we come together for the first time to be special. Something brand new for both of us."

He unzipped her jacket and repositioned his hands so only one layer separated them from the high, firm globes of her breasts. She made a harsh, groaning sound and recaptured his cock, rubbing harder.

Juan reached down and disentangled her fingers. "Your touch

feels amazing, but I don't want to come yet, and if you do that for very much longer, I will."

Desire turned her eyes a deep, mossy green. "What do you want to do right now?"

"Look at you. I want to see the body I've imagined in my fantasies."

She grinned and took a step back from him. Hooking fingers beneath her top, she pulled it over her head. The vest she hadn't bothered to unzip left at the same time. She wasn't wearing a bra. Juan stared at the perfection spread before him. She had broad shoulders for a woman, shapely with lean muscles. Her breasts were tipped with strawberry-colored nipples. They were hard, pebbled, and as big as silver dollars.

He surged forward and claimed both breasts, filling his hands with them. "But I don't have everything off," she protested. "Neither do you."

Juan bent his head and suckled a breast. The nipple fluttered against his tongue, and his cock jerked against his belly. He told it to stand down. Its turn would come, but not until he'd savored Aura's lush body. She buried her fingers in his hair as he lashed his tongue from one breast to the other and back again.

"I've dreamed about your hair," she murmured. "It's like wheat sheaves glowing on a summer day. Gold, but with these subtle red highlights."

He raised his mouth from her breasts. "Did you stop with my hair?" he teased.

"Oh hell, no, but you should leave a girl a bit of privacy." She caught the edges of his top and dragged it over his head. Once he was naked from the waist up, she took a step back, and he felt the heat of her gaze as she took him in.

He had an attack of self-consciousness at her frank contemplation. None of his lovers had ever bothered to take the time to study at him. Not like she was doing.

"Were you a pirate in a former life?" She ran a fingertip gently over the worst of his scars.

"It would have been a lot more fun than how I got all those marks. That one was an unruly shark in a diving incident. The others"—he shrugged—"came from a variety of accidents and occasional knife fights in seedy bars."

"What happened to the shark?"

"I killed him."

"Better than him killing you." Aura moved to the waistband of his pants.

"Hang on," Juan said. "Let me get rid of my boots." Bending, he toed first one and then the other off. When he glanced at her feet, he saw she wore slippers. "Smart cookie." He pointed at her feet.

"It's not as calculating as you might think." She winked, flicking her lush lashes his way. "I stopped in my cabin for the slippers before I came up here mostly because my feet were tired. Those Muck boots get heavy when you wear them all day."

"Wellingtons."

"Where I come from, they're called Muck boots. Company used to be in Washington. Or maybe it was Oregon, but none of that matters. You took those boots off for a reason, fellow."

His breath accelerated, and his heart slammed against his ribs as she slid the waist of his trousers down his legs. They pooled around his feet, and he stepped out of them. All that remained were his shorts. She curved her fingers over the ridged flesh jutting from his body, and he pushed into her touch and her warmth.

"Nice," she murmured. "Why didn't you tell me you were hung like a donkey?"

He laughed. "Would it have mattered? I wanted you to love me for my mind, wench."

She laughed too, and the musical tones warmed his soul. Letting go of him abruptly, she gave his shorts a shove, and they joined his pants on the floor. He moved them aside and reached for her thick, woolen trousers. His fingers shook a little as he undid the snap and the zipper, and levered them down her legs.

Because he knelt in front of her, the musk of her center hit him like a fine-tuned aphrodisiac. He fastened his mouth over her mound and worked her panties out of the way. They slipped partway down her legs, but he was too busy to worry about them. He licked her swollen nub, teasing it with his tongue and sucking the slick globe while he drove two fingers between her legs, hunting for the dark, hidden mysteries of her body.

She writhed against him, panting and moaning, and tangled her hands in his hair again. He sank his fingers inside her and upped the ante with his tongue. She thrust her hips against his mouth, and he felt her muscles contract, gripping his fingers. He swirled his tongue around her nub and then sucked hard. She dissolved around him in a flood of scorching heat, but he kept the stimulation flowing until he was sure her orgasm had played itself out.

Color made beautiful patterns across her breasts and face when he looked up at her. He got to his feet, so aroused he was surprised his legs cooperated. "About that chart table…"

"Grand idea," she got out between heaving breaths, and stepped away from her pants and slippers. Pushing her underwear the rest of the way down, she got rid of it too and glided across the bridge to the generous, elevated table.

The movement of her hips mesmerized him, and he couldn't have not followed her if he'd tried. Maybe she'd used magic to ensorcel him. If she had, he welcomed it. She spread herself over the chart table, chest down. The cheeks of her ass parted, framing her sex with its halo of spiky, golden curls.

A woman had never been so alluring, and he'd never been more aroused. Juan didn't recognize the sounds that emerged from him. He'd never made any of them before. Desperation, hunger, lust all rolled into one, and he rushed forward. Grasping his cock, he positioned it at her entrance. Her labia were hot and slippery, and he slid slowly inside.

She rotated her hips at first. As he got deeper, she thrust backward, claiming more of him each time. Juan concentrated on breathing. Just breathing until the urgency spiraling out of control receded a little. He bent low over her body and wrapped his arms around her, settling one hand over a breast and the other over the slick, swollen nub between her legs.

He tasted her on his lips. The sweet musk of her passion inflamed him each time he inhaled. He nuzzled her neck, stringing kisses wherever his lips connected with tantalizing flesh. When he thought he could move without exploding, he withdrew very slowly and then pressed into her again, equally slowly. She thrashed beneath him, moaning and urging him to go faster, deeper. After far too short a time, his carefully choreographed lovemaking fell apart. He thrust hard, fast, deep, glorying in the sensations spilling through him. As he plunged into her, he rubbed her clit. She jammed her fingers over his and showed him what she needed. Smaller circles, more pressure.

He rode a ragged edge of control, determined to love her until she crested again. His release could wait. It had to. Her vault tightened around him, and he upped the pace and the pressure. Where his mouth contacted her shoulder, he bit her. She screamed as orgasm took her. The rhythmic contractions around his cock drove him mad. No reason to wait any longer. Even if he'd wanted to, it was too late. White-hot gouts of semen juddered from him. He came hard and for so long it felt like he'd been transported to another world.

He lay across her for delicious moments while the world came back into focus. "Darling, my darling," he crooned. "It will be better next time. I promise. It's been so long, I—"

She jackknifed beneath him until they lay on their sides on the chart table, facing one another. Reaching between them, she cradled his still-hard cock in one hand. "Anything better would damn near kill me." She wrapped her other arm around his neck and kissed him hard.

Juan kissed her back. They might have drowsed for a while until he startled awake. "Jesus. The ship. I have to check everything."

She murmured sleepily, and he jumped to his feet, dragging on discarded clothing as he assessed the various instruments. Luckily, nothing had gone to hell while he was otherwise occupied. Juan winced. He'd never shirked his duty to any ship he'd been on. A grin started in his belly and spread to his mouth. He and Aura would just have to make love when he wasn't on duty.

How difficult could that be?

"Is everything okay?"

When he turned, she was getting dressed. "Yeah. All fine. I didn't expect it not to be. Sailing is a lot like flying. Extended periods of boredom punctuated by moments of sheer terror. Things don't often turn to crap, but when they do, it happens damned fast."

Aura shrugged into her jacket. "The goddess owed us this one."

"Got your order in before you accosted me and lured me away from my post?" He chuckled.

"You might say so, except you seduced me. Time to go." She pointed out the windows. "Dawn's not far off. I might turn into a pumpkin."

He closed the distance to her and hugged her tight. "Be my pumpkin, and all will be well."

She trained luminous eyes on his face. "I'm happy. So happy it hurts."

"Me too. I'll do my damnedest to make certain we stay that way." He hesitated before adding, "Rowana would be happy for us."

Aura's green eyes grew soft and wistful. "Indeed she would. I'm going to head for the galley. Since I'm up, I'll get coffee and breakfast going for everyone."

"Sounds great. See you very soon."

The door to the bridge flew open, and Viktor strode in. He stopped after three paces and stared from one to the other of them before winking lewdly. "Appears I timed this well."

"I'm sure I have no idea what you mean." Juan stared his old friend down.

"Ha! You can play innocent, but the bridge reeks of sex. I'm glad you two finally stopped dancing around your attraction, though."

Aura cleared her throat. "Reeks, huh? I was just on my way to the galley. If you're up, it means I can tap Ketha to help me with breakfast." Chuckling softly, she slipped out the door.

Viktor crossed to Juan and slapped him on the back. "Excellent. You let me know if you'd like a shipboard wedding."

Juan laughed. "Ship's captain and all that rot."

"Right you are, mate." Viktor strode to the wheel. "Where are we? Halfway to Bora Bora by now?"

"Very funny. The course you set is still active."

Viktor's expression turned serious. "We need to have a major meeting right after breakfast and determine if my choice is majority rule."

"What if it's not?" Juan asked, curious. Viktor had never been one to take kindly to intercession from others where decisions for one of his ships were concerned.

Viktor shrugged. "We'll do what most of us want to. I'll be damned if I'll take us into another debacle like the one on Arctowski without full assent from everyone."

Juan nodded. "I'm glad you didn't drown yesterday, *amigo*."

"You know what, mate? Me too." Viktor made his way to the wheel and settled his hands over its polished surface. "If you're willing to stay up for a few more minutes, grab your notebook and let's get a list of destinations cooking."

21

HIJACKED BY THE FUTURE

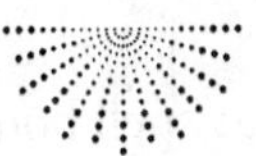

AURA'S first stop was the cabin across the hall from the bridge where Viktor and Ketha slept. She knocked and then pushed the door open. "Rise and shine, sleepyhead."

Ketha rolled over and groaned. Slitting her eyes, she said, "Really? What the fuck are you doing up so early?"

"Maybe I never went to bed," Aura countered.

Ketha's eyes widened, and she bolted to a sitting position, pushing tangled sheets and a duvet aside. "I sense dirt. Spill. Is it Juan? Did you—?"

"It is, and we did." Heat rose to Aura's face, but she didn't look away.

"Thought so. It always smells like sex in here, but the scent got a whole lot stronger when you came into the cabin."

Aura snorted. "Viktor commented on the same thing. Except about the bridge."

Ketha snickered. "That man. Of course, he'd notice. He's a fiend in bed." She raised her brows into twin question marks. "Tell me everything, sweetie. I want details."

"I'll talk once we're in the kitchen making breakfast," Aura countered.

Ketha snorted. "You drive a hard bargain, sister, but who could resist an offer like yours?"

"I don't know. Lots of people who weren't perverts at heart." Aura watched as Ketha tossed clothes on and gathered her hair into a tangled queue without bothering to brush it.

"Ready." Ketha stuffed her feet into the sheepskin slippers that were ubiquitous. Along with thick, terrycloth robes, they'd been in every cabin.

"Have you consulted your spell book lately?" Aura asked.

"No. Why?"

"How about if we bring it along to the galley? We'll be alone, and you can hunt for wisdom while I try to locate prophecies matching whatever you find."

"Not a bad idea." Ketha pulled a closet open and rummaged in the bottom, coming up with a thick book covered in cracked black leather. She tucked it under one arm. "Too bad I didn't take the time to do this before yesterday." Bitterness lined her words.

Aura wound her fingers around Ketha's upper arm. "You cannot blame yourself for Rowana's death."

"Why not?" Ketha's golden eyes shot darts, but anguish wasn't far from the surface. "I'm a seer. Reading the future well enough to keep us alive is my job."

"Prophecies are mine. I'm sure there's one out there relating to what's happening around us."

"Let go." Ketha tried to pull her arm away, but Aura held fast.

"Later this morning, we'll decide where we're going next. Maybe you and I will come up with something critical to push the decision in one direction or another."

Ketha yanked free of Aura's grip. "What exactly do you suppose we'll find? Nothing as specific as the sorcerer who could bend protoplasm to his bidding will be in here." She tapped the book's cover.

Aura chewed her lower lip. "Of course not, but maybe we can tease out the long-term effect the Cataclysm had on manifestations of evil. Take those Vamps in stasis, for example. Or the priest possessed by the demon."

"You're thinking they're all indicators of the same underlying problem?" Ketha frowned.

"Yes. I spent a lot of yesterday trying to work out an explanation, but every pathway had its own set of drawbacks. Nothing was a perfect fit."

"Looking beyond glitches, what'd you come up with?"

Aura shrugged. "Not much beyond the Cataclysm feeding new life into every wicked thing in this world and others. Abominations and monstrosities not seen in our lifetimes, but that were likely more common when your book was originally written."

"Or back when all those prophecies were conceived."

"Exactly." Aura took a measured breath. "We've had it pretty easy. Or we did before the Cataclysm. Modern life didn't recognize magic. It made it impossible to be Shifters openly, but it offered options for us to explore other opportunities. Ones not available hundreds of years ago."

Ketha twisted her mouth into a bitter expression. "We might have been better off with less book learning and a stronger grasp of how magic weaves into the warp and weft of the world. I've been trying to figure out how the hell that mage inserted his own ley lines so they appeared real."

Aura led the way into the corridor and kept her voice low so they wouldn't wake anyone as they moved through the ship. "It was simple illusion. In the first place, no one without magic would ever adopt a psychic view. So they'd never know the difference."

"People without magic wouldn't have seen either set of lines, which means he had to be expecting us." Ketha glanced sidelong at her.

"Not necessarily. I don't see how he could have known we'd show up. I'm less certain about the faux ley lines. Maybe what he did weakened the real ones. Or would have if they'd been in place long enough." They trotted down one more flight of stairs to Deck Three and the galley.

Ketha pushed the swinging door to the dining room open and held it while Aura walked through. Aura did the same for the galley door. Ketha set the magical book on one of the stainless-steel food preparation tables and turned slowly. "A dynamic balance point has to exist."

"Between good and evil?" Aura poured water into an industrial-sized coffee maker and added beans after she'd ground them.

Ketha nodded. "Right. What if the balance point is far more sensitive than we believed? We always knew good counterbalanced evil, and vice versa. What if the tipping point between the two is far less robust than we suspected?"

Aura thought about it. "Which would mean it wouldn't take much energy to tilt the scales in one direction or the other."

"Exactly," Ketha went on. "Stay with me here. Removing Vamps from the equation—more or less—left a void. It wouldn't have been hard to fill since it was already carved out."

With coffee underway, Aura plugged two large electric kettles in for tea water. "Vampires may have been bastards, but they weren't particularly magical," she murmured, thinking out loud. "So whatever jumped into the breach could do a whole lot of damage—if they truly wielded dark power. I feel like an idiot."

"Why?" Ketha trained her unnerving gaze on Aura.

"Maybe because I spent all those years, first in college and then teaching, congratulating myself because our ancestors defeated evil, drove it underground." She shook her head. "Hell, it was only taking a break, a breathing spell while it waited for an auspicious time to return. The Cataclysm provided that opportunity. Its malevolence would have been a huge drawing card. And then, I thought we'd done a good thing getting rid of Vampires. Maybe they were a necessary placeholder keeping something far worse at bay."

"I just got a chill, which means we're onto something." Ketha waved her hands over the spell book, chanting in Gaelic. Moments dragged past before the book fell open, pages riffling as whatever magic powered it decided what to show Ketha.

Aura wanted to stand over the book, urge it to divulge its secrets, but one Shifter was enough. Besides, the book wouldn't communicate with anyone but Ketha, so Aura rustled through bins and bags of powdered eggs, powdered cheese, and dried vegetables, sorting what she needed for an omelet.

Magic simmered around Ketha, a blue-white shroud partially obscuring both her and the book. The hum of her chanting was unsettling and soothing by turns. Time dribbled past. Enough for Aura to pop several pans of eggs into one of the large wall ovens. She started on cornbread to occupy herself while Ketha paid out magic.

What the hell was taking so much time?

Or maybe it wasn't long at all. She had no clue how Ketha's particular brand of magic worked since she'd only seen its end point, not its process—except when they fought the Cataclysm. The bread joined the eggs in the oven, and Aura washed her mixing bowls and utensils. She was drying her hands when the low hum of Ketha's power receded.

Still clutching the dish towel, Aura turned to face the other Shifter, waiting. The shroud turned to particles of light right before it vanished. Ketha lifted her hands from the place the spell book had opened to. Her face was set in lines of grim determination, and she straightened from her hunched-over posture as if the motion cost her.

She appeared so distraught, Aura hurried to her side and drew her into a hug, dish towel and all. "It can't be that bad."

"Yeah it can." Ketha hugged her back before letting go. "Evil's on the loose, exactly as we suspected, but there's history. Important background material I'd never have guessed on my own." She looked askance at Aura. "You'll appreciate this next part."

Aura wanted to shake words out of her friend. Instead, she hung the towel back on its hook, waiting.

"Darkness was the original condition here on Earth," Ketha said. "All the biblical crap is nonsense. God—or goodness—was *not* here first. Bad shit was. Over millennia, it's ebbed and flowed. Skipping a few million years, the last time it gained a staunch toehold was during Hitler's Reich. It was extending its reach again under the perfectly hideous president we had in the US. when the Cataclysm struck. After that, it forgot about seducing the president into piling one bad decision atop another, and went for the gusto."

Aura swallowed hard. "What, exactly, does *went for the gusto* mean?"

Ketha sent a penetrating glance Aura's way. "That, my dear, is the line of demarcation between my magic and yours. Does any of this remind you of a prophecy?"

"No, but keep talking. Maybe something will come to me. Did the book offer any insight into where we should go next?"

Ketha nodded. "Indeed it did. You know the bunch of Shifters and Vamps who spawned this mess?"

"What about them? If I ever get my hands on them, they're dogmeat. The Shifters, anyway. This whole disaster was their idea."

"Well, they weren't precisely in Siberia, but on an island off the Far East Siberian coast. It's where we need to go, if we're to have a prayer of living in a world not ruled by darkness."

"What do we do when we get there?" Aura sucked in a tight breath.

"Cast magic to close the gateway."

"You're talking in riddles," Aura muttered. "What gateway?"

"Yeah, I suppose I am. The primary gateway. When Vampires intervened midway and blasted the Shifters' spell to shreds, it opened a portal. An easy route from Hell and every other border-world for demons, trolls, sorcerers, wizards, and whatever else lives in places like that. Creatures who'd yearned to sow misery finally had a free ride, a way to access Earth. Counter to our earlier hypotheses, whether Vamps were still a contender wouldn't have mattered very much. Their nastiness is trivial compared with what's loose in the world now."

Aura's stomach twisted sourly, and her appetite fled. "I'm guessing it's why a hell horde was in the church in Grytviken. And how the dark mage ended up in residence at Arctowski."

Ketha nodded. "I believe so. Once they breached the primary veil and entered Earth's environment, they could travel wherever suited them."

Aura's thoughts pedaled in tired circles. "But we closed the gateway in the church."

Ketha squared her shoulders. "Doesn't matter. They'll crop up elsewhere until we dismantle the primary gateway."

"Are you certain that will do it?" Aura stared hard at her friend.

Muscles rippled when Ketha ground her teeth together. "No, but it's the only direction the spell book offered."

A shudder racked Aura, followed by one more. What hope did they have against an army of darkness?

Ketha's gaze had never left her. "Forgive me for pilfering from your mind, but I harbor the same sense of futility." Sadness filled her eyes. "Just because something feels impossible doesn't excuse us from trying, though."

"What happens if we don't?" Aura shook her head. "Never mind. It's a prophecy question. I need to do some hunting. At least now I have a leg up. I'll start with end-of-the-world ones and widen my search from there. Funny thing."

"What? None of this feels the least bit humorous to me."

"I wasn't fond of Raziel when he dropped out of nowhere and lent his magic to our cause, but right about now, I'd love to have ten of him."

"Know what you mean." Ketha snapped the book shut.

The smells of breakfast filled the galley. Aura picked up the towel and removed the omelet pans from the oven. A glance at the cornbread told her it wasn't done yet.

"Guess that settles where we're going," she said.

"Some of us," Ketha spoke cautiously. "I wouldn't blame Boris and his crew if they opted to leave somewhere between here and Wrangel Island."

"How do you know some of us won't want to leave as well?"

"I don't, but it's not an option. We need every Shifter. Bottom line is we need as much good magic as we can lay our paws and talons on to counteract whatever we find on Wrangel. The fissure has had ten years to establish itself, and it's not going down without a hell of a struggle."

Juan breezed into the kitchen, whistling a merry tune Aura didn't recognize. "Smells great in here." He made a beeline for Aura and hugged her.

After a momentary pause, she hugged him back.

He let go and stared from her to Ketha. "Jesus. What happened? You two look like someone walked over your graves."

Aura cut to the chase. "Can we sail to a place called Wrangel Island?"

"Sure. We've been there before. It's in the Russian Arctic. But why would we want to?"

Ketha filled him in with a few well-chosen words.

"Mmph, there goes everyone's free choice," he muttered. "Viktor's not going to like having to backpedal on his promise about democratic process."

"Viktor's preferences are the least of our problems," Ketha said. "I'll go talk with him, so he's not surprised." Scooping up the book, she plodded out of the galley.

Aura opened the oven and removed both tins of cornbread, setting them on the ledge. "Boris and them don't have to sign on for Wrangel Island," she said.

"I don't see any alternative." Juan walked close and put his arms around her. "We barely have enough manpower to run this bucket of bolts. It's doubly true for extended, blue water stretches."

Aura leaned into his embrace and threaded her arms around his waist. He smelled wonderful. Wild things, greenery, the sharp tang of the sea, and musky undernotes from their lovemaking.

"I haven't studied a map," she said, "but I believe we'll sail right past McMurdo and then turn north from there. It gives us lots of places to stop. You want crew. I'm hoping for more Shifters or other magical beings on our side of the line. Good magic, not the destructive variety."

He cradled one side of her face. "We'll figure things out, but we will need to top out our storage tanks. McMurdo is a likely spot for that. Boris said they had barrels of biodiesel at Arctowski, but we're not returning there. We'll backtrack to Ushuaia first. Or Christchurch. It's closer to McMurdo."

Aura extricated herself from his embrace. "I could hug you forever, but I want to get breakfast out on the tables. Maybe you could run up to the bridge and get everybody moving toward the dining room."

"No maybe about it. I can definitely spread the word about breakfast." He plucked a cup off a hook and held it under the coffeepot's spigot. Once it was full, he sipped appreciatively. "Mmmm. Tastes good. Nothing like my first jolt of caffeine in the morning."

"You Argies and your coffee." She grinned.

"Yup. Black, bitter, and thick enough to stand a spoon."

Aura watched him. She opened her mouth but wasn't certain how to phrase what she wanted to say, so she closed it.

"Spit it out," he urged. "It's easier that way."

She rolled her eyes. "How do you know I wanted to say anything?"

"It's written all over your face. I might be new to magic, but I've been reading men's faces for twenty years. It's helped me weed the bad apples off my ships before they did too much damage."

"Ketha's job is done." Aura stood straighter. "Mine is only beginning."

Juan drained his cup and set it on the ledge. "Explain."

"She used her spell book to determine what we face. I need to locate which prophecy addresses our situation. It will tell us the outcome."

"Maybe. Unless it's one of those six unfinished ones."

"Yeah, then we'll have to wing it."

He tipped her chin with his index finger until she had to meet his gaze. "It was how we faced the Cataclysm, and that turned out all right. We have to believe this will too."

Every major failed military campaign in history marched across her mind, mocking her. Those generals and commandants had high hopes too.

Juan shook his head. "Uh-uh. We take this one day at a time. One difficulty at a time. It will take us a month to transit the globe south to north. Maybe more. Depends how things go. What we run into. What we run out of, where we can't continue until we resupply."

"*Remember what I said about his common sense and experience being more useful than all your book learning,*" her cat spoke up.

"I heard that." Juan grinned. "Tell your bond animal thank you."

"Tell it yourself," she countered. The corners of her mouth twitched until she grinned back. "I shouldn't be smiling. Nothing much to be happy about. For all I know, none of us will survive."

He smoothed his thumbs over her cheekbones. "There's a lot to be happy about. You and me, for instance. No matter what happens, we found each other."

Remorse smote her. "You're way too important to forget, and I didn't. Not really. I was focused way ahead."

"Too far ahead." He kissed the tip of her nose. "I suppose not going to Wrangel Island isn't an option."

"It's not. It might buy us another few months. Maybe as much as a couple of years, but eventually evil would reign. Everywhere would look like Arctowski, replete with monsters and evil overlords."

Juan angled his head, a thoughtful expression on his face. "It's the same decision Rowana faced. Where she sacrificed herself in hopes her companions would make it out alive."

Aura hadn't viewed events in quite the same way, but Juan nailed it. "Thank you."

"For what?" This time he placed butterfly kisses on both her cheeks.

"Reminding me courage is grace under pressure."

"Hemingway said that. I read all his books through my years at sea." Juan let go of her. "I'm off to herd everyone to the dining room before the food gets cold."

She gripped his arm. "I love you."

Juan's hazel eyes glowed with pleasure. He settled his lips over hers, the kiss sharp and sweet, before hustling out of the galley.

Aura turned back to the cooling pans of food and began cutting it into portions. She'd face whatever fate threw in their path. Her ivory-tower life hadn't been much of a proving ground, but it had taught her how to think through problems.

"We all have our strengths," she told her cat.

"Indeed, we do, and you and Juan are stronger together." Her bond-mate sounded insufferably smug.

"I love you too," she said.

"I never doubted it for a moment." The cat hesitated. *"I'll miss Ro and her eagle."*

"Aw, sweetie. So will I."

A deep, sad purr rumbled from her belly. Aura opened her mouth and let it reverberate through the galley.

"No matter what happens"—she stood tall—"Rowana will not

have died for nothing. We'll do everything in our power to thrust evil back into the shadows and force it to remain there."

"Yes," the cat chimed in. *"We will. I'll be with you every step of the way."*

You've reached the end of *Twisted*, book two of Bitter Harvest. Please leave a review for *Twisted*. Doesn't have to be fancy. A sentence or two would be just great. Reviews make such a huge difference. Thanks in advance!

Stay tuned for *Abandoned*, next book in the series. Read on for a sample chapter.

ABOUT THE AUTHOR

Ann Gimpel is a USA Today bestselling author. A lifelong aficionado of the unusual, she began writing speculative fiction a few years ago. Since then her short fiction has appeared in several webzines and anthologies. Her longer books run the gamut from urban fantasy to paranormal romance. Once upon a time, she nurtured clients. Now she nurtures dark, gritty fantasy stories that push hard against reality. When she's not writing, she's in the backcountry getting down and dirty with her camera. She's published over fifty books to date, with several more planned for 2018 and beyond. A husband, grown children, grandchildren, and wolf hybrids round out her family.

Keep up with her at www.anngimpel.com or http://anngimpel.blogspot.com

If you enjoyed what you read, get in line for special offers and pre-release special reads. Newsletter Signup!

ABANDONED: BOOK DESCRIPTION

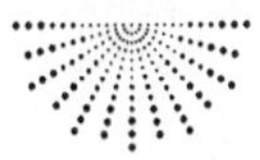

RECCO MISSES his cozy lab and well-organized veterinary clinic, but ten years as a Vampire stripped him of any illusions. Life is done handing him everything he wants. He could rail against fate —which never bought him much—or suck it up and keep going. Defeating the Cataclysm broke Vampirism's hold on him, though. Even better, it threw Zoe square in his path and kicked open the door for him to bond with a wolf.

When Zoe left Ireland for a visiting professorship in Wyoming, she assumed she'd be home in a year. She didn't factor in being trapped by the Cataclysm and scratching and clawing for everything from food to air clean enough to breathe. She's a very different woman now. And not one she likes all that well—or even recognizes some days. A rotten sailor, she never imagined she'd end up on a ship.

In a world with few choices, evil runs rampant and none of the old rules apply. Darkness stalks the ship. Harsh and ruthless, it blocks them at every turn.

ABANDONED, CHAPTER ONE:
BORROWED TROUBLE

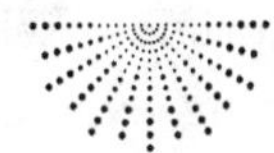

Zoe Seisyll lurched from one side of the generous galley to the other, compensating for the motion of the ship. She was alone in the stainless-steel kitchen that ran behind *Arkady's* dining room, but it was her turn to prepare the evening meal. The beginnings of biscuits spread before her. Half the dough was shaped into rough circles. The other half still sat in an enormous mixing bowl. Back before the Cataclysm, *Arkady* had been home to as many as sixty passengers and a sizeable crew, which explained the industrial sized pans and cookware.

She flexed her fingers, coated with cornmeal, flour, powdered eggs, powdered milk, and enough water to hold it all together. Maybe focusing on her hands would drive the infernal song from her head. The elusive mix of chords that mocked her, slipping away before she could identify their origins.

"Och, and I brought it on myself," she muttered.

Zoe adored music. She played guitar and piano passably well, and could hold her own on the flute. Cooking and singing went together like old, cherished friends, and she'd been deep into an Irish folk tune when the discordant melody intruded.

The one she hadn't been able to get out of her head from a few weeks after they fought the Cataclysm. Not for long, anyway. Whenever she gave in and hummed or sang anything, she rarely got away with it. When she did, her victory was brief.

Aye, verra brief.

Her mind voice was thick with the brogue from her native Northern Ireland. She'd spent nearly as much time in Scotland, so her speech held hints of both accents, something that had confused folk in the U.K., many of whom amused themselves by placing wagers about her origins. When she'd taken a visiting professor position in Wyoming, everyone there chalked her up as a Brit. Or God forbid, an Aussie.

No self-respecting U.K. native would ever make a mistake like that, but to North Americans, everyone from across the Atlantic— or the Pacific—sounded alike.

She swallowed a snort and plunged her hands back into the dough, working on autopilot until three pans of cornmeal biscuits were ready for the waiting oven. Popping them inside, she set a mental timer for fifteen minutes. At least the jarring music in her mind had fallen silent. It was like the intruder knew the moment she let her guard down, waiting in in the wings to pounce when she was vulnerable.

The worst part was it killed the spontaneous joy she'd always taken in music.

Moving to the sink, she rinsed her bowl and her hands. Something about the eerie melody was familiar, but it was unsettling enough she always tuned it out before she could identify it. A knee-jerk reaction to unpleasantness. She perched on a three-legged stool to wait until the biscuits were ready to rescue from the ovens but was too antsy to sit still.

A quick tour through the pantry identified other items to add to dinner preparations. It was too early in the day to do much more than get the biscuits done, though. No point wasting electricity keeping a casserole hot for hours. Everything on the ship was generator powered, but those generators required fuel. The scent of warm cornmeal wafted through the kitchen, comforting and reminiscent of home.

Aye, home. Is aught left of it?

She rolled her shoulders back and stood straighter. No point thinking about Belfast or the family she'd left behind. Parents, aunts, uncles, cousins. She'd never meant to be gone forever. Her plan had been a one year visiting professorship at the University of Wyoming. Their offer included full access to newly excavated Native American settlements and the expectation of several research papers in prestigious journals. Journals that were already lined up and anxiously awaiting her impressions—and her photos.

Definitely a career-making move, and one that would have guaranteed the offer of a full professorship when she returned to Queen's University in Belfast.

Even with all that, she'd hedged about going until the university in Wyoming sweetened the pot by offering to underwrite her travel and living expenses. Zoe would have been a fool to refuse what was any archaeologist's dream. Once she'd gotten her visa squared away and moved into a cozy cottage walking distance from the campus in Laramie, she'd been delighted to meet Aura MacKenzie, another Shifter who was also a history professor.

Aura had introduced her to the local Shifter pack, and Zoe's doubts about the wisdom of traveling so far from home evaporated—

The smell of almost-overcooked biscuits sent her flying to the ovens, mitt in hand. She pulled the pans out, thanking all the bloody saints she'd gotten to them in time, and turned off the oven. They had sufficient supplies on *Arkady*, but it didn't mean she could ruin an entire batch of anything daydreaming. Their food stocks wouldn't last forever. Between now and then, they had to figure out a way to resupply.

She located cooling racks and stacked the pans atop them. Wisps of the eerie, haunting melody were back, but she didn't want to dig any deeper. Something about the song drew her to the restless ocean churning beneath the ship's hull.

Had something followed her from Ushuaia?

Worse, had she done something wrong during their group incantation to defeat the Cataclysm and absorbed some of its fell energy?

No point borrowing trouble.

The corners of her mouth twisted into a grimace. Her long-dead grandma had been partial to that phrase.

Zoe arranged the rest of her dinner preparations in a neat row and left the galley intent on layering up, so she could spend some time out on deck. She trotted up the stairs to the corridor leading to her cabin and let herself inside the small, neat space. Bunks ran beneath the porthole and at right angles along the back wall. A small desk and chair were the only other furniture in the room.

She flipped the duvet into place to cover her unmade bed with its rumpled sheets and pulled gear from one of the cabin's many closets. Because this boat had ferried tourists through the world's polar regions, it held a full complement of cold weather clothing, saving the passengers from packing bulky gear on long transoceanic flights.

Zoe stepped into thick black trousers and an insulated red jacket that she zipped to her chin. Red waterproof bibs came next. Followed by knee-high Wellingtons and a weatherproof rust-colored parka. She tugged a woolen hat over her head, before snugging the parka's hood into place, and stuffed her hands into fluffy down mitts. After a quick glance at her Tarot deck and a few magical accoutrements—mostly gemstones—she'd hung onto through her years in Ushuaia, she felt guilty. Maybe her time would be better spent immersing herself in chasing the intrusive song to its roots.

I won't be outside for long, she promised herself. *Only enough to clear my head.*

Before she could overthink her decision, she trudged out of

her cabin and along the corridor to the first door leading outside. The ship had a million doors and almost as many staircases. She supposed they'd been placed strategically to maximize safety, but things like insurance companies were part of the old world order.

None of that mattered anymore, and maybe the demise of things like insurance companies was one of the plusses. No one to bail you out when you fucked up meant you were a hell of a lot more careful.

Cold hit her like an unyielding wall after the ship's interior warmth. Her first full breath stuck in her throat, making her gasp, and she buried her nose and mouth in the parka's neck ruff.

Zoe walked mindlessly. She started to hum, but cut it off fast. For once the marauding melody didn't insert itself. After a while, she wrapped her arms around herself in a feeble attempt to preserve her body's heat. Icy wind cut through her layers of clothing, and sleet stung her face. The cold air searing her lungs was clean, though. A welcome counterpart to the years she and eleven other Shifters had been trapped in Ushuaia wondering what was going to kill them first. A marauding Vampire or tainted air and water.

Years ago, Aura had talked her into joining their group on a trip to the tip of South America. At the time, it sounded like quite the adventure, and it occurred during a week when the university was closed for one of many U.S. holidays. The Shifters had planned to harness the power of an eclipse, something that would have enhanced their Earth-linked magic. Except the eclipse never happened. Instead, a spell gone bad imprisoned them at the ass end of the earth.

She pushed past the chill leaching into her bones and strode briskly from deck to deck, covering a familiar pathway. She tried to get outdoors as much as she could, but foul weather had kept her inside the last two days. Her coyote had pitched a right fit at the confinement.

"Better?" she asked her bondmate and picked up the pace.

"Yes." The word held a grudging tone.

Zoe waited. After twenty years, she knew better than to argue —or cajole—her bond animal into anything. That strategy never worked.

"What happens after this McMurdo place?" the coyote asked.

"Depends what we find there." Zoe was hedging, but she didn't want to break the news about a blue water voyage that could take a month or better. For some reason, the coyote hated water—or maybe it was the combination of water, cold, and being stuck in a small space. She tried a different tack. *"Before we left Ireland, you enjoyed our jaunts in those little boats I used to rent."*

"That was different, and you know it. How can you compare a sunny afternoon when we'd spend an hour or two within sight of land to this? Everything here is white or gray. It's unnatural. I miss green and trees."

She gave up on telepathy—the coyote would hear her either way—and chose not to mention that most of their sailing time around the British Isles had scarcely been under sunny skies. It had been green, though. A byproduct of incessant rain. "What bothers you most?" She channeled a thread of magic to her feet before her circulation shut down entirely.

"All of it."

"Could you narrow that down?" Zoe reached the sixth deck and reversed course. Clouds the color of hammered pewter boiled across the horizon, limiting vision to fifty yards. Wind ripped at her, pushing her first one way, and then another.

"I assumed when we defeated the Cataclysm and left Ushuaia the world wouldn't be quite so hostile." The coyote yipped, wistful and somber.

"We all hoped that." Zoe sent warm thoughts inward.

"What have we encountered so far?" the coyote demanded, not mollified by her attempt to soothe it. Without waiting for her to reply, it kept right on talking. *"Four reluctant shifters. A mad priest. Demons. Vampires—that apparently aren't all dead yet. An evil dark mage—"*

"I know all those things. I was there too," she cut in. "Goddammit. This is hard enough without you cataloging all the bad shit. Besides, the men made peace with their bond animals, so at least that part is on its way to being fixed."

A vicious blast of wind chopped sideways. She gripped a nearby railing with her mitten-clad hand, but her booted feet slipped on icy metal risers. A quick blast of magic kept her upright.

"What's wrong?" she repeated a variant of her earlier question and hustled to the next deck down. "It's not like you to be such a pessimist."

"I want forests. I want you to shift so we can run and I can hunt." Rather than petulant, the coyote's words were bittersweet, as if it were bidding farewell to a life it figured was gone forever.

Zoe chose her words carefully. "You can have those things. But not with me right now. In the special world you share with the bond animals, nothing has changed. My feelings wouldn't be hurt if you retreated there to roam."

"Really?"

"Really," she reassured her bondmate.

"But what if another wicked mage shows up? And you need my magic to strengthen yours?"

"I have a feeling you'd know. No matter where you were." Caring and gratitude for the coyote tracked from her toes to her head. Its last bondmate had died in a bloody skirmish during the first World War, and it had always blamed itself for not keeping its human partner safe from the shrapnel that had torn him to bits.

Wars had been simpler then. At least they'd had beginnings and ends. Winners and losers. Not anymore. From the time a magical barricade trapped them inside Ushuaia, they'd fought an amorphous enemy. One without defined boundaries that was a magnet for evil. Zoe shivered and set her teeth together to keep them from chattering.

They'd fought Vampires too, but they were pikers in the evil department. Nowhere near as daunting as demons or powerful mages. Besides, Vamps seemed to be on their way out. The battle against the Cataclysm had paved the way for them to lose their fangs and welcome a bond animal if they chose to do so.

Zoe broke into a shambling trot. Perpetually cold outside. Stifling heat within. She reminded herself it was good to have choices. Any choices at all. Those years in Ushuaia hadn't offered much in the way of alternatives. She'd spent most of that time helping humans survive and avoiding Vampires.

She burrowed deeper into her parka, shielding her eyes from blowing snow with one hand. It might be cold out here on deck, but at least it wasn't claustrophobic. They'd been en route from Antarctica's Palmer Peninsula to McMurdo Research Station for the past week. Between pack ice that had surrounded the ship—and forced them to slow down—and storms that blew up out of nowhere, their progress hadn't been as brisk as they'd hoped.

Or as Viktor and Juan had hoped, she corrected herself. They were the only ones who actually knew anything about sailing a ship as large as *Arkady*. As she'd recently reminded her bondmate, she'd done her share of piloting skiffs and day sailors in the murky zone where Scotland and Ireland were separated by the Irish Sea, but that experience scarcely prepared her for a three-hundred-foot-long vessel.

Vik and Juan had parceled out tasks, training the rest of them as fast as they could, but the ship's array of instrumentation was daunting. Zoe doubted anything as prosaic as sitting down with an instruction manual would be sufficient to teach her the basics of what she needed to know. Guiding *Arkady* required years of hands-on practice. *Sailing for Dummies* wouldn't cut it.

"There you are," sounded from behind her.

Zoe spun to face Ketha, a wolf shifter and seer, who was also Viktor's wife. "Here I am," she agreed, surprised by how flat and hard the words sounded.

Ketha had tossed a parka over her tall, slender frame. Dark hair shot with red and gold streamed around her, tossed by the wind, and her golden eyes held a worried cast. "Is something wrong?"

Zoe choked on a groan at the memory of what she'd dragged out of her coyote by asking the same question.

Ketha grappled with her parka hood with one bare hand. Clearly, she hadn't expected to remain outside very long.

"Come on." Zoe trotted twenty feet and yanked the first door she came to open. "You're not dressed to be out here."

"Judging from how white your skin is, neither are you," Ketha retorted, but she dove through the door Zoe held for her.

"My skin is always white. 'Tis an Irish redhead's curse."

"Looks like frostbite to me." Ketha stopped in the long corridor spanning Deck Three and turned to look askance at Zoe. "Och, sure and ye've a wee bit of Scots blood too, lassie."

A laugh bubbled from Zoe's belly. Ketha had a quirky optimism, and it was impossible to remain annoyed with her. "Drop the brogue, sweetie."

"But I speak Gaelic," Ketha protested.

"Aye, but it doesn't translate well when you pretend you were born on the old side of the Atlantic."

"North America is every bit as old, but that's not why I came hunting for you. We could use your archeology skills."

Zoe frowned. "Why? Surely you didn't unearth any pot shards or strips of fabric or bits of buildings for me to examine."

"Yes and no."

"Equivocate, why don't you?" Zoe rolled her eyes and hustled down the corridor to her cabin. "You may as well come on in and tell me what's going on while I ditch some of these clothes. I'll cook if I keep all these layers on."

Ketha followed her into her cabin and pushed the door shut. "What do you know about genetic blends?"

Zoe unzipped her parka and slung it over a hook next to the

door. Next she toed off the Arctic Pac boots so she could get out of her bibs. "By genetic blends, do you mean two species that aren't normally associated with one another?" Ketha nodded, so Zoe went on. "You're the microbiologist. Why ask me?"

Ketha laid her parka on one of the bunks and settled next to it. "I didn't mean on a cellular level. What I was fishing for was evidence—and it can be anecdotal—of beings not explainable by any normal selection process."

"Do you mean mythical creatures? Like the Phoenix? Or Selkies?"

"More like Gryphons since they're a mix of eagles and lions."

"Ah." Zoe unhooked the bibs and stepped out of them, hanging them next to the jacket. Once she'd stuffed her feet into slippers, she perched on the bed catty-corner to Ketha's. "And you'd be asking this, why?"

Ketha blew out a tight breath and stretched out fingers that had rounded into fists. "We've been at this for the last two days. Ever since the weather turned to shit and lab time was about the only avenue open to us—"

"Who's us?"

"Karin, Recco, Daide, and me."

Zoe nodded. It made sense. Karin was an MD, and the two men had been veterinarians before being turned into Vampires. Courtesy of the standoff with the Cataclysm, they were Shifters now.

"Go on." Zoe made come along motions with one hand.

Ketha pressed her lips into a thin line. "You know how Karin's first evaluation yielded unrelated bits of genetic material?"

"Yeah. And we figured the dark mage bound the protoplasm to his liking when he created those impossible animals."

"Exactly. Well, the unrelated DNA strings are there, but there's more. We've checked it nine different ways—except it feels like a hundred—and we keep coming up with the same result."

Zoe leaned forward and rested a hand on Ketha's knee. "You

don't have to justify yourself to a jury of your overeducated peers. This is only me. I don't need the runup. What'd you find?"

"Something truly ancient. It's made up of archaea, but they're arranged in an intelligent fashion. I've never seen anything like it. Never read about it, either."

Zoe culled through her memory. "Those are what? Some kind of ameba, right?"

"Not exactly. Ameba have a cellular nucleus, and these don't. Archaea are the oldest, simplest, single cell organisms. The original building blocks of life. They're a type of prokaryote, and they date back three and a half billion years that we know of." She stopped to take a measured breath. "I'm here to ask you to generate a list of possibilities."

Zoe got to her feet and clasped her hands behind her as she covered the distance to the door and back again, stopping in front of Ketha. "So you have a microscopic piece of…of something. And you want me to come up with a list of everything that used to live in this neck of the woods millions—or billions—of years ago? Without the Internet or access to textbooks?"

Ketha opened her mouth, but Zoe held up a hand. "Archaeologists are exactly like any other scientific discipline. We have areas of specialization. Mine was native and indigenous peoples. I had colleagues who fell in love with the polar regions, but I only spend one summer there."

The hopeful look on Ketha's face folded in on itself. "Damn but I miss libraries and my collections of scientific journals. This could be the find of the millennium. A sentient prehistoric creature that migrated to Antarctica before the continent turned into nature's icebox."

"How did you get from prokaryotes arranged in unusual ways to a sentient prehistoric creature?"

Ketha screwed her mouth into a grimace. "Bit of a leap, eh? That's why I'm here. I was hoping you might have relevant information that could feed into figuring this out."

"I understand it's important," Zoe said, picking her words with care. "I'm not blowing you off, just cautioning you this isn't exactly my area of expertise. I'll try to remember what I can, and I'll ask my bond animal. It's one of the older ones. Have you asked Juan what his mountain lion remembers? It wasn't one of the first Shifters, but it wasn't far removed from them, either."

"Grand idea. Ashamed I didn't think of it first." Ketha jumped to her feet, snapped up her parka, and headed for the door.

A blast of discordant music rocked Zoe. The timing couldn't be accidental. "Did you hear that?" she demanded.

Ketha pulled her hand away from the door latch and turned to face Zoe. "Hear what?"

"It sounds like a five-year-old pounding the flats of both hands on a keyboard."

"Fascinating. Do you think something is trying to communicate with you?" Ketha skewered Zoe with troubled eyes. "Have you heard it before?"

"Aye, that I have. 'Tis so unpleasant, I've always shut it down before it had a chance to be more than annoying."

Ketha screwed her face into a reprimand. "When were you going to get around to telling the rest of us about this toddler piano player?"

"Skip the lecture. I told you now. I was worried maybe I'd brought a piece of the Cataclysm along with us. I hoped it would go away. I—"

"Sorry. I was way too harsh. There might be a connection between my tissue sample in the lab and whatever is singing to you."

Zoe rolled her eyes. "That's another really big stretch."

Ketha rolled her eyes back and squeezed Zoe's shoulder. "When you have no fucking idea what you're dealing with, no idea is too fantastic to discard out of hand. I'm going back to the lab."

"I'll see if I can remember any of the legends unique to the poles."

"Good woman." Ketha pulled the door open and left at a quick pace.

Zoe stepped into the bathroom long enough to sluice water over her face, and then she sat at the desk and pulled paper and a pencil from its top drawer.

"Monsters from the North and South Poles, huh?" she muttered and cleared her mind.

It didn't take long before her eidetic memory regurgitated materials she'd studied during a long-ago summer spent above the Arctic circle researching the Inuit and the hunter-gatherer forbearers of Scandinavians. She stared at the page centered in front of her, stabbed her pencil onto it, and began to write.

Adlet: A type of werewolf with the upper body of a man and the hindquarters of a wolf.

Keelut: Evil earth spirit that takes the form of a large, hairless black dog...

www.ingramcontent.com/pod-product-compliance
Lightning Source LLC
Chambersburg PA
CBHW071234190726

48292CB00007B/2287